COMING THROUGH SLAUGHTER

Michael Ondaatje

Buddy Bolden

Published by
House of Anansi Press Limited
1800 Steeles Avenue West
Concord, Ontario
L4K 2P3

First published in 1976
by House of Anansi Press Limited

Canadian Cataloguing in Publication Data

Ondaatje, Michael, 1943-
Coming through slaughter

ISBN 0-88784-517-7

1. Bolden, Buddy, ca. 1868-1931 - Fiction. I.Title.

PS8529.N33C6 1991   C813'.54   C91-094352-4
PR9199.3.053C6 1991

Cover design: Leslie Styles

Printed and bound in Canada

$12.95

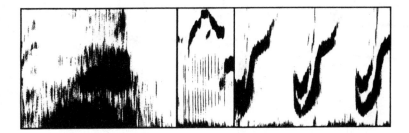

Three sonographs — pictures of dolphin sounds made by a machine that is more sensitive than the human ear. The top left sonograph shows a "squawk." Squawks are common emotional expressions that have many frequencies or pitches, which are vocalized simultaneously. The top right sonograph is a whistle. Note that the number of frequencies is small and this gives a "pure" sound — not a squawk. Whistles are like personal signatures for dolphins and identify each dolphin as well as its location. The middle sonograph shows a dolphin making two kinds of signals simultaneously. The vertical stripes are echolocation clicks (sharp, multi-frequency sounds) and the dark, mountain-like humps are the signature whistles. No one knows how a dolphin makes both whistles and echolocation clicks simultaneously.

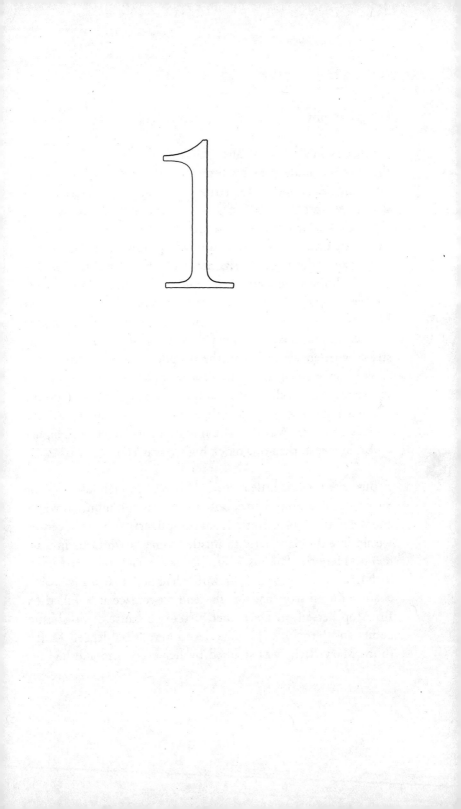

*

His geography.

Float by in a car today and see the corner shops. The signs of the owners obliterated by brand names. Tassin's Food Store which he lived opposite for a time surrounded by DRINK COCA COLA IN BOTTLES, BARG'S, or LAURA LEE'S TAVERN, the signs speckled in the sun, TOM MOORE, YELLOWSTONE, JAX, COCA COLA, COCA COLA, primary yellows and reds muted now against the white horizontal sheet wood walls. This district, the homes and stores, are a mile or so from the streets made marble by jazz. There are no songs about Gravier Street or Phillips or First or The Mount Ararat Missionary Baptist Church his mother lived next door to, just the names of the streets written vertically on the telephone poles or the letters sunk into pavement that you walk over. GRAVIER. A bit too stylish for the wooden houses almost falling down, the signs the porches and the steps broken through where no one sits outside now. It is further away that you find Rampart Street, then higher up Basin Street, then one block higher Franklin.

But here there is little recorded history, though tales of 'The Swamp' and 'Smoky Row', both notorious communities where about 100 black prostitutes from pre-puberty to their seventies would line the banquette to hustle, come down to us in fragments. Here the famous whore Bricktop Jackson carried a 15 inch knife and her lover John Miller had no left arm and wore a chain with an iron ball on the end to replace it — killed by Bricktop herself on December 7, 1861, because of his 'bestial habits and ferocious manners'. And here 'One-legged Duffy' (born Mary Rich) was stabbed by her boyfriend and had her head beaten in with her own wooden leg. 'And gamblers carrying cocaine to a game'.

History was slow here. It was elsewhere in town, in the brothel district of Storyville, that one made and lost money — the black whores and musicians shipped in from the suburbs and the black customers refused. Where the price of a teenage virgin was $800 in 1860, where Dr Miles (who later went into the Alka Seltzer business) offered cures for gonorrhea. The women wore Gloria de Dijon and Marshall Neil roses and the whores sold 'Goofer Dust' and 'Bend-Over Oil'. Money poured in, slid around. By the end of the Nineteenth Century, 2000 prostitutes were working regularly. There were at least 70 professional gamblers. 30 piano players took in several thousand each in weekly tips. Prostitution and its offshoots received a quarter of a million dollars of the public's money a week.

Tom Anderson, 'The King of the District', lived between Rampart and Franklin. Each year he published a Blue Book which listed every whore in New Orleans. This was the guide to the sporting district, listing alphabetically the white and then the black girls, from Martha Alice at 1200 Customhouse to Louisa Walter at 210 North Basin, and then the octoroons. The Blue Book and similar guides listed everything, and at any of the mansions you could go in with money and come out broke. No matter how much you took with you, you would lose it all in paying for extras. Such as watching an Oyster Dance — where a naked woman on a small stage danced alone to piano music. The best was Olivia the Oyster Dancer who would place a raw oyster on her forehead and lean back and shimmy it down all over her body without ever dropping it. The oyster would criss-cross and move finally down to her instep. Then she would kick it high into the air and would catch it on her forehead and begin again. Or at 335 Customhouse (later named Iberville), the street he went crazy on, you could try your luck with French Emma's '60 Second Plan'. Whoever could restrain his orgasm with her for a whole minute after penetration was excused the $2 payment. Emma allowed the odd success to encourage others but boasted privately that there was no man she couldn't win. So no matter how much you took in you came out broke. Grace Hayes even had a pet raccoon she had trained to pick the pockets of her customers.

Anderson was the closest thing to a patron that Bolden had, giving him money for the family and sending him, via runner boys, two bottles of whisky a day. To the left of Canal Street was Dago Tony who, at the height of Bolden's popularity, sponsored him as well sending him Raleigh Rye and wine. And to the left of Canal are also the various homes of Bolden, still here today, away from the recorded history – the bleak washed out one-storey houses. Phillips, First, Gravier, Tassin's Food Store, taverns open all day but the doors closed tight to keep out heat and sunlight. Circle and wind back and forth in your car and at First and Liberty is a corner house with an overhang roof above the wooden pavement, barber stripes on the posts that hold up the overhang. This is N. Joseph's Shaving Parlor, the barber shop where Buddy Bolden worked.

⁂

He puts the towel of steam over a face. Leaving holes for the mouth and the nose. Bolden walks off and talks with someone. A minute of hot meditation for the customer. After school, the kids come and watch the men being shaved. Applaud and whistle when each cut is finished. Place bets on whose face might be under the soap.

✳

N. Joseph's Shaving Parlor. One large room with brothel wallpaper left over from Lula White's Mahogany Hall. Two sinks with barber chairs in front of them, and along the wall several old donated armchairs where customers or more often just visitors sat talking and drinking. Pausing and tense when the alcohol ran out and drinking from the wooden coke racks until the next runner from Anderson or Dago Tony arrived, the new bottle travelling round the room including the half-shaved customer and the working Bolden, the bottle sucked empty after a couple of journeys, Bolden opening his throat muscles and taking it in so he was sometimes drunk by noon and would cut hair more flamboyantly. Close friends who needed cuts and shaves would come in early, well before noon.

In the afternoon a stray customer might be put in the chair and lathered by someone more sober and then Bolden would fight back into the room protesting loudly to his accusers that he had nerves of steel, and so cut hair once more, or whatever came in the way. Humming loud he would crouch over his sweating victim and cut and cut, offering visions of new styles to the tilted man. He persuaded men out of ten year mustaches and simultaneously offered raw steaming scandal that brought up erections in the midst of their fear. As the afternoon went on he elaborated long seductions usually culminating in the story of Miss Jessie Orloff's famous incident in a Canadian hotel during her last vacation. So friends came early to avoid the blood hunting razors of the afternoon. At 4 o clock in any case the shop closed down and he slept.

It was a financial tragedy that sleep sobered Bolden up completely, that his mind on waking was clear as an empty road and he began to casually drink again although never hard now for he played in the evenings. He slept from 4 till 8. His day had begun at 7 when he walked the kids a mile to school buying them breakfast along the way at the fruit stands. A half hour's walk and another 30 minutes for them to sit on the embankment and eat the huge meal of fruit. He taught them all he was thinking of or had heard, all he knew at the moment, treating them as adults, joking and teasing them with tall tales which they learned to sift down to the real. He gave himself completely to them during the walk, no barriers as they walked down the washed empty streets one on either side, their thin cool hands each holding onto a finger of his. Eventually they knew the politics of the street better than their teachers and he in turn learned the new street songs from them. By 8 they were at school and he took a bus back to Canal, then walked towards First, greeting everybody on his way to the shop.

What he did too little of was sleep and what he did too much of was drink and many interpreted his later crack-up as a morality tale of a talent that debauched itself. But his life at this time had a fine and precise balance to it, with a careful allotment of hours. A barber, publisher of *The Cricket,* a cornet player, good husband and father, and an infamous man about town. When he opened up the shop he was usually without customers for an hour or so and if there were any there they were usually 'spiders' with news for *The Cricket.* All the information he was given put unedited into the broadsheet. Then he cut hair till 4, then walked home and slept with Nora till 8, the two of them loving each other when they woke. And after dinner leaving for Masonic

Hall or the Globe or wherever he was playing. Onto the stage.

He was the best and the loudest and most loved jazzman of his time, but never professional in the brain. Unconcerned with the crack of the lip he threw out and held immense notes, could reach a force on the first note that attacked the ear. He was obsessed with the magic of air, those smells that turned neuter as they revolved in his lung then spat out in the chosen key. The way the side of his mouth would drag a net of air in and dress it in notes and make it last and last, yearning to leave it up there in the sky like air transformed into cloud. He could see the air, could tell where it was freshest in a room by the colour.

And so arrived amateur and accidental with the band on the stage of Masonic Hall, bursting into jazz, hurdle after hurdle. A race during which he would stop and talk to the crowd. Urging the band to play so loud the music would float down the street, saying 'Cornish, come on, put your hands through the window'. On into the night and into blue mornings, growing louder the notes burning through and off everyone and forgotten in the body because they were swallowed by the next one after and Bolden and Lewis and Cornish and Mumford sending them forward and forth and forth till, as he could see them, their bursts of air were animals fighting in the room.

*

With the utmost curiosity and faith he learned all he could about Nora Bass, questioning her long into the night about her past. Her body a system of emotions and triggers he got lost in. Every hair she lost in the bath, every dead cell she rubbed off on a towel. The way she went crazy sniffing steam from a cup of coffee. He was lost in the details, he could find no exact focus towards her. And so he drew her power over himself.

Bolden could not put things in their place. What thrilled him beyond any measure was that she, for instance, believed in the sandman when putting the children to bed whereas even the children didn't.

Quick under the covers, the sandman's coming down the street.
Where where show us.
He's just stopped to get a drink. And the children groaned inwardly but went to bed anyway. For three years a whore before she married Bolden she had managed to save delicate rules and ceremonies for herself.

But his own mind was helpless against every moment's headline. He did nothing but leap into the mass of changes and explore them and all the tiny facets so that eventually he was almost completely governed by fears of certainty. He distrusted it in anyone but Nora for there it went to the spine, and yet he attacked it again and again in her, cruelly, hating it, the sure lanes of the probable. Breaking chairs and windows glass doors in fury at her certain answers.

Once they were sitting at the kitchen table opposite each other. To his right and to her left was a window. Furious at something he drew his right hand across his body and lashed out. Half way there at full speed he realised it was a window he would be hitting and braked. For a fraction of a second his open palm touched the glass, beginning simultaneously to draw back. The window starred and crumpled slowly two floors down. His hand miraculously uncut. It had acted exactly like a whip violating the target and still free, retreating from the outline of a star. She was delighted by the performance. Surprised he examined his fingers.

Nora's Song

Dragging his bone over town. Dragging his bone over town.
Dragging his bone over town. Dragging his
bone over town. Dragging his bone
over and over dragging his bone over town.
Then and then and then and then
dragging his bone over town

                            and then

dragging his bone home.

＊

Dude Botley

Monday nights at Lincoln Park was something to see, especially when the madams and pimps brought their stables of women to hear Bolden play. Each madam had different colour girls. Ann Jackson featured mulatto, Maud Wilson featured high browns, so forth and so on. And them different stables was different colours. Just like a bouquet.

Bolden played nearly everything in B-Flat.

＊

Nora Bass came home to find a man on her front step. Immaculate. Standing up as she approached, not touching her.

Hello Webb, come on in.
Thanks. Buddy must be out.
She half laughed. Buddy! And then looked quizzical at him.
Then shook her head.
Yeah, you better come in Webb.

Alcohol burning down his throat as she tells him that Buddy went, disappeared, got lost, I don't know Webb but he's gone.
How long?
5 or 6 months.
Nora opening out the curtains so the light falls over him, the cup with the drink in front of his face, between them, shielding him from the story, gulping more down.

Jesus why didn't you tell me before, let me know.
I don't know you Webb, Buddy knows you, why didn't *he* tell you.
You should have told me.
You're a cop Webb.
He's not safe by himself, he's gone lost, with nothing – the *Cricket,* the band, the kids.
He didn't say anything.
He stands up and goes towards her.
Who was he with.
I don't know.
Tell me.

He has covered her against the window, leaning very close to her, like a lover.

You're shaking Webb.

He won't last by himself Nora, he'll fall apart. He's not safe by himself.

Why are you shaking?

He needs you Nora, who was he with last?

Crawley. Another cornet. He was playing with him in Shell Beach, north of here, never came back.

Just like that?

Just like that.

I could find him. Tell me about Crawley.

She moves his arm away holding the cloth of his sleeve and goes to the door, opens and leans against it. She is a mask, her hand against the handle, he almost doesn't realise what she is doing, then walks to the door, angry at her coldness.

Do you want me to?

Looking hard at him.

I'm not going to hire you Webb.

Jesus I don't want your fucking money!

I don't want your fucking compassion Webb. If you look for him then do it for yourself, not for me.

I'm very fond of him.

I know that Webb.

He's a great talent.

Silence from her, lifting her hand and moving it across the small dark living room and its old wallpaper and few chairs like a tired showman.

Most of the cash went down his throat or was given away. You never did find your mother either did you? What? ... No.

Sad laugh over her face as Webb moves past her. Webb steps backward off the doorstep with his hands in his pockets.

Are you with anybody now? Long silence. No. He'll come back Nora. When he married you, before you two went to my cabin in Pontchartrain, he phoned and we talked for over an hour, he needs you Nora, don't worry he'll be back soon.

Nora closing the door more, narrow, just to the width of her face. Webb grins encouragement and walks slowly backwards down the four steps to the pavement. He has remembered the number of steps. He is wrong. Bolden will take two more years before he cruises home. Her door closes on him and he turns. Spring 1906.

He went down to Franklin and bought bananas. Hungry after seeing Nora. Webb got off the bus as soon as he saw the first grocery store and bought six bananas, then a pound of nectarines. Put them in the large pocket of his raincoat and walked on downtown following the direction of the bus towards Lincoln Park. It was still about 8 in the morning. He ate watching the travel of people going both ways. For those who saw him it looked as if he had nothing to do. As it was he was trying to place himself casually in a mental position that was so high and irrelevant he hoped to stumble on the clues that were left by Bolden's disappearance.

It looked as if Bolden had no notion he was *not* coming back when he left for Shell Beach. Webb took much more seriously than others of his profession sudden actions and off hand gestures. Always found them more dangerous, more determined. Also he had discovered that Bolden had never spoken of his past. To the people here he was a musician who arrived in the city at the age of twenty-two. Webb had known him since fifteen. He could just as easily be wiping out his past again in a casual gesture, contemptuous. Landscape suicide. So perhaps the only clue to Bolden's body was in Webb's brain. Sleeping in childhood stories and now thrown into the future like an arrow. To be finished when they grew up. What was Bolden's favourite story? Whose moment of terror did he want to witness, Webb thought as he began the third banana.

Don't go 'way nobody

Careless love

2.19 took my babe away ·

Idaho

Joyce 76

Funky Butt

Take your big leg off me

Snake Rag

Alligator Hop

Pepper Rag

If you don't like my potatoes why do you dig so deep?

All the whores like the way I ride

Make me a pallet on your floor

If you don't shake, don't get no cake.

✿

The Cricket existed between 1899 and 1905. It took in and published all the information Bolden could find. It respected stray facts, manic theories, and well-told lies. This information came from customers in the chair and from spiders among the whores and police that Bolden and his friends knew. *The Cricket* studied broken marriages, gossip about jazzmen, and a servant's memoirs told everyone that a certain politician spent twenty minutes each morning deciding which shirt to wear. Bolden took all the thick facts and dropped them into his pail of sub-history.

Looked at objectively *The Cricket* contained excessive reference to death. The possibilities were terrifying to Bolden and he hunted out examples obsessively as if building a wall. A boy with a fear of heights climbing slowly up a tree. There were descriptions of referees slashed to death by fighting cocks, pigs taking off the hand of a farmer, the unfortunate heart attack of the ninety year old Miss Bandeen who opened her door one night to let in her cats and let in someone's pet iguana instead. There was the freak electrocution of Kenneth Stone who stood up in his bathtub to straighten a crooked lightbulb and was found the next morning by his brother Gordon, the first reaction of Gordon being to turn the switch off so that Kenneth fell stiff to the floor and broke his nose. Whenever a celebrated murder occurred Bolden was there at the scene drawing amateur maps. There were his dreams of his children dying. There were his dreams of his children dying. There were his dreams of his children dying. And then there was the first death, almost on top of him, saved by its fictional quality and nothing else.

Bolden's marriage to Nora Bass had been a surprise to most of his friends. Webb, in Pontchartrain, continuing his career as police detective, received a long phone call from Bolden with the news. Webb offered them his cabin which they could use during the next month, so Bolden and Nora went there. Eventually, after three weeks, Nora's mother drove up for a visit in her Envictor, her suitcase full of whisky. Since the death of Mr Bass she had two overwhelming passions – the drawings of Audubon, and an old python she had bought second-hand, retired from a zoo. And since the death of Mr Bass all her daughters had slipped successively into the red light district. Bolden in fact had slept with each of Nora's sisters in his time. Now he was formally married to one of them, the veil of suspicion had been removed from the mother's eyes, and the two of them would hold great drunk conversations together. A sparky lady. She would lecture him on the world of animals while he listened morosely studying her body for betrayals of her daughter's physical characteristics. The final stages of an evening's drunkenness would see her reaching into her suitcase to bring out the copies of Audubon drawings. Hardly able to talk around a slur now she'd interpret the damned birds, *damned,* as she saw them, for she was sure John James Audubon was attracted to psychologically neurotic creatures. She showed him the drawing of the Purple Gallinule which seemed to lean over the water, its eyes closed, with thoughts of self-destruction. You don't know that! Shut up, Buddy! She showed him the Prophet Ibis, obviously paranoid, that built its nest high up before floods came, and the Cerulean Wood Warbler drunk on Spanish Mulberry, and her favourite – the Anhinga, the Water Turkey, which she said would sit in the tree tops till disturbed and then plummet down into the river leaving hardly a ripple and swim off with just its eyes and beak cresting water – or if disturbed further would hide by submerging completely and walk along the river bottom, forgetting to breathe, and so drown. That's how they catch water turkeys, she said, scare them under water and then net their bodies when they float up a few minutes later, did you know that? Bolden shook his head. You tell a good story Mrs Bass but I don't believe you, you crazy woman, you're drunk you know that – you crazy woman. A week later Mrs Bass went for a drive and never came back. After lunch Buddy and Nora set out walking. They found the Envictor two miles down the road. Mrs Bass was sitting at the wheel and had been strangled.

There was much curiosity on Bolden's part. They had been away from news for nearly a month, god knew if there was a famous murderer in the area. His mind went into theories. Eventually he decided to take the car and drive to Pontchartrain and tell Webb about it. Nora refused to be left with a strangler around. They drove with the dead Mrs Bass in the front seat settling carefully into rigor mortis. At the turns however she would sometimes fall over onto Bolden's lap like a valuable statue, so Nora got in the front and Mrs Bass was put in the back seat. Covered with a tarp for diplomacy. Bolden parked outside the police station and asked for Webb. Nora went to a restaurant to get a meal.

Listen we've got a dead body outside.
What!
Yeah. Nora's mum. Strangled. We brought her in.
Other cops looked round. Webb took his feet off the desk and stood up.
Listen if you murdered her you should get rid of the body, you should've buried her, don't try to bluff it out.
Hell Webb, we didn't kill her, I liked the old lady, but it looks suspicious, she has a lot of cash we're gonna get, so how would it look if we buried her?

Right, and you can't claim the money without the body, so you'd *have* to bluff it.

We didn't do it you bastard.

Ok Ok I believe you, where's the body?

In the back seat. Under the tarp.

Ok go with Belddax here and bring it in.

Minutes later Belddax rushed in. Webb asked where Bolden was.

He's running down the road, sir.

What!

Someone stole the car.

This crisis deflated with investigation. Search parties went out looking for the car as well as a strangler in the Hill district. After two weeks nothing had been found. The Boldens who would have been reasonably wealthy had no chance of a will until the body was located. Advertisements were placed in *The Cricket* and the Pontchartrain papers for a lost Envictor and the goods therein. A year later Bolden got a letter from Webb.

Buddy –

I've solved the murder if not the disappearance. Not everyone agrees with me, and I wouldn't have thought of it if not for last week's newspaper. Enclosed.

> *St Tropez. France*
> The flamboyant and controversial 'dancer' Isadora Duncan died yesterday in another one of those dramatic situations that seemed to follow her all her life. Riding with a friend in his Bugatti, her silk scarf caught in the back wheel of the

moving car and strangled her before the driver realised what was happening. The British Automobile Association has given out frequent warnings that this is a common danger to motorists. Miss Duncan was 49. For more of her life see 'SCARF' page 17.

You see what I'm getting at don't you. The old lady's pet snake is near her, taking in the breeze. Its tail somehow gets caught in a rear wheel. It quickly hangs onto the one thing close to it, her neck, this strangles her. After the car comes to a halt the snake who has been stretched badly but not killed uncoils and slides away. No trace of a weapon. If the snake was human it wouldn't get much more than manslaughter ... Sometimes Bolden I think I am a genius.

Webb

There were his dreams of his children dying.

❋

The other kid came in with the news he's dead, sobbing, and he jumped and ran in one movement and caught the boy's shoulders WHO IS he heard himself weep out loud and being told floated into the kitchen picked up the wood handled knife with the serrated edge and pushed it again and again into his left wrist, then the open hand which was numb already, through the door and the police amazed at him his white shirt bloody looking at the cops who brought the news he'd always imagined each night – hit by a car, god. After the boy's words he hadn't heard a thing but his own screaming, went past the cop and leaned over the hot metal of the hood of the police truck, his face and his wet arm on it.

*

Crawley was losing weight and looking pale. He was fasting and the lines in his face were exaggerated. He sat in his chair drinking distilled water from a large bottle while Webb sat on the edge of the bed trying to get information. Now 10 a.m. He had got to him just before he started practising.

Give me half an hour. I'll be out by 10.30.
Who you?
I've just come from Nora. We're trying to find Buddy.

He tried offering Crawley a banana.

Banana, hell, I'm dieting. Just this special water.
Go on, take one, you look sick.
I can't. Jesus I'd like to. Do you know I haven't had a shit for a week?
How's your energy?
Slow … this time I'm aiming for the tail of shit.
The tail of shit.
Yeah … got to it once before. If you don't eat you see you finally stop shitting, naturally. And then about two weeks after that you have this fantastic shit, it comes out like a tornado. It's all the crap right at the bottom of your bowels, all the packed in stuff that never comes out, that always gets left behind.
Yeah? When did you last see Bolden?
Like someone removing a poker that's been up your arse all your life. It's fantastic. Then you can start eating again – is that a nectarine? I'll have a nectarine.
What was he doing when you last saw him?
He was on a boat.
Shit man, Bolden hated boats.
Listen, he was on a *boat*.

＊

While Webb is talking to Crawley, this is what Bolden sees:

The woman is cutting carrots. Each carrot is split into 6 or 7 pieces. The knife slides through and hits the wood table that they will eat off later. He is watching the coincidence of her fingers and the carrots. It began with the colour of the fingers and then the slight veins on the carrot magnified themselves to his eyes. In this area of sight the fingers have separated themselves from her body and move in a unity of their own that stops at the sleeve and bangle. As with all skills he watches for it to fail. If she thinks what she is doing she will lose control. He knows that the only way to catch a fly for instance is to move the hand without the brain telling it to move fast, interfering. The silver knife curves calm and fast against carrots and fingers. Onto the cuts in the table's brown flesh.

＊

'The only thing I can tell you Webb is about the last time I saw him. Last fall. He had never been on a boat before. Though god knows he's lived against the river all his life. But he was never on it. Anyway, the two of us and a couple of others went up to Shell Beach. We were supposed to play for three nights there. Usually we didn't play together but we liked each other's way and got on. There was very little money in the Shell Beach thing and each of the band was billeted with organisers. Bolden was to stay with a couple called the Brewitts — a pianist and his wife. You may have heard of him, Jaelin Brewitt, he used to be popular about five years ago...'

Spanish Fort, Shell Beach, Lake Pontchartrain,
Milneburg, Algiers, Gretna.
— All considered New Orleans suburbs.

[Milenburg Joys!]

Bolden lost himself then. Jaelin's wife, Robin, was very much part of the Shell Beach music world too, small enough in itself, but they got good musicians in and often. When he saw her he nearly fainted. After a party he went home with the Brewitts and pretended he was hungry so they wouldn't go to bed. Bolden was never much of an eater but he lied that he hadn't eaten for two days and so they sat there for three hours and he forced himself to eat and eat, taking twenty minutes with an egg squashed in a bowl and a drink in the hand. They sat till all tiredness was gone, the three of them, and about five in the morning they stood and groaned and went to bed. Then Bolden did a merciless thing. For the first time he used his cornet as jewelry. After the couple had closed their door, he slipped in a mouthpiece, and walked out the kitchen door which led to an open porch. Cold outside. He wore just his dark trousers and a collarless white shirt. With every sweet stylised gesture that he knew no one could see he aimed for the gentlest music he knew. So softly it was a siren twenty blocks away. He played till his body was frozen and all that was alive and warm were the few inches from where his stomach forced the air up through his chest and head into the instrument. Music for the three of them, the other two in bed, not saying a word.

Next morning Crawley was on the beach while Bolden got into the boat, a day cruiser, bobbing on the crowded Sunday water. He began to yell something at Crawley. Crawley called back. Bolden a hundred feet out with the Brewitts. They were shouting back and forth in musical terms. Crawley knew he was saying goodbye to his friend. He was saying goodbye to his friend.

'That was it ... I went back into town later that afternoon, he didn't show for the last two performances and didn't show at the train. I went over to the Brewitts the next day and Robin said he wasn't there. No one has seen or heard of him playing anywhere since. Shortly afterwards I heard the Brewitts had moved and haven't been seen either. It's been a case of everyone looking for Bolden and me saying I last saw him with the Brewitts and then people looking for the Brewitts. Nora didn't believe that. *Bolden,* she said, *on a boat* !'

＊

He woke up and his mouth was parched. He didn't know what hour it was. The previous night of drink and talk with the Brewitts had made him lose the order of time. There was sunlight over part of the bed, his arm. He got some pants on and started down the hall towards the Brewitts' kitchen. Robin came round the corner at the other end. She was naked except for the sheet wrapped round her waist and trailing at her feet. Her long black hair on her shoulders and down her back. In each hand she was carrying a glass of orange juice, one for herself and one for Jaelin, walking back to their bedroom. She saw him and stopped, awkward, not knowing what to do. She looked at each of the glasses in her hands, then at him, and smiling shrugged. He stood still, where he was, as she walked past him, as she mouthed 'Morning' to him.

Webb twenty and Bolden seventeen when they worked in fun-fairs along the coast. Being financially independent for the first time they spend all their money on girls, and sometimes on women. They take rooms, stock beer, and gradually paste their characters onto each other. They spend a week alone building up the apartment in Pontchartrain. It is during this time that Webb and Bolden get to know each other. Afterwards, busy with women, their friendship is a public act of repartee, bouncing jokes off each other in female company. They live together for two years.

So Webb wanted to focus on that one week. And it was difficult for in that era, that time, it was Webb who was the public figure, Bolden the side-kick, the friend who stayed around. If others spoke of the two of them it was usually with surprise at what Webb could see in Bolden. The two of them after work busy with their own hobbies, Webb's curiosity making him move serene among his growing collection of magnets and Bolden practising for hours, strengthening his mouth and chest as he blew violently into a belled cornet. So the constant noise in Webb's ears was the muted howl in the other room. Till coming into Webb's room with beer and sweating Bolden would collapse in an armchair and say 'Tell me about magnets, Webb'. And Webb who had ten of them hanging on strings from the ceiling would explain the precision of the forces in the air and hold a giant magnet in his hands towards them so they would go frantic and twist magically with their own power and twitch and thrust up and swivel as if being thrashed jerking until sometimes the power that Webb held from across the room would break one of the strings and Webb would put his magnet at his foot and drag the smaller piece invisibly towards him or sometimes throw the magnet across the room halfway up the strings and the tied pieces of metal would leap up and jointly catch it in their smooth surfaces like a team of acrobats. Bolden would applaud and then they would drink.

After two years Bolden had gone to New Orleans and Webb stayed in Pontchartrain. Since then it was Bolden the musician that Webb heard stories of. It was Bolden who had jumped up, who had swallowed everything Webb was. Webb left with the roots of Bolden's character, the old addresses they passed through. A month after Bolden had moved Webb went to the city and, unseen, tracked Buddy for several days. Till the Saturday when he watched his nervous friend walk jauntily out of the crowd into the path of a parade and begin to play. So hard and beautifully that Webb didn't even have to wait for the reactions of the people, he simply turned and walked till he no longer heard the music or the roar he imagined crowding round to suck that joy. Its power.

*

Frank Lewis

It was a music that had so little wisdom you wanted to clean nearly every note he passed, passed it seemed along the way as if travelling in a car, passed before he even approached it and saw it properly. There was no control except the *mood* of his power ... and it is for this reason it is good you never heard him play on recordings. If you never heard him play some place where the weather for instance could change the next series of notes — then you *should* never have heard him at all. He was never recorded. He stayed away while others moved into wax history, electronic history, those who said later that Bolden broke the path. It was just as important to watch him stretch and wheel around on the last notes or to watch nerves jumping under the sweat of his head.

But there was a discipline, it was just that we didn't understand. We thought he was formless, but I think now he was tormented by order, what was outside it. He tore apart the plot — see his music was immediately on top of his own life. Echoing. As if, when he was playing he was lost and hunting for the right accidental notes. Listening to him was like talking to Coleman. You were both changing direction with every sentence, sometimes in the middle, using each other as a springboard through the dark. You were moving so fast it was unimportant to finish and clear everything. He would be describing something in 27 ways. There was pain and gentleness everything jammed into each number.

Where did he come from? He was found before we knew where he had come from. Born at the age of twenty-two. Walked into a parade one day with white shoes and red shirt.

Never spoke of the past. Simply about which way to go for the next 10 minutes.

God I was at that first parade, I was playing, it was a very famous entrance you know. He walks out of the crowd, struggles through onto the street and begins playing, too loud but real and strong you couldn't deny him, and then he went back into the crowd. Then fifteen minutes later, 300 yards down the street, he jumps through the crowd onto the street again, plays, and then goes off. After two or three times we were waiting for him and he came.

Shell Beach Station. From the end of the track he watched Crawley and the rest of the band get on the train. They were still half-looking around for him to join them from someplace, even now. He stood by a mail wagon and watched them. He watched himself getting onto the train with them, the fake anger relief on their part. He watched himself go back to the Brewitts and ask if he could stay with them. The silent ones. Post music. After ambition. As he watched Crawley lift his great weight up onto the train he could see himself live with the Brewitts for years and years. He did not have any baggage with him, just the mouthpiece in his pocket. He could step on the train or go back to the Brewitts. He was frozen. He woke to see the train disappearing away from his body like a vein. He continued to stand hiding behind the mail wagon. Help me. He was scared of everybody. He didn't want to meet anybody he knew again, ever in his life.

*

He left the station, went down to the small loin district of Shell Beach. Bought beer and listened to poor jazz in the halls. Listening hard so he was playing all the good notes in his brain his mouth flourishing whenever the players missed or avoided them. Had a dollar, less now. Enough for seven beers. Wearing his red shirt black trousers shoes. Stayed in the halls the whole day avoiding the bright afternoon sun which he could see past the open door of the bar, watching the band get replaced by others, ignoring the pick-ups who stroked his neck as they passed the tables. Dead crowd around him. He sat frozen. Then when his money was finished he went down to the shore and slept. Tried to sleep anyway, listening to the others there talk — where to hustle, the weather in Gretna. He took it in and locked it. In the morning he stole some fruit and walked the roads. Went into a crowded barber shop and sat there comfortable but didn't allow himself to be shaved walking out when it was his turn. Always listening, listening to the wet fluid speech with no order, unfinished stories, badly told jokes that he sober as a spider perfected in silence.

For two days picking up the dirt the grime from the local buses before he was thrown off, dirt off bannisters, the wet slime from toilets, grey rub of phones, the alley shit on his shoe when he crouched where others had crouched, tea leaves, beer stains off tables, piano sweat, trombone spit, someone's smell off a towel, the air of the train station sticking to him, the dream of the wheel over his hand, legs beginning to twitch from the tired walking when he lay down. He collected and was filled by every noise as if luscious poison entering the ear like a lady's tongue thickening it and blocking it until he couldn't be entered anymore. A fat full king. The hawk its locked claws full of salmon going under greedy with it for the final time. Nicotine from the small smokes he found burning into his nails, the socks thick with dry sweat, the nose blowing out the day's dirt into a newspaper. Asking for a glass of water and pouring in the free ketchup to make soup. Sank through the pavement into the music of the town of Shell Beach.

And then finding home in the warm gust of soup smells that came through pavement grids from the subterranean kitchens which kept him in their heat, so he travelled from one to another and slept over them at night drunk with the smell of vegetables, saved from the storms that came purple over the lake while he sat in the rain. Warm as a greenhouse over the grid, the heat waves warping, disintegrating his body. The shady head playing with the perfect band.

＊

The ladies had come and visited them in their large brown painted apartment and their taste for women, diverse at first, became embarrassingly similar, both liking the tall brown ladies, bodies thin and long and winding, the jutting pelvis when naked. The relationships often moved over from Webb to Bolden or the other way.

Webb training in the police force, three years older, and Bolden a barber's apprentice emphasizing his ability to be an animated listener. Later on, after he moved, he continued listening at N. Joseph's Shaving Parlor. Here too he reacted excessively to the stories his clients in the chair told him, throwing himself into the situation, giving advice that was usually abstract and bad. The men who came into N. Joseph's were just as much in need of confession or a sense of proportion as a shave and Bolden freely gave bizarre advice just to see what would happen. He was therefore the perfect audience to these songs and pleas. Just take the money and put it on the roosters. Days later furious men would rush in demanding to speak to Bolden (who was then only twenty-four for goodness sake) and he would have to leave his customer and *that* man's flight of conversation, take the angered one into Joseph's small bathroom and instead of accepting guilt quickly suggest variations. Five minutes later Bolden would be back shaving a neck and listening to other problems. He loved it. His mind became the street.

Two years later Webb once more made a silent trip to New Orleans, partly to see how his friend was doing, partly to do with a Pontchartrain man being murdered there. Amazed from a distance at the blossoming of Bolden, careful again not to meet him. He finished the case in two days trying hard to keep out of Buddy's way for the man had died while listening to Bolden play. Two men had been standing at the bar separated by a third, a well dressed pianist. Buddy was on stage. Man A shot Man B with a gun, the pianist Ferdinand le Menthe between them leaning back just in time and disappearing before the first scream even began. Bolden seeing what happened changed to a fast tempo to keep the audience diverted which he had almost managed when the police arrived. Tiger Rag.

On his last night Webb went to hear Bolden play. Far back, by the door, he stood alone and listened for an hour. He watched him dive into the stories found in the barber shop, his whole plot of song covered with scandal and incident and change. The music was coarse and rough, immediate, dated in half an hour, was about bodies in the river, knives, lovepains, cockiness. Up there on stage he was showing all the possibilities in the middle of the story.

*

Among the cornet players that came after Bolden the one who was closest to him in volume and style was Freddie Keppard.

'When Keppard was on tour with the Creole Band, the patrons in the front rows of the theatre always got up after the first number and moved back.'

✻

He found himself on the Brewitts' lawn. She opened the door.
For a moment he looked right through her, almost forgot to
recognize her. Started shaking, from his stomach up to his
mouth, he could not hold his jaws together, he wanted to get the
words to Robin or to Jaelin clearly. Whichever one answered the
door. But it was her. Her hand wiping the hair off her face. He
saw that, he saw her hand taking her hair and moving it. His
hands were in his coat pockets. He wanted to burn the coat it
stank so much. Can I burn this coat here? That was not what he
wanted to say. Come in Buddy. That was not what he wanted to
say. His whole body started to shake. He was looking at one of
her eyes. But he couldn't hold it there because of the shake. She
started to move towards him he had to say it before she reached
him or touched him or smelled him had to say it. Help me.
Come in Buddy. Help me. Come in Buddy. Help me. He was
shaking.

Back then, Webb, there was the world of the Joseph Shaving Parlor. The brown freckles suspended in the old barber-shop mirror. This is what I saw in them. Myself and the room. Nora's plant that came as high as my shoulder. The front of the empty chair, the fake silver roller for the head to rest on. The wallpaper of Louisiana birds behind me.

The Joseph Shaving Parlor was the one cool place in the First and Liberty region. No one else within a mile could afford plants, wallpaper. The reason was good business. And the clue to good business, Joseph knew, was *ice.* Ice against the window so it fogged and suggested an exotic curtain against the heat of the street. The ice was placed on the wood shelf that sloped downwards towards the window at knee level. The ice changed shape all day before your eyes. Each morning I walked along Gravier to pick up the blocks of it and carried them into the parlor and slid them onto the slope. By 3.45 they had melted and drained through the boards into the waiting pails. At 4.00 I carried these out and threw the filmy water over the few plants to the side of the shop. The only shrubs on Liberty. The rest of the day I cut hair.

Cut hair. Above me revolving slowly is the tin-bladed fan, turning like a giant knife all day above my head. So you can never relax and stretch up. The cut hair falls to the floor and is swept by this thick almost liquid wind, which tosses it to the outskirts of the room.

I blow my nose every hour and get the hair-flecks out of it. I cough them up first thing in the morning. I spit out the black fragments onto the pavement as I walk home with Nora from work. I find pieces all over my clothes even in my underwear. I go through the evenings with the smell of shaving soap up to my elbows. It is there in my fingers as I play. The layers of soap all day long have made another skin over me. The cleanest in town. I can look at a face and tell how long ago it was shaved. I work with the vanity of others.

I see them watch their own faces for the twenty minutes they sit below me. Men hate to see themselves change. They laugh nervously. This is the power I live in. I manipulate their looks. They trust me with the cold razor at the vein under their ears. They trust me with liquid soap cupped in my palms as I pass by their eyes and massage it into their hair. Dreams of the neck. Gushing onto the floor and my white apron. The men stumbling with no more sight to the door and feeling even through their pain the waves of heat as they go through the door into the real climate of Liberty and First, leaving this ice, wallpaper and sweet smell and gracious conversation, mirrors, my slavery here.

❊

So many murders of his own body. From the slammed fingernail to the sweat draining through his hair eventually bleeding brown into the neck of his shirt. That and Nora's habit of biting the collars of his shirt made him eventually buy them collarless. There was a strange lack of care regarding his fingers, even in spite of his ultimate nightmare of having hands cut off at the wrists. His nails chewed down and indistinguishable from the callouses of his fingers. He could hardly feel his lady properly anymore. Suicide of the hands. So many varieties of murder. After his child died in his dream it was his wrist he attacked.

✳

I need a picture.
Thought you knew him.
I need it to show around.
Still – *shit* man who has pictures taken.
Bolden did, he mentioned one. Perhaps with the band.
You'll have to ask them. Ask Cornish.

But Cornish didn't have one though he said a picture had been taken, by a crip that Buddy knew who photographed whores. Bellock or something.

Bellocq.

He went down to the station and looked in the files for Bellocq's place. They knew Bellocq. He was often picked up as a suspect. Whenever a whore was chopped they brought him in and questioned him, when had he last seen her? But Bellocq never said anything and they always let him go.

Bellocq was out so he broke in and searched the place for the picture. Hundreds of pictures of whores in the cabinets. Naked and clothed, with pets or alone. Sad stuff. To Webb the only difference between these and morgue files was the others were dead. But there was nothing of Bolden. He sat down in the one comfortable armchair and eventually fell asleep. Buddy what the hell are you doing out there. You don't know what you're doing do ya. Hope Bellocq has the picture. I can't even remember what you look like too well. I'd recognize you but in my mind you're just an outline and music. Just your bright shirts that have no collars are there. Something sharp.

Something sharp was at his heart. Pressing. As he opened his eyes it pushed deeper and he jerked back into the chair. Bellocq was peering into his face out of the darkness. It must have been around two in the morning. Bellocq was still holding the camera case with his left hand and with the right hand the tripod, leaning his own chest against it so the three iron points were hard against Webb's body. Watch out man. Bellocq pressed harder.

What do you want. I've got no money.
I need a photograph.
None for sale.
Do you remember Bolden. He disappeared. I'm a friend. Trying to find him. Cornish told me you took a picture of the band.
Why don't you leave him, he's a good man.
I know I told you he was a friend. Can you take that hook off me and turn a light on in here. I'd like to talk to you.

Bellocq swung the tripod to his side in an arc. He didn't touch the lights or sit down but leaned against the tripod as if it were a crutch. You've got a nerve coming in here like this. Just like a cop.

Webb wanted Bellocq to talk. Bellocq began to walk around the room. He could hardly see the features on the small figure as it moved around him. There was something wrong with his legs and the tripod was now his cane. He had put the camera away carefully on a shelf. He walked round Webb several times expecting him to talk but the other was silent.

Cornish? He used to be in Bolden's band?

Yes.

Shitty picture.

Doesn't matter. I just need a picture with him in it.

I wouldn't want it getting around. Coughing over his tripod.

How'd you get to take it?

Long story. He knew some of the girls I used to do. He used to screw a lot and being famous they let him in. He used some of them to get stories for *The Cricket*. He paid them for that but not for the fucking. He was a kind man. He didn't treat you like a crip or anything. We'd talk a lot. It was him who got the girls to let me photograph them. They didn't like the idea at first. What was his real name?

Charlie.

Yeah. Charlie … So I took the picture but I was using old film and it's no good.

Can I see it?

Don't have a print.

Make me one will you.

Ten minutes later he bent over the sink with Bellocq, watching the paper weave in the acid tray. As if the search for his friend was finally ending. In the thick red light the little man tapped the paper with his delicate fingers so it would be uniformly printed, and while waiting cleaned the soakboard in a fussy clinical way. The two of them watching the pink rectangle as it slowly began to grow black shapes, coming fast now. Then the sudden vertical lines which rose out of the pregnant white paper which were the outlines of the six men and their formally held instruments. The dark clothes coming first, leaving the space that was the shirt. Then the faces. Frank Lewis looking slightly to the left. All serious except for the smile on Bolden. Watching their friend float into the page smiling at them, the friend who in reality had reversed the process and gone back into white, who in this bad film seemed to have already half-receded with that smile which may not have been a smile at all, which may have been his mad dignity.

That's the best I can get. Keep the print.

Bellocq dried his hand of the acid by brushing it through his hair. Habit. From the window he watched the man who had just left waving the print to dry it as he walked. He hadn't asked him to stay longer. Lot of work tonight. He turned to the sink. He made one more print of the group and shelved it and then one of just Bolden this time, taking him out of the company. Then he dropped the negative into the acid tray and watched it bleach out to grey. Goodbye. Hope he don't find you.

He brought out the new film and proceeded to make about ten prints until they were all leaning against the counter, watching him. He hadn't told the man that much about Bolden. Hadn't told him he had pictures of Nora before she and Buddy were married. He looked in the files and found a picture of Nora Bass, five years younger. He hadn't seen her since the wedding — though it was no real wedding, just a party marriage. Buddy, who had given him free haircuts at Joseph's when there was no one there to disturb their talking. Sometimes late into the night, when he wasn't playing, Bolden would pull the blinds down and turn on the light of the shop so no one could look in and would warn him always about the acid in his hair. Except for cops this person tonight had been the first one here since Buddy. Not even Nora had come. He dropped her into the acid. No more questions. Watching the mist spill into her serious face.

*

The photographs of Bellocq. HYDROCEPHALIC. 89 glass plates survive. Look at the pictures. Imagine the mis-shapen man who moved round the room, his grace as he swivelled round his tripod, the casual shot of the dresser that holds the photograph of the whore's baby that she gave away, the plaster Christ on the wall. Compare Christ's hands holding the metal spikes to the badly sewn appendix scar of the thirty year old naked woman he photographed when she returned to the room — unaware that he had already photographed her baby and her dresser and her crucifix and her rug. She now offering grotesque poses for an extra dollar and Bellocq grim and quiet saying No, just stand there against the wall there that one, no keep the petticoat on this time. One snap to quickly catch her scorning him and then waiting, waiting for minutes so she would become self-conscious towards him and the camera and her status, embarrassed at just her naked arms and neck and remembers for the first time in a long while the roads she imagined she could take as a child. And he photographed that.

What you see in his pictures is her mind jumping that far back to when she would dare to imagine the future, parading with love or money on a beautiful anonymous cloth arm. Remembering all that as she is photographed by the cripple who is hardly taller than his camera stand. Then he paid her, packed, and she had lost her grace. The picture is just a figure against a wall.

*

Some of the pictures have knife slashes across the bodies. Along the ribs. Some of them neatly decapitate the head of the naked body with scratches. These exist alongside the genuine scars mentioned before, the appendix scar and others non-surgical. They reflect each other, the eye moves back and forth. The cuts add a three-dimensional quality to each work. Not just physically, though you can almost see the depth of the knife slashes, but also because you think of Bellocq wanting to enter the photographs, to leave his trace on the bodies. When this happened, being too much of a gentleman to make them pose holding or sucking his cock, the camera on a timer, when this happened he had to romance them later with a knife. You can see that the care he took defiling the beauty he had forced in them was as precise and clean as his good hands which at night had developed the negatives, floating the sheets in the correct acids and watching the faces and breasts and pubic triangles and sofas emerge. The making and destroying coming from the same source, same lust, same surgery his brain was capable of.

Snap. Lady with dog. Lady on sofa half naked. Snap. Naked lady. Lady next to dresser. Lady at window. Snap. Lady on balcony sunlight. Holding up her arm for the shade.

＊

There were things Bellocq hadn't told him. He knew for he looked up from the street and saw the photographer in the window. He continued walking, the damp picture in his hand.

The connection between Bellocq and Buddy was strange. Buddy was a social dog, talked always to three or four people at once, a racer. He had no deceit but he roamed through conversations as if they were the countryside not listening carefully just picking up moments. And what was strong in Bellocq was the slow convolution of that brain. He was self-sufficient, complete as a perpetual motion machine. What could Buddy have to do with him?

The next day Webb knew more about Bellocq. The man worked with a team of photographers for the Foundation Company—a shipbuilding firm. Each of them worked alone and they photographed sections of boats, hulls that had been damaged and so on. Job work. Photographs to help ship designers. Bellocq, with the money he made, kept a room, ate, bought equipment, and paid whores to let him photograph them. What had Bolden seen in all this? He would have had to take time and care. Bellocq seemed paralysed by suspicions. He had let Buddy so *close*.

Webb walked around Bellocq for several days. Bellocq with his stoop, and his clothy hump, bent over the sprawled legs of his tripod. Not even bent over but an extension for he didn't have to bend at all, being 4 foot 11 inches. Bellocq with hair at the back of his head down to his shoulders, the hair at the front cut in a fringe so no wisps would spoil his vision. Bellocq sleeping on trains as he went from town to town to photograph ships, the plates wrapped carefully and riding in his large coat pockets. Something about the man who carries his profession with him always, like a wife, the way Bolden carried his mouthpiece even in exile. This is the way Bellocq moved. E.J. Bellocq in his worn, crumpled suits, but uncrumpled behind the knees.

In the no-smoker carriages his face through the glass, the superimposed picture, windows of passing houses across his mouth and eyes. Looking at the close face Webb understood the head shape, the blood vessels, the quiver to the side of the lip. Face machinery. HYDROCEPHALIC. His blood and water circulation which was of such a pattern that he knew he would be dead before forty and which made the bending of his knees difficult. To avoid the usual splay or arced walk which was the natural movement for people with this problem, he walked straight and forward. That is he went high on the toe, say of his right leg, which allowed the whole left leg enough space to move forward directly under his body like a pendulum, and so travel past the right leg. Then with the other foot. This also helped Bellocq with his height. However he did not walk that much. He never shot landscapes, mostly portraits. Webb discovered the minds of certain people through their bodies. Or through the perceptions that distinguished them. This was the stage that Bellocq's circulation and walk had reached.

＊

In the heat heart of the Brewitts' bathtub his body exploded. The armour of dirt fell apart and the nerves and muscles loosened. He sank his head under the water for almost a minute bursting up showering water all over the room. Under the surface were the magnified sounds of his body against the enamel, drip, noise of the pipe. He came up and lay there not washing just letting the dirt and the sweat melt into the heat. Stood up and felt everything drain off him. Put a towel around himself and looked out into the hall. The Brewitts were out so he walked to his room lay down on the bed and slept.

When Robin came in he was on his back asleep, bedclothes and towel fallen off. She let her hair down onto his stomach. Her hair rustled against the black curls of his belly, then her mouth dropping its tongue here and here on his flesh, he slowly awake, her tongue the flesh explorer, her cool spit, his eyes watching her kneel over the bed. Then moving her face up to his mouth his shoulder.

Stay with us.
Does this change things?
Don't you think so? Don't you think Jaelin would think so?
I wouldn't feel different if I was him.
I can't do things that way Buddy.
She put her mouth at the hollow of his neck.
Your breath feels like a fly on me, about three or four of them on me.
Talk about the music, what you want to play.
You know Bellocq had a dog I'd watch for hours. It would do

nothing, all day it would seem to be sitting around doing nothing, but it would be *busy*. I'd watch it and I could see in its face
that it was becoming aware of an itch on its ribs, then it would
get up and sit in the best position to scratch, then it would
thump away, hitting the floor more often than not.

Who was Bellocq.

He was a photographer. Pictures. That were like ... windows.
He was the first person I met who had absolutely no interest in
my music. That sounds vain don't it!

Yup. Sounds a bit vain.

Well it's true. You'd play and people would grab you and grab
you till you began to — you couldn't help it — believe you were
doing something important. And all you were doing was steal-
ing chickens, nailing things to the wall. Everytime you stopped
playing you became a lie. So I got so, with Bellocq, I didn't trust
any of that ... any more. It was just playing games. We were
furnished rooms and Bellocq was a window looking out.

Buddy —

She refused then to take off her clothes. She lay on top of him,
kissing him, talking quietly to him. He could feel the material of
her clothes all over his naked body, as if he were wearing them.
His eyes closed. It could have been a sky not a ceiling above
him.

Don't lean on that arm. Sorry. It got broken once.

She was conscious that while they spoke his fingers had been
pressing the flesh on her back as though he were plunging them
into a cornet. She was sure he was quite unaware, she was sure
his mind would not even remember. It was part of a conversation held with himself in his sleep. Even now as she lay against
his body in her red sweater and skirt. But she was wrong. He
had been improving on *Cakewalking Babies*.

Passing wet chicory that lies in the field like the sky.

❊

She. Again in the room, now in the long brown dress. Brown
and yellow, no buttons no shoes and the click of the door as she
leans against the handle, snapping shut so we are closed in with
each other. The snap of the lock is the last word we speak.
Between us the air of the room. Thick with past and the ghosts
of friends who are in other rooms. She will not move away from
the door. I am sitting on the edge of the bed looking towards the
mirror. With her hands behind her. I must get up and move
through the bodies in the air. To the first slow kiss in the cloth of
her right shoulder into the skin of her neck, blowing my nerv-
ousness against the almost cold hair for she has been walking
outside. My fingers into her hair like a comb till the hair is tight
against the unused nerves between my fingers. The taste the
pollen in her right ear, the soft circuit of her hearing wet with my
spit that I send to her like a ship and suck back and swallow. This
soft moveable limb on the side of her head.

I press myself into her belly. Her breath into my white shirt.
Her cool breath against my sweating forehead so I can feel the
bubbles evaporate. I lift her arms and leave them empty above us
and bend and pull the brown dress up to her stomach and then
up into her arms. Step back and watch her against the corner of
my room her hands above her holding the brown dress she has
lifted over her head in a ball. Turns her back to me and leans her
face now against the dress she brings down to her face. Cool
brown back. Till I attack her into the wall my cock cushioned
my hands at the front of the thigh pulling her at me we are hardly
breathing her crazy flesh twisted into corners me slipping out
from the move and our hands meet as we put it in quick *christ*
quickly back in again. In. Breathing towards the final liquid of

the body, the liquid snap, till we slow and slow and freeze in this corner. As if this is the last entrance of air into the room that was a vacuum that is now empty of the other histories.

Lying here. Kept warm by her dress and my shirt over us. I am dry and stuck to her thigh. Joined by the foam we made. By the door, and the light and the air from the hall comes under the door. Sniff it. She hasn't taken one step further into my room. Dear Robin. I remember when I shook against you. The flavour of mouth. We are animals meeting an unknown breed. The reek, the size, where to find the right softness. Against this door. Coiled into each other under the brown and white cloth. Trying to come closer than that. A step past the territory.

✣

Webb had spoken to Bellocq and discovered nothing. Had spoken to Nora, Crawley, to Cornish, had met the children — Bernadine, Charlie. Their stories were like spokes on a rimless wheel ending in air. Buddy had lived a different life with every one of them.

Webb circled, trying to understand not where Buddy was but what he was doing, quite capable of finding him but taking his time, taking almost two years, entering the character of Bolden through every voice he spoke to.

In fact Bellocq was more surprised than anyone when Buddy Bolden left. He had pushed his imagination into Buddy's brain, had passed it awkwardly across the table and entertained him, had seen him take it in return for the company, not knowing the conversations were becoming steel in his only friend. They had talked for hours moving gradually off the edge of the social world. As Bellocq lived at the edge in any case he was at ease there and as Buddy did not he moved on past him like a naïve explorer looking for footholds. Bellocq did not expect that. Or he could have easily explained the ironies. The mystic privacy one can be so proud of has no alphabet of noise or meaning to the people outside. Bellocq knew this but never bothered applying it to himself, he did not consider himself professional. Even his photographs were more on the level of fetish, a joyless and private game. Bellocq thought of this. Aware it was him who had tempted Buddy on. Buddy who had once been enviably public. And then this small almost unnecessary friendship with Bellocq. Bellocq had always thought his friend to be the patronising one, now he discovered it was himself.

*

Jaelin and Robin. Jaelin and Robin. Jaelin and Robin and Bolden. Robin and Bolden. There was this story between them. There was this deceit and then there was this honour between them. He wanted to tell that to Webb later.

The silence of Jaelin Brewitt understood them all. His minimal stepping out the door saying he would be back the next day. And he would be back not before the next day. All three of them talking for hours about things like the machinery of the piano, fishing, stars. This year, he told Bolden, there is a new star, the Wolf Ryat star. It should be the Wolf Star Bolden said it sounds better. It sounds better yes but that's not its real name. There were two people who found it. Someone called Wolf and someone called Ryat, Jaelin Brewitt said. There was that story between them. Later both of them realised they had been talking about Robin.

*

There is only one photograph that exists today of Bolden and the band. This is what you see.

Jimmy Johnson on bass   Bolden   Willy Cornish on valve trombone   Willy Warner on clarinet

Brock Mumford on guitar   Frank Lewis on clarinet

As a photograph it is not good or precise, partly because the print was found after the fire. The picture, waterlogged by climbing hoses, stayed in the possession of Willy Cornish for several years.

✳

The fire begins with Bellocq positioning his chairs all the way round the room. 17 chairs. Some of which he has borrowed. The chairs being placed this way the room, 20′ by 20′, looks like it has a balcony running all the way around it. Then he takes the taper, lights it, stands on a chair, and sets fire to the wallpaper half way up to the ceiling, walks along the path of chairs to continue the flame until he has made a full circle of the room. With great difficulty he steps down and comes back to the centre of the room. The noise is great. Planks cracking beneath the wallpaper in this heat as he stands there silent, as still as possible, trying to formally breathe in the remaining oxygen. And then breathing in the smoke. He is covered, surrounded by whiteness, it looks as if a cloud has stuffed itself into the room.

Horror of noise. And then the break when he cannot breathe calm and he vomits out smoke and throws himself against the red furniture, against the chairs on fire and he crashes finally into the wall, only there is no wall any more only a fire curtain and he disappears into and through it as if diving through a wave and emerging red on the other side. In an incredible angle. He has expected the wall to be there and his body has prepared itself and his mind has prepared itself so his shape is constricted against an imaginary force looking as if he has come up against an invisible structure in the air.

Then he falls, dissolving out of his pose. Everything has gone wrong. The wall is not there to catch or hide him. Nothing is there to clasp him into a certainty.

Under the sunlight. I am the only object between water and sky. There can be either the narrow dark focus of the eye or the crazy chaos of white, that is the eyes wide, wishing to burn them out till they are stones.

In the late afternoon I walk back along the shore to the small house and it is against me dark and shaded. Robin and her friends. I am full of the white privacy. Collisions around me. Eyes clogged with people. Yesterday Robin in the midst of an argument flicked some cream on my face. Without thinking I jumped up grabbing the first thing, a jug full of milk, and threw it all over her. She stood by the kitchen door half laughing half crying at what I had done. She stood there frozen in a hunch she took on as she saw the milk coming at her. Milk all over her soft lost beautiful brown face. I stood watching her, the lip of the jug dribbling the rest onto the floor.

Jaelin and the others in the room silent. I very gently placed the jug on the table, such a careful gesture for I wanted her to see I was empty of all the tension. Then getting one of the big towels and placing it over her wet shirt. And then like a wise coward leaving the house till late evening when they had all gone to bed. When I got back she was still in the living room, almost asleep in the armchair.

Let's go for a swim. I want to get the milk out of my hair.
I'm sorry, try and forget it.
No I won't forget it, Buddy, but I know you're sorry.
Well it's just as well it happened.

Yeah, you'll be better for a few days. But which window are you going to break next, which chair.

Don't talk Robin.
You expect to come back and for me to say nothing? With Jaelin here?
Look you're either Jaelin's wife or my wife.
I'm Jaelin's wife and I'm in love with you, there's nothing simple.
Well it should be.
How do you think he feels. He said nothing, even when you went out. Do you really expect me to say nothing.
Yes. I'm sorry, you know that.
Ok ... let's swim Buddy.

She grins. And there is my grin which is my loudest scream ever.

In the water like soft glass. We slide in slowly leaving our clothes by the large stone. Heads skimming along the surface.

As long as I don't hurt you or Jaelin.
As long as I don't hurt you or Jaelin she mimics. Then beginning to imitate loons and swimming deeper, her head sliding away from me. Below our heads all the evil dark swimming creatures are waiting to brush us into nightmare into heart attack to suck us under into the darkness into the complications. Her loon laugh. The dull star of white water under each of us. Swimming towards the sound of madness.

See Tom Pickett.
Why?
Cos he, cos Buddy cut him up.
Why Pickett?
Go ask him.
Where'll I find him?
Don't know.
Tell me, Cornish.
Try Chinatown. Opium.
Was that why?
No.
Ok I'll find him.

Then as Webb is almost out of the door, Cornish saying

Listen what he'll tell you is true. I saw his face afterwards. You won't believe it but it's true.
Thanks Willy.

After a day he found Pickett in the room of flies. The air damp and thick. He had to practically sweep the flies off his face and hair.

Don't kill one you bastard or you'll be out, in fact get out'f here, willya.
What the fuck is all this. Not the dope but this mess. The flies.
I invite them in, ok? If you don't like it get out.

Cornish wouldn't know about this or Cornish would have told him. Cornish would never come here. Webb could hardly breathe without one going in his nose or into his mouth. Early evening and the windows closed, no breeze, just Tom Pickett and open food on plates around the room.

You're the first to come here since I started. Don't tell others.
I came to talk about Buddy.
I guessed. That's what everyone wants to talk about.

Pickett lying on the floor bed while Webb stood over him.

He did this. Pickett clapped his hands near his face so the flies left it for a moment and then settled back. Five or six scars cut into his cheeks. Pickett had been one of the great hustlers, one of the most beautiful men in the District.

Did they try to arrest him, is that why he went?
No.
Why did he go?
Don't know. I don't think it was this you see, he accepted what he did, he could do this and forgive himself. Shame wasn't serious to him.
How did it happen?
The flies moved over the roads on his face.

Nine o clock. Storm rain outside. *Cricket* work finished. Don't want to think. The kid has been around with the bottle and I haven't opened it yet. I watch the wall behind me in the mirror. Alone. Want to think.

Tom Pickett walks in. Black trousers and white shirt, the thunderstorm making it stick to his skin. Got time for a good haircut, Buddy? I think he said that, something like that. I was looking at the shirt speckled with long water drops, making it brown there. I get up and give him a small towel to dry his hair, unscrew the top and hand the bottle to him. Jesus it hasn't been touched, you sick? Shrug and point to the chair for him to sit in. Tells me, as always, exactly what he wants. Beautiful people are very conservative. And puts his feet up on the sink as usual. I lay the towel over his shirt and knot it at the back of his neck. He passes the bottle to me and I put it away.

'I started talking about his mood which was so quiet you know so fuckin strange for him and he still wouldn't say much. I guess if you want to find out what happened you should find out why he was like that. After a while I threw in a few cracks about the band playing too much and he didn't say much about that either. He was cutting the hair then, he was doing what I told him. But he was ... tense, you know. I started telling him this joke about, jesus I still remember what it was, aint that something? It was about the guy who is feeling good but everybody he meets tells him he looks terrible, well anyway he just said he'd heard it, so I shut up. I could see him in the mirror all the time. Then we started talking, I wasn't pushing him now. About my pimping. We always did that. That was our one real connection. Usually it was good talk cos even though he wasn't involved with the money he was a great hustler. I don't know if you knew that.'
'Yes.'
'Well he always had a sense of humour about it. He didn't come on like a preacher. So I was going on casual about trade, he'd done the left side of my head, and then he starts shouting at me, I mean real filth. So I thought it was a game right and I joked back. I thought he was joking. I started to heckle him about Nora and me, smiling at him in the mirror all the time and then

he slips the towel round behind my neck and pulls back, pulls my neck back over the chair. He got his left arm under my chin – like this – then he opens the razor with his other hand, flicks it open in a movement like he was throwing it away and puts it in my shirt and slits it open in a couple of places. Once the shirt's open he starts shaving me up and down my front taking the hairs off. I wasn't moving or saying anything. Thought I'd keep still. Then he slices off my nipple. I don't think he meant to, was probably an accident. But that got me shouting. Then he lets go my neck and starts shaving my face very fast now small cuts now I was crying from the pain and the tears were going into the cuts, then I got my thumb into the wrist with the razor and got free, that's when I got really badly cut on the face, this one here. But I got loose and took a small chair against him.'

Right on my head. But I still have the razor and we stand looking at each other. The blood drooling off his chin onto the wet shredded shirt. He takes a quick look at himself in the mirror and the tears just rush out of his face. I am exhausted, sorry for him. Got no anger at him now. I'm finished I'm empty but I can't tell him. What the hell is wrong with me? And Pickett's face is hard waiting to come for me, looking around the room. With the chair he got me on the head with, he moves sideways to the sink. With the other hand he lifts the leather strop that has the metal hook on the end of it. He sways it out to the left and then sends it back slowly to the right and lands the hook in the centre of the mirror. $45. It falls onto the towel he has placed in the sink before. In large pieces which is what he wanted. I stand with the razor at the back of the room.

He picks up a large piece of mirror and skims it hard across the room at me. It hits the wall to the left of my shoulder but it came really fast and it scares me. I know he will slice me. He takes the next piece and jerks it at me twenty feet away and it comes straight for me. My neck. Is coming for me I'm dead I can't. Move. And then catches on a muscle of air and tilts up crashing above my head. Door opens near me. Nora. What! Stay back. And I run to him before he can get more and wave him from the sink with the razor. He holds me back with the chair in his left hand, with the right he swings the strop gets me hard on the left elbow. Broken. Just like that, no pain yet but I know it is broken. He swings the chair but it is too heavy for speed and I avoid it. Swings the strop and gets me on the knee. Numb but I can move it. Next time he swings the chair I drop the razor and wrestle it from him and push him backwards now able to keep the strop off but my left hand still dead. See Nora in another mirror. The parlor is totally empty except for the two of us and Nora shouting in a corner at the back screaming to us that we're crazy we're crazy.

Pickett's face swelled now, he cannot see too well over the puffs. Balance. His strop and my chair. I won't swing the chair. If I go off balance he will go for the head. My knee is stumbling, pain coming through. Can't feel my arm. Pickett swings and the strop tangles in the chair. I push hard hard he goes back the wood almost against his face that he doesn't want me to touch. Push again and he goes over the ice through the front window. A great creak as the thing folds over him like a spider web, he goes through, the hook of the strop pulls the chair and me frantic I won't let go and I come through too over the ice and glass and empty frame. And we are on the street.

Liberty. Grey with thick ropes of rain bouncing on the broken glass, Pickett on the pavement and now me too falling on the bad arm he kicks but there is no pain it could be metal. We scramble apart. Three feet between us, still joined by strop and chair, the rain thick and hard. His shirt which was red in the parlor now bloated and pink, the spreading cherry at his nipple. Exhausted. Silent. Battle of rain all around us. Nora screaming through the open window stop stop then climbs out herself and runs to the rack of empty coke bottles and starts throwing them between us. Smash Smash Smash. And some which don't break but roll away loud and we still don't move. Then she aims them at Pickett. Hits him on the foot and he steps back unconcerned still watching me then hits him on the side of the head and he gasps for she has hit a cut, the blood down his face. Shakes himself and drops the strop, moves backwards his hand over his eye, and then lopes down the street shouting out I tried to kill him.

So he leaves me Tom Pickett. Goes to tell my friends I have gone mad. Nora walking to me slowly to tell me I am mad. I put the chair down and I sit in it. Tired. The rain coming into my head. Nora into my head. Tom Pickett at the end of Liberty shouts at me shaking his arms, waving at me, my wife's ex-lover, ex-pimp, sit facing Tom Pickett who was beautiful. Nora strokes my arm, don't tell her I can't feel her fingers. Her anger or her pity. The rain like so many little windows going down around us.

*

Brock Mumford

'He was impossible during that time, before he went. I had a
room on the fourth floor. Room 119A, where we were yesterday.
I was avoiding people. A lot of fuss about Buddy at this time.
Band was breaking up and I was being used as the go-between,
made to decide who was being unfair *this* time *that* time. So I
just stopped going out during the day cos I'd be sure to run into
one of them. Buddy was always shouting. In any argument he'd
try to overpower you with yelling.

The last time I saw him ... The door downstairs was locked. Bell
rang, I didn't want to answer and I just lay on the mattress
smoking. Then minutes later he is tapping on the window, he
had walked along the roof. In fact it was quite easy to do though
he seemed so proud of himself I didn't tell him that. You took
anything away from him in those days and he'd either start
shouting or would go into a silent temper. He was a child really
– though most of the time, and this is important, he was right. A
lot of people wanted to knock him down at that time. The
Pickett incident had made him unpopular. Buddy didn't leave at
the peak of his glory you know. No one does. Whatever they say
no one does. If you are at the peak you don't have time to think
about stopping you just build up and up and up. It's only a few
months later when it wears off – usually before anyone else
realises it has worn off – that you start to go, if you are the kind
that goes. But he was still playing fine....

He came in through the window and sat down on the foot of the
bed I was lying on, and started talking right away. Just like you.

He sat down and he talked, god he talked, just complaining. It was about Frank Lewis or something. Someone had passed him on the street and not spoken, probably hadn't seen him. He went on and on. Then I started in saying how I was fed up too, that I didn't want to be judge any more to all these fights. I had my own problems. This was the first time I'd said this you know and I thought he might be interested but within a minute he started to show how bored he was of it. You know, just irritated, looking around the room, sniffing, clucking, as if he'd heard too much of this sort of thing. So I shut up and he went on. Then left about an hour later. By this time even I wasn't listening. Went out of the window saying they were probably watching the door.'

*

IF Nora had been with Pickett. Had really been with Pickett as he said. Had jumped off Bolden's cock and sat down half an hour later on Tom Pickett's mouth on Canal Street. Then the certainties he loathed and needed were liquid at the root.

Nora and others had needed the beautiful Pickett that much. To see her throwing bottles at Pickett in the rain to brush him away gave her a life all her own which he, Bolden, had nothing to do with. He was aware the scene on the street included a fight which did not include him. Pickett earlier so confident he knew her thoroughly, her bones, god he knew even the number of bones she had in her body.

Bolden imagined it all, the wet deceit as she hunched over him and knelt down under him or drank him in complex kisses. The trouble was you could see all the way through Pickett's mind, and so the moment he had said he had been fucking Nora Bolden believed him. In the very minute he was screening his laughter at Pickett's fantasies he believed him. Tom Pickett didn't have the brain to have fantasies.

He called Cornish. Everybody's ear. Made him drink and listen to him. LISTEN! Drinking so much the rhetoric of fury at everyone disintegrated into repetition and lies and fantasies. He dreamt up morning encounters between Nora and the whole band. Towards 4 o clock in the morning both of them were frozen with drinks in their hands, unable to move. Bolden was lying across three chairs muttering up to the ceiling.

Well I got to go Charlie.

NO! Don't go just tell me what you think of the bitch.

Well you don't know that, she's a beautiful lady Charlie.

Well what the hell – he mimicked – I'm a beautiful. Bursting into peals of laughter and sliding arms first onto the floor in order to laugh more fully. And then as Cornish had finally reached the door, Bolden on the floor saying, You know ... in spite of everything that happens, we still think a helluva lot of ourselves! And more laughter till Cornish was gone and his chest and his throat were tired from it.

He lay there crucified and drunk. Brought his left wrist to his teeth and bit hard and harder for several seconds then lost his nerve. Flopped it back outstretched. Going to sleep while feeling his vein tingling at the near chance it had of almost going free. Ecstasy before death. It marched through him while he slept.

*

For a while after that Frankie Dusen the trombonist took over some of Bolden's players. They called themselves the Eagle Band. Bunk Johnson, seventeen years old, took his place. And Bolden arrived at Lincoln Park and saw him playing there, up front centre, and just turned around and walked back through the crowd who stepped aside to let him pass. Dude Botley followed him and tells this story which some believe and which others don't believe at all.

'He steps out of the park like a rooster ignoring everybody, everything and goes up Canal. I trail him back to the barber shop. There's wood planks all over the broken glass window and he just rips one out and climbs in, steps off the ice-shelf onto the floor and paces around his arms out to the side like he's doing a cakewalk. I watch from across the street and soon he's just sitting there in one of the chairs looking into a mirror. Pretty dark there, not much light. There's light in the back of the shop and it pours in all over the floor of the shaving parlor and Bolden is restless as a dog in the chair. He shouldn't be there because he don't work there any more. This is about eight at night and I'm on the other side of the road shuffling to keep warm because it's cold and I should be dancing. I can even hear Lincoln Park over the streets.

I see him walk to the back of the parlor where the light is and he come back with a bottle and the cornet. He try first to drink but he begin crying and he put the bottle in the sink. The tears came to my eyes too. I got to thinking of all the men that dance to him and the women that idolize him as he used to strut up and down the streets. Where are they now I say to myself. Then I hear

Bolden's cornet, very quiet, and I move across the street, closer. There he is, relaxed back in a chair blowing that silver softly, just above a whisper and I see he's got the hat over the bell of the horn ... Thought I knew his blues before, and the hymns at funerals, but what he is playing now is real strange and I listen careful for he's playing something that sounds like both. I cannot make out the tune and then I catch on. He's mixing them up. He's playing the blues and the hymn sadder than the blues and then the blues sadder than the hymn. That is the first time I ever heard hymns and blues cooked up together.

There's about three of us at the window now and a strange feeling comes over me. I'm sort of scared because I know the Lord don't like that mixing the Devil's music with His music. But I still listen because the music sounds so strange and I guess I'm hypnotised. When he blows blues I can see Lincoln Park with all the sinners and whores shaking and belly rubbing and the chicks getting way down and slapping themselves on the cheeks of their behind. Then when he blows the hymn I'm in my mother's church with everybody humming. The picture kept changing with the music. It sounded like a battle between the Good Lord and the Devil. Something tells me to listen and see who wins. If Bolden stops on the hymn, the Good Lord wins. If he stops on the blues, the Devil wins.'

4763 Callarpine Street. Where the Brewitts live.

Webb arrived in front of the house at 7.30 in the morning. He slept in the parked car till 9. Till he thought they would be awake. There would be Bolden and there would be Robin Brewitt. And maybe Jaelin Brewitt. Ugly trees on the lawn, he went by the side of the house and climbed the stairs to the first floor. Knocked at the door. No reply. He went into the apartment, could see no one. He knocked on a door in the hall and looked in. Robin Brewitt asleep in bed.

What?
Sorry. I'm looking for Buddy.
He's up somewhere. Maybe the bathroom.

He nodded and closed the door quietly. Went down the hall. Knocked on the bathroom door.

Yep!

And went in and found him.

He sat on the edge of the tub where his friend was having a bath. At first Bolden was laughing. He couldn't get over it. He wanted to know how. Webb gave him all the names. Nora. Cornish. Pickett. Bellocq. Bellocq! Yes Bellocq's dead now, killed himself in a fire. What do you mean killed himself in a fire? He started a fire round himself.

They could hear Robin through the wall in the kitchen. And that's Robin Brewitt? Bolden nodded into the water. And Jaelin Brewitt comes and goes. Bolden nodded. And your music. Haven't played a note for nearly two years. Thought about it? A little. You could train in the Pontchartrain cabin. I don't want to go back, Webb. You want to go back Buddy, you want to go back. Webb on the edge of the enamel talking on and on, why did you do all this Buddy, why don't you come back, what good are you here, you're doing nothing, you're wasting, you're —

Till Bolden went underwater away from the noise, opening his eyes to look up through the liquid blur at the vague figure of Webb gazing down at him gesturing, till he could hardly breathe, his heart furious wanting to leap out and Bolden still holding himself down not wishing to come up gripping the side of the tub with his elbows to stop him to stop him o god jesus leave me alone his eyes staring up aching, if Webb reaches down and tries to pull him up he will never come up he knows that, air! his heart empty overpowers his arms and he breaks up showering Webb, gulping everything he possibly can in.

Breathing hard, yes ok Webb ok ok ok. Hunched and breathing hard looking at the taps while Webb on his right tried to brush the wetness off his suit beginning to talk again and Buddy hardly listening to him, listening past him to Robin and the morning kitchen noises that he knew he would lose soon. Webb was releasing the rabbit he had to run after, because the cage was open now and there would always be the worthless taste of worthless rabbit when he finished.

Robin hit the door. Is he staying for breakfast, Buddy?

Silence. Like a huge, wild animal going round and round the bathroom. Just before he closed his eyes he saw her standing, years ago, holding two glasses of orange juice. Yes. He's staying for breakfast.

Train Song

Passing wet chicory that lies in the fields like the sky.

Passing wet chicory that lies in the fields like the sky.

Passing wet chicory lies

like the sky,

like the sky like the sky like the sky

passing wet sky chicory

passing wet sky chicory lies

*

When he left we sat with the remains of breakfast. The two of us knew at precisely the same time. When Webb was here with all his stories about me and Nora, about Gravier and Phillip Street, the wall of wire barrier glass went up between me and Robin. And when he left we were still here, still, not moving or speaking, in order to ignore the barrier glass. God he talked and sucked me through his brain so I was puppet and she was a landscape so alien and so newly foreign that I was ridiculous here. He could reach me this far away, could tilt me upside down till he was directing me like wayward traffic back home.

Here. Where I am anonymous and alone in a white room with no history and no parading. So I can make something unknown in the shape of this room. Where I am King of Corners. And Robin who drained my body of its fame when I wanted to find that fear of certainties I had when I first began to play, back when I was unaware that reputation made the room narrower and narrower, till you were crawling on your own back, full of your own echoes, till you were drinking in only your own recycled air. And Robin and Jaelin brought me back to that open fright with the unimportant objects.

He came here and placed my past and future on this table like a road.

This last night we tear into each other, as if to wound, as if to find the key to everything before morning. The heat incredible, we go out and buy a bag of ice, crack it small in our mouths and spit it onto each other's bodies, her tongue slipping it under the skin of my cock me pushing it into her hot red fold. But we are already travelling on the morning bus tragic. Like the ice melting in the heat of us. Dripping wet on our chest and breasts we approach each other private and selfish and cold in the September heatwave. We give each other a performance, the wound of ice. We imagine audiences and the audiences are each other again and again in the future. 'We'll go crazy without each other you know.' The one lonely sentence, her voice against my hand as if to stop her saying it. We follow each other into the future, as if now, at the last moment we try to memorize the face a movement we will never want to forget. As if everything in the world is the history of ice.

Morning. Water has dried tight on my chest and stomach. I wake up crucified on my back in this bed. There is no need to turn. Blue cloud light in the room. There is no need to turn my head for Robin is gone. Already my body has unbuckled out into the space she left. Bending my left hand over my body and then crashing it down as hard as I can on her half of the bed. And it bounces against the sheet. And as I knew, she's gone.

He went to Webb's cottage on Lake Pontchartrain on a bus. His hands dead on his thighs and his body leaning against the window, the wet weather outside and this woman on his right in the dark dress who smiled as she took the seat, scribbling something on paper that she is hunched over. Her legs twitching now and then as if her brain is there.

He tried to take in the smell of her. The taste of her mouth in the next hotel room they passed along the road. He knew the shape of her body. As she would stand in front of him, the small breasts cold in the room, the heart of her. He went with her for months into the relationship, awkward first fights, the slow true intimacy, disintegration after they exchanged personalities and mannerisms, the growing tired of each other's speed. All this before they went one more mile — as she wrote on and he thought on into the heart and mind of her, not even glancing at her as she got off alone at Milneburg for she was an old friendship now and he could guess the expressions, her face for all the moments. Accidental lust on the bus carrying her new into his dead brain so even months later, years later, pieces of her body and character returned. What he wanted was cruel, pure relationship.

✳

Got here this afternoon. Walk around remembering you from the objects I find. Books, pictures on the wall, nail holes in the ceiling where you've hung your magnets, seed packets on the shelf above the sink – the skin you shed when you finish your vacations. Re-smell your character.

Not enough blankets here, Webb, and it's cold. Found an old hunting jacket. I sleep against its cloth full of hunter sweat, aroma of cartridges. I went to bed as soon as I arrived and am awake now after midnight. Scratch of suicide at the side of my brain.

Our friendship had nothing accidental did it. Even at the start you set out to breed me into something better. Which you did. You removed my immaturity at just the right time and saved me a lot of energy and I sped away happy and alone in a new town away from you, and now you produce a leash, curl the leather round and round your fist, and walk straight into me. And you pull me home. Like those breeders of bull terriers in the Storyville pits who can prove anything of their creatures, can prove how determined their dogs are by setting them onto an animal and while the jaws clamp shut they can slice the dog's body in half knowing the jaws will still not let go.

All the time I hate what I am doing and want the other. In a room full of people I get frantic in their air and their shout and when I'm alone I sniff the smell of their bodies against my clothes. I'm scared Webb, don't think I will find one person who will be the right audience. All you've done is cut me in half, pointing me here. Where I don't want these answers.

*

I go outside and piss in your garden. When I get back onto the porch the dog is licking at the waterbowl trying to avoid the yellow leaves floating in it. With all the time in the world he moves his body into perfect manoeuvering position so he can get his tongue between the yellow and reach the invisible water. His tongue curls and captures it. He enters the house with me, the last mouthful pouring out of his jaws. Once inside he rushes around so the cold night air caught in his hair falls off his body.

The dog follows me wherever I go now. If I am slow walking he runs ahead and waits looking back. If I piss outside he comes to the area, investigates, and pisses in the same place, then scratches earth over it. Once he even came over to the wet spot and covered it up without doing anything himself. Today I watched him carefully and returned the compliment. After he had leaked against a tree I went over, pissed there too, and scuffed my shoe against the earth so he would know I had his system. He was delighted. He barked loud and ran round me excited for a few minutes. He must have felt there had been a major breakthrough in the spread of hound civilization and who knows he may be right. How about that Webb, a little sensa humour to show you.

*

Tired. Sulphur. When you're tired, the body thick, you smell sulphur. Bellocq did that. Always. Two in the morning three in the morning against the window of the street restaurant he'd rub a match on the counter and sniff it in. Ammonia ripping into his brain. Jarring out the tiredness. And then back to his conversations about everything except music, the friend who scorned all the giraffes of fame. I said, You don't think much of this music do you? Not yet, he said. Him watching me waste myself and wanting me to step back into my body as if into a black room and stumble against whatever was there. Unable then to be watched by others. More and more I said he was wrong and more and more I spent whole evenings with him.

The small tired man sitting on the restaurant bench or the barber chair never saying his scorn but just his boredom at what I was trying to do. And me in my vanity accusing him at first of being tone deaf! He was offering me black empty spaces. Revived himself with matches once an hour, wanted me to become blind to everything but the owned pain in myself. And so yes there is a need to come home Webb with that casual desert blackness.

Whatever I say about him you will interpret as the working of an enemy and what I loved Webb were the possibilities in his silence. He was just *there*, like a small noon shadow. Dear Bellocq, he was so short he was the only one who could stretch up in the barber shop and not get hit by the fan. He didn't rely on anything. He trusted nothing, not even me. I can't summarize him for you, he tempted me out of the world of audiences where I had tried to catch everything thrown at me. He offered mole comfort, mole deceit. Come with me Webb I want to show you something, no come with me I want to *show* you something. You come too. Put your hand through this window.

You didn't know me for instance when I was with the Brewitts, without Nora. Three of us played cards all evening and then Jaelin would stay downstairs and Robin and I would go to bed, me with his wife. He would be alone and silent downstairs. Then eventually he would sit down and press into the teeth of the piano. His practice reached us upstairs, each note a finger on our flesh. The unheard tap of his calloused fingers and the muscle reaching into the machine and plucking the note, the sound travelling up the stairs and through the door, touching her on the shoulder. The music was his dance in the auditorium of enemies. But I loved him downstairs as much as she loved the man downstairs. God, to sit down and play, to tip it over into music! To remove the anger and stuff it down the piano fresh every night. He would wait for half an hour as dogs wait for masters to go to sleep before they move into the garbage of the kitchen. The music was so uncertain it was heartbreaking and beautiful. Coming through the walls. The lost anger at her or me or himself. Bullets of music delivered onto the bed we were on.

Everybody's love in the air.

*

For two hours I've been listening to a radio I discovered in your cupboard of clothes. Under old pyjamas. You throw nothing away. Nightshirts, belts, some coins, and sitting in the midst of them all the radio. The wiring old. I had to push it into a socket, nervous, ready to jump back. But the metal slid in and connected and the buzz that gradually warmed up came from a long distance away into this room.

For two hours I've been listening. People talking about a crisis I missed that has been questionably solved. Couldn't understand it. They were not being clear, they were not giving me the history of it all, and I didn't know who was supposed to be the hero of the story. So I've been hunched up on the bed listening to voices, and then later on Robichaux's band came on.

John Robichaux! Playing his waltzes. And I hate to admit it but I enjoyed listening to the clear forms. Every note part of the large curve, so carefully patterned that for the first time I appreciated the possibilities of a mind moving ahead of the instruments in time and waiting with pleasure for them to catch up. I had never been aware of that mechanistic pleasure, that trust.

Did you ever meet Robichaux? I never did. I loathed everything he stood for. He dominated his audiences. He put his emotions into patterns which a listening crowd had to follow. My enjoyment tonight was because I wanted something that was just a utensil. Had a bath, washed my hair, and wanted the same sort of clarity and open-headedness. But I don't believe it for a second. You may perhaps but it is not real. When I played parades we would be going down Canal Street and at each intersection people would hear just the fragment I happened to be playing and it would fade as I went further down Canal. They would not be there to hear the end of phrases, Robichaux's arches. I wanted them to be able to come in where they pleased and leave when they pleased and somehow hear the germs of the start and all the possible endings at whatever point in the music that I had reached *then*. Like your radio without the beginnings or endings. The right ending is an open door you can't see too far out of. It can mean exactly the opposite of what you are thinking.

An abrupt station shut down. Voices said goodnight several times and the orchestra playing in the background collapsed into buzz again, a few yards away from me in your bedroom.

*

My fathers were those who put their bodies over barbed wire. For me. To slide over into the region of hell. Through their sacrifice they seduced me into the game. They showed me their autographed pictures and they told me about their women and they told me of the even bigger names all over the country. My fathers failing. Dead before they hit the wire.

There were three of them. Mutt Carey, Bud Scott, Happy Galloway. Don't know what they taught me for the real teachers never teach you craft. In a way the stringmen taught me more than Carey and his trumpet. Or Manuel Hall who lived with my mother in his last years and hid his trumpet in the cupboard and never touched it when anyone was around. It was good when you listened to Galloway bubble underneath the others and come through slipping and squealing into neighbourhoods that had nothing to do with the thumper tunes coming out of the rest. His guitar much closer to the voice than the other instruments. It swallowed moods and kept three or four going at the same time which was what I wanted. While the trumpet was usually the steel shoe you couldn't get out of because you led the music and there was an end you had to get to. But Galloway's guitar was everything else that needn't have been there but was put there by him, worshipful, brushing against strange weeds. So Galloway taught me not craft but to play a mood of sound I would recognize and remember. Every note new and raw and chance. Never repeated. His mouth also moving and trying to mime the sound but never able to for his brain had lost control of his fingers.

In mirror to him Carey's trumpet was a technician — which

went gliding down river and missed all the shit on the bottom. His single strong notes pelting out into the crowds, able to reach any note that he wished for but always reaching for the purest. He was orange juice he was exercise, you understand. He was a wheel on a king's coach. So that was technique.

Drawn to opposites, even in music we play. In terror we lean in the direction that is most unlike us. Running past your own character into pain. So they died eventually maybe suiciding for me or failing because of a lost lip who knows. Climbing over them still with me in the sense I have tried all my life to avoid becoming them. Galloway in his lovely suits playing his bubble music under shit bands — so precise off the platform so completely alone in his music he wished to persuade no one into his style, and forgotten by everyone who saw him. A dull person off stage. And he'd lie and make himself even duller to keep people away from him. Who remembers him? Even I forgot him for so long until now. Till you ask these questions. He slipped back into my memory as accidentally as a smell. All my ancestors died drunk or lost but Galloway continued to play till he died and when he failed to show up was replaced. Had a stroke during breakfast at sixty-five and was forgotten. So immaculate when he fell against his chair even the undertaker could not improve on him.

So I suppose I crawled over him.

And Scott who kept losing his career to neurotic women.

And Carey who lost his hard lip too young and slept himself to death with the money he made. Floating around the bars to hear good music, having a good time and then died. Attracted to opposites again, to the crazy music he chose to die listening to, bitching at new experiments, the chaos, but refusing to leave the table and go down the street and listen to captive jazz he himself had generated. A dog turned wild in pasture.

He was my father too in the way he visited me and Nora at the end. Not liking my music damning my music but moving in for a month or so before he died, trying to make passes at my pregnant wife by getting up early in the morning when she got up and I was still in bed or in a bath. Perhaps even hurt by me not bothering to be jealous because I took my time getting downstairs. We would fight about everything. Even the way I held the cornet or shouted out in the middle of numbers. And still he'd come every night and listen and be irritated and enjoy himself tremendously. And then one morning in the room he shared with my first kid he stayed in bed and shook and shook, unable to move anything except for those massive shoulders. Arms struck dead. Get the sweat out of my eyes get the sweat out of my eyes fuckit I'm going to die, and then dead in the middle of a shake. I leaned over his wet body and put an ear to his mouth wanting more than anything then to hear his air, the swirl of air in him but there was none. His open mouth was an old sea-shell. I turned my head slowly and kissed the soft old lips. I then went over the barbed wire attached to his heart.

The black dog I picked up a few miles south of your place has snuggled against me. No woman for over a month has been as close to my body as he is tonight. I got up to make a drink and returned to find him sitting on the sofa where my warmth had been. Dogs on your furniture, Webb. He is quite dirty and I'll bathe him tomorrow. Just dusty for the most part but there are pointed knots of mud under the belly – probably collected by going through wet evening grass. He is not used to living in houses I can tell, although he immediately climbs onto furniture. He is not used to softness and every few hours throughout the night he moves from chair to sofa and finally finds the floor to be the answer. I came back into the room and he looked up expecting me to reclaim my place. I've snuggled against his warmth. Have just bent over and notice his claws are torn.

The heat has fallen back into the lake and left air empty. You can smell trees across the bay. I notice tonight someone has moved in over there. One square of light came on at twilight and changed the gentle shape of the tree line, making the horizon invisible. Was annoyed till I admitted to myself I had been lonely and this comforted me. The rest of the world is in that cabin room behind the light. Everyone I know lives there and when the light is on it means they are there. Before, every animal noise made me suspect people were arriving. Rain would sound like tires on the gravel. I would run out my heart furious and thumping only to be surrounded by a sudden downpour. I would stand shaking, getting completely wet for over a minute. Then come in, strip all my clothes off and crouch in front of the fire.

Webb I'm tired of the bitching tonight. The loneliness. I really wanted to talk about my friends. Nora and Pickett and me. Robin and Jaelin and me. I saw an awful thing among us. And that was passion could twist around and choose someone else just like that. That in one minute I knew Nora loved me and then, whatever I did from a certain day on, her eyes were hunting Pickett's mouth and silence. There was nothing I could do. Pickett could just stand there and he had her heart balanced on his tongue. And then with Robin and me — Jaelin stood there far more intelligent and sensitive and loving and pained and it did nothing to her, she had swerved to me like a mad compass, aimed east east east, ignoring everything else. I knew I was hurting him and I screwed her and at times humiliated her in front of him, everything. We had no order among ourselves. I wouldn't let myself control the world of my music because I had no power over anything else that went on around me, in or around my body. My wife loved Pickett, I think. I loved Robin Brewitt, I think. We were all exhausted.

*

From the very first night I was lost from Robin.

The cold in my head and the cough woke me. Walking round your house making hot water grapefruit and Raleigh Rye drinks. That was the first night that was four weeks ago. And now too my starving avoiding food. Drunk and hungry in the middle of the night in this place crowded with your furniture and my muttering voice. Robin lost. Who slid out of my heart. Who has become anonymous as cloud. I wake up with erections in memory of Robin. Every morning. Till she has begun to blur into Nora and everybody else.

What do you want to know about me Webb? I'm alone. I desire every woman I remember. Everything is clear here and still I feel my brain has walked away and is watching me. I feel I hover over the objects in this house, over every person in my memory — like those painted saints in my mother's church who seem to always have six or seven inches between them and the ground. Posing as humans. I give myself immaculate twenty minute shaves in the morning. Tap some lotion on me and cook a fabulous breakfast. Only meal of the day. So I move from the morning's energy into the later hours of alcohol and hunger and thickness and tiredness. Trying to overcome this awful and stupid clarity.

After breakfast I train. Mouth and lips and breathing. Exercises. Scales. For hours till my jaws and stomach ache. But no music or tune that I long to play. Just the notes, can you understand that? It is like perfecting 100 yard starts and stopping after the third yard and back again to the beginning. In this way the notes jerk forward in a spurt.

Alone now three weeks, four weeks? Since you came to Shell Beach and found me. Come back you said. All that music. I don't want that way any more. There is this other path I beat the bushes away from with exercise so I can walk down it knowing it is just stone. I've got more theoretical with no one to talk to. All suicides all acts of privacy are romantic you say and you may be right, as I sit here at 4.45 in the middle of the night, sky beginning to emerge blue through darkness into the long big windows of this house. Here's an early morning ant crossing the table ...

Three days ago Crawley visited me. I made you promise not to say where I was but you sent him here anyway. He came in his car, interrupted my thinking and it has taken me a couple of days to get back. With a girl fan he came in his car and played some music he's working on, while she was silent and touching in the corner. I could have done without his music, I could have done with her body. Music quite good but I could have finished it for him, it was a memory. I wanted to start a fight. I was watching her while he was playing and I wanted the horn in her skirt. I wanted her to sit with her skirt on my cock like a bandage. My old friend's girl. What have you brought me back to Webb?

The day got better with the opening of bottles and all of us were vaguely drunk by the time they left and me rambling on as they were about to leave, leaning against the driver's window apologizing, explaining what I wanted to do. About the empty room when I get up and put metal onto my mouth and hit the squawk at just the right note to equal the tone of the room and that's all you do. Pushing all that into the car as if we had a minute to live as if we hadn't talked rubbish all day.

You learn to play like that and no band will play with you, he says.

I know. I want to get this conversation right and I'm drunk and I'm making it difficult.

Shouting into his car, standing on the pebble driveway, the sweat on me which is really alcohol gone through me and bubbled out. I said I didn't want to be a remnant, a ladder for others. So Crawley knowing, nodding. I ask him about Nora, tells me that she's living with Cornish. And I've always thought of her as sad Nora, and my children, all this soft private sentiment I forgot to explode, the kids who grow up without me quite capable, while I sit out this drunk sweat, thinking along a stone path. I am terrified now of their lost love. I walk around the car put my head in to kiss Crawley's girl whose name I cannot even remember, my tongue in her cool mouth, her cool circling answer that gives me an erection against the car door, and round the car again and look at Crawley and thank him for the bottles he brought. His brain with me for two days afterwards.

Alcohol sweat on these pages. I am tired Webb. I put my forehead down to rest on the booklet on the table. I don't want to get up. When I lift my head up the paper will be damp, the ink spread. The lake and sky will be light blue. Not even her cloud.

Interviewer: To get back to Buddy Bolden —
John Joseph: Uh-huh.
Interviewer: He lost his mind, I heard.
John Joseph: He lost his mind, yeah, he died in the bug house.
Interviewer: Yes, that's what I heard.
John Joseph: That's right, he died out there.

Travelling again. Home to nightmare.

The earth brown. Rubbing my brain against the cold window of the bus. I was sent travelling my career on fire and so cruise home again now.

Come. We must go deeper with no justice and no jokes.

All my life I seemed to be a parcel on a bus. I am the famous fucker. I am the famous barber. I am the famous cornet player. Read the labels. The labels are coming home.

＊

Charlie Dablayes Brass Band

The Diamond Stone Brass Band

The Old Columbis Brass Band

Frank Welch Brass Band

The Old Excelsior Brass Band

The Algiers and Pacific Brass Band

Kid Allen's Father's Brass Band

George McCullon's Brass Band

And so many no name street bands
… according to Bunk Johnson.

*

So in the public parade he went mad into silence.

This was April 1907, after his return, after staying with his wife and Cornish, saying *sure* he would play again, had met and spoken to Henry Allen and would play with his band in the weekend parade. Henry Allen snr's Brass Band.

The music begins two blocks north of Marais Street at noon. All of Henry Allen's Band including Bolden turn onto Iberville and move south. After about half a mile his music separates from the band, and though the whole procession is still together Bolden is now stained untouchable, powerful, an 8 ball in their midst. Till he is spinning round and round, crazy, at the Liberty-Iberville connect.

By eleven that morning people who had heard Bolden was going to play had already arrived, stretching from Villiere down to Franklin. Brought lunches and tin flasks and children. Some bands broke engagements, some returned from towns over sixty miles away. All they knew was that Bolden had come back looking good. He was in town four days before the parade.

On Tuesday night he had come in by bus from Webb's place. A small bag held his cornet and a few clothes. He had no money so he walked the twenty-five blocks to 2527 First Street where he had last lived. He tapped on the door and Cornish opened it. Frozen. Only two months earlier Cornish had moved in with Bolden's wife. Almost fainting. Buddy put his arm around Cornish's waist and hugged him, then walked past him into the living room and fell back in a chair exhausted. He was very tired

from the walk, the tension of possibly running into other people. The city too hot after living at the lake. Sitting he let the bag
slide from his fingers.

Where's Nora?
She's gone out for food. She'll be back soon.
Good.
Jesus, Buddy. Nearly two years, we all thought –
No that's ok Willy, I don't care.

He was sitting there not looking at Cornish but up at the ceiling,
his hands outstretched his elbows resting on the arms of the
chair. A long silence. Cornish thought this is the longest time
I've ever been with him without talking. You never saw Bolden
thinking, lots of people said that. He thought by being in motion. Always talk, snatches of song, as if his brain had been a
fishbowl.

Let me go look for her.
Ok Willy.

He sat on the steps waiting for Nora. As she came up to him he
asked her to sit with him.

I haven't got time, Willy, let's go in.

Dragging her down next to him and putting an arm around her
so he was as close to her as possible.

Listen, he's back. Buddy's back.

Her whole body relaxing.

> Where is he now?
> Inside. In his chair.
> Come on let's go in.
> Do you want to go alone?
> No let's go in, both of us Willy.

She had never been a shadow. Before they had married, while she worked at Lula White's, she had been popular and public. She had played Bolden's games, knew his extra sex. When they were alone together it was still a crowded room. She had been fascinated with him. She brought short cuts to his arguments and at times cleared away the chaos he embraced. She walked inside now with Willy holding her hand. She saw him sitting down, head back, but eyes glancing at the door as it opened. Bolden not moving at all and she, with groceries under her arm, not moving either.

⁙

The three of them entered a calm long conversation. They talked in the style of a married couple joined by a third person who was catalyst and audience. And Buddy watched her large hip as she lay on the floor of the room, the hill of cloth, and he came into her dress like a burglar without words in the family style they had formed years ago, with some humour now but not too much humour. Sitting against her body and unbuttoning the layers of cloth to see the dark gold body and bending down to smell her skin and touching with his face through the flesh the buried bones in her chest. Writhed his face against her small breasts. Her skirt still on, her blouse not taken off but apart and his rough cheek scraping her skin, not going near her face which he had explored so much from across the room, earlier. When Cornish had still been there.

They lay there without words. Moving all over her chest and arms and armpits and stomach as if placing mines on her with his mouth and then leaned up and looked at her body glistening with his own spit. Together closing up her skirt, slipping the buttons back into their holes so she was dressed again. Not going further because it was friendship that had to be guarded, that they both wanted. The diamond had to love the earth it passed along the way, every speck and angle of the other's history, for the diamond had been earth too.

*

So Cornish lives with her. Willy, who wanted to be left alone but became the doctor for everyone's troubles. Sweet William. Nothing ambitious on the valve trombone but being the only one able to read music he brought us new music from the north that we perverted cheerfully into our own style. Willy, straight as a good fence all his life, none to match his virtue. Since I've been home I watch him and Nora in the room. The air around them is empty so I see them clear. They are for me no longer in a landscape, they are not in the street they walk over, the chairs disappear under them. They are complete and exact and final. No longer the every-second change I saw before but like statues of personality now. Through my one-dimensional eye. I left the other in the other home, Robin flying off with it into her cloud. So I see Willy and Nora as they are and always will be and I hunger to be as still as them, my brain tying me up in this chair. Locked inside the frame, boiled down in love and anger into dynamo that cannot move except on itself.

I had wanted to be the reservoir where engines and people drank, blood sperm music pouring out and getting hooked in someone's ear. The way flowers were still and fed bees. And we took from the others too this way, music that was nothing till Mumford and Lewis and Johnson and I joined Cornish and made him furious because we wouldn't let him even finish the song once before we changed it to our blood. Cornish who played the same note the same way every time who was our frame our diving board that we leapt off, the one we sacrificed so he could remain the overlooked metronome.

So because Willy was the first I saw when I got back I pretended to look through his eyes, the eyes Nora wanted me to have. So everyone said I'd changed. Floating in the ether. They want nothing to have changed. Unaware of the hook floating around. A couple of years ago I would have sat down and thought out precisely why it was Cornish who moved in with her why it was Cornish she accepted would have thought it out as I set the very type it was translated into. *The Cricket*. But I shat those theories out completely.

There had been such sense in it. This afternoon I spend going over four months worth of *The Cricket*. Nora had every issue in the bedroom cupboard and while she was out and the kids stayed around embarrassed to come too close and disturb me (probably Nora's advice — why doesn't she still hate me? Why do people forget hate so easily?) I read through 4 months worth of them from 1902. September October November December. Nothing about the change of weather anywhere but there were the details of the children and the ladies changing hands like coins or a cigarette travelling at mouth level around the room. All those contests for bodies with children in the background like furniture.

I read through it all. Into the past. Every intricacy I had laboured over. How much sex, how much money, how much pain, how much sweat, how much happiness. Stories of riverboat sex when whites pitched whores overboard to swim back to shore carrying their loads of sperm, dog love, meeting Nora, marriage, the competition to surprise each other with lovers. *Cricket* was my diary too, and everybody else's. Players picking up women after playing society groups, the easy power of the straight quadrilles. All those names during the four months moving now like waves through a window. So I suppose that was the crazyness I left. Cricket noises and Cricket music for that is what we are when watched by people bigger than us.

Then later Webb came and pulled me out of the other depth and there was nothing on me. I was glinting and sharp and cold from the lack of light. I had turned into metal at my mouth.

Second Day

By breakfast the next day Cornish still hadn't returned so Buddy walked the kids to school, he was quiet but got them talking. Soon however numerous friends of his kids joined them on the walk. They were the ones who began conversations now and though the dialogue took him in there were codes and levels he was not allowed to be a part of as the group bounced loud and laughing towards the embankment. Hands in his pockets he strolled alongside them, his two kids dutifully sticking with him.

Hey Jace — this is my dad.
Oh yeah? Hi.

As they hit the embankment he impressed all by answering three complex dirty jokes in a row. Riddles he had heard years ago. Dug into his mind for further jokes he knew would be appreciated and which spread like rabies the minute they got into school.

Stanley, what's that note you're passing — bring it here.
It's a question Miss.
Bring it here.

Handed to her silently, creeping back to his desk.

What's this ... What's the diffrence, difference is spelled wrong Stanley, what's the difference between a nun praying and a young girl taking a bath? ... Well Stanley, stand up, what's the difference?

Rather not say Miss.

Come on come on, you know I like riddles.

You sure Miss.

Of course. As long as it's clever.

Oh it's clever Miss, Charles' dad told it.

Go on then.

Well. One has hope in her soul and one has soap in her —
STANNNNNLLLLLEEEEEEEEEEEEEEEEEEEEEEY!

By the time they reached the school Bolden was a hero. He raked his memory for every pun and story. Finding out who the teachers were he revived old rumours about them. He suggested various tricks to drive a teacher out of the room, various ways to get a high temperature and avoid classes. As they approached the school the kids began to run from him fast into the yard to be the first there with the hoard of new jokes. He combed his fingers through his son's hair, kissed his daughter, and walked back. He avoided the areas he knew along Canal. Eventually he cut into Chinatown and asked about Pickett. No one knew of him, no one.

A guy with scars on his cheek, right cheek.

He was directed to the Fly King.

He was home then four days before the street parade. The first evening with Nora and Willy Cornish. The first night with Nora. The second morning with the children, late morning (perhaps) with Pickett. Pickett should not have been that difficult to find. He had at one time been a power. His room was on Wilson. Chinatown however was a terrible maze.

But Bellocq had been there photographing the opium dens, each scene packed with bunks that had been removed from sleeping compartments of abandoned trains, his pictures full of grey light which must have been the yellow shining off the lacquered woodwork. Cocoons of yellow silence and outside the streets which were intricate and convoluted as veins in a hand. Two squares between Basin and Rampart and between Tulane and Canal through which Bellocq had moved, never lost, and taken his photographs.

So Bolden had probably been there before, with him.

Parading around alone. I walk to Gravier north past Chinatown and then cut back to Canal, near Claiborne. Along the water. The mist has flopped over onto the embankment like a sailing ship. Others walking disappear into the white and the mattress whores have moved off their usual perch to avoid being hidden by the mist. They walk up and down, keep moving like sentries to show they haven't got broken ankles. The ones that have stand still and try to hide it. A quarter a fuck. The mist has helped them tonight. Normally now the pimps are out hunting the mattress whores with sticks. When they catch them they break their ankles. Women riddled with the pox, remnants of the good life good time ever loving Storyville who, when they are finished there, steal their mattress and with a sling hang it on their backs and learn to run fast when they see paraders with a stick. Otherwise they drop the mattress down and take men right there on the dark pavements, the fat, poor, the sadists who use them to piss in as often as not because the disease they carry has punched their cunts inside out, taking anything so long as the quarter is in their hands.

So their lives have become simplified by seeing all the rich and healthy as dangerous, and they automatically run when they see them. The ones who can run. The others drop their mattress and lie down and flick their skirts up, spread their legs with socks on, these ones who don't care who it is that's coming. If it's a pimp he's gonna check her for a swollen foot so she can't slip back to Storyville. These broken women so ruined they use the cock in them as a scratcher. The women who are called gypsy feet. And the ones not caught yet carrying their disease like coy girls into and among the rocks and the shallows of the river where the pimps in good shoes won't follow. But those who are lame thrusting their fat foot at you, immune from the swinging stick that has already got them swelled and fixed in a deformed walk, gypsy foot gypsy foot.

For them it is a good night. Standing like grey angels on the edge of the mist, stepping backward and invisible when they hear a fast rich walk. Like mine. God even mine, me with a brain no better than their sad bodies, so sad they cannot afford to feel sorrow towards themselves, only fear. And my brain atrophied and soaked in the music I avoid, like milk travelling over the border into cheese. All that masturbation of practice each morning and refusing to play and these gypsy feet wanting to play you but drummed back onto the edge of the water by your rich sticks and your rich laws. Bellocq showed me pictures he took of them long ago, he was crying, he burned the results. Thighs swollen and hair fallen out and eyelids stiff and dead and those who had clawed through to the bones on their hips. Rales. Dear small dead Bellocq. My brain tonight has a mattress strapped to its back.

Even with me they step into the white. They step away from me and watch me pass, hands in my coat pockets from the cold. Their bodies murdered and my brain suicided. Dormant brain bulb gone crazy. The fetus we have avoided in us, that career, flushed out like a coffin into the toilets and into the harbour. The sum of the city. To eventually crash into the boats going out to sea. Walk over the driblets of manure of the gypsy foot whores, they don't eat much, what they can beg or take from the half-formed weeds along the embankment. Salt in their pockets for energy. There is no horror in the way they run their lives.

Came home with just his face laughing at the jokes. Refused to enlarge stories as he used to. They noticed that, those who had known him before.

There were younger ones around now who had heard of him who wished to revive him but he easily turned conversations back onto them and their lives. Perhaps they were the eventual catalysts. Maybe. As it was they gradually heard of him being back and brought bottles of Raleigh Rye to leave on the doorstep, and Bolden just smiling and bringing the bottles in to Nora in the kitchen but not touching the cap, not drinking, not wishing to, now. Just talked gently and slowly with Nora, watching Nora get meals as he sat in the kitchen as if she was a sister he had never met since they were kids. And sleeping a lot.

On the third day old friends came in, shy, then too loud as they entertained him with the sort of stories he loved to hear, stories he could predict now. He sat back with just his face laughing at the jokes. It was like walking out of a desert into a park of schoolchildren. No one mentioned Pickett until he did and then there was silence and Bolden laughing out loud for the first time. And everyone in the room watching Buddy, waiting for any expression to move across his face, even a nerve.

No those visitors hadn't bothered him much. He liked to think of Pickett running down the road holding his scars like a dying dog. He still remembered the metal of the strop touch the mirror and both of them watching it fall, like a chopped sheet into the basin. No it was to Nora that the pain came, the people in the house watching him. Buddy's mind slipped through them. She saw him there and saw he wasn't even in the room, the only real muscle was his wink at her as some story was ending and she could see him getting his fucking grin ready. She wanted to collect everybody and kick them out of the room. Screw his serenity. Buddy knowing what he owed her and hadn't given her.

That night Willy Cornish went out again. Buddy was walking and came in at ten. It was after midnight when he wanted to go to sleep. One of the kids cried and without thinking he went into their room and lay on the edge of the bed his arm around the child. Act from the past. Charles jnr probably too old to want this. The cry was part of his sleep and he wasn't awake, just nuzzled into his father's body. Did Cornish do this?

He fell asleep, his fingers against his son's spine under the shirt. About an hour later he woke up and realised where he was. Took his jacket off and lay back in the old flannel shirt Nora had found for him to wear. Then heard Nora's 'Buddy' close to him and saw her sitting on Bernadine's bed, leaning forward. He got up and moved towards her.

You ok?
She shook her head slowly.
Is Willy out there?
No. He won't come back tonight Buddy.
Must be late.
1.30. I don't know.
He put his hand to the side of her face against her ear.
Please talk, Buddy.

He helps her off the bed and walks with her into the living room, his red arm loose over her shoulder.

She is on the sofa, he is in the chair. She lifts her knees up so her chin is resting on them. She is gazing at the floor between them.

Still love you Buddy ... I'm sorry. Not like it was before because I don't know you anymore but I care about you, love you as if you weren't my husband. I'm just sorry about this ... I feel sorrier for William. Jesus that red shirt on you, you look fabulous, you look really well aint that crazy that's all I can think of ... you look like a favourite shirt I lost.

They start giggling and soon are laughing across at each other.

Stop it Bolden, snorting back her laugh, we should be having a serious conversation.

His mouth on his wife's left ear. Feeling his wife's hands between their bodies unbuttoning the front of her dress. His own hands waiting and then into the cave of his wife's open dress, round to touch her back and sliding back to cover the breasts of his wife. His fingers recognizing the nipples, the appendix scar. He lies back with his head in her lap. Looking up at her. The home of his wife's mouth coming down on him.

*

With Bellocq on the street.

Walking with him to introduce him to whores. But I don't want you there when I do it. Ok Ok. Cos otherwise let's just go home. He was scared of Bolden's presence for the first time. He staggered at Buddy's side with the camera. You're sure? I just don't want you hanging round, just introduce me and say what I want. I know Bellocq I know. Yeah. Well you know what I mean.

He pulled Bellocq up the steps, the camera strapped across his back like a bow. He had seen it so often on his friend that whenever he thought of him his body took on an outline which included the camera and the tripod. It was part of his bone structure. A metal animal grown into his back. He pulled him up the steps, through the doors. You've got to get up these stairs man. Bellocq already exhausted began to climb them with Bolden. Man what a wallpaper, giggling as he climbed along the carpet runners that would take him to the paradise of bodies. He brushed his free hand against the blue embossed wallpaper. He saw a photograph of a girl sitting against it, alone on the stairs, no one around. Maybe a plate of food. The wallpaper would come out light grey. Up one flight, then another, his legs starting to ache. This ain't no joke is it man? No. One more and we're there.

Let me go in and talk to her first. Her? I thought I was going to meet them all. Yeah yeah but I just want to talk to Nora first ok.

He left Bellocq outside resting on the top steps carefully removing the camera off its sling. Listen I've got this friend who wants photographs of the girls. Same price as a fuck you know that Buddy. Ok, but I want to tell you about him first. Willya call the others in I don't want to say this more than once. He wasn't sure how to explain it. He wasn't even sure himself what Bellocq wanted to do. Listen this guy's a ship photographer – a burst of laughter – and just for himself, nothing commercial, he wants to get pictures of the girls. I don't know how he wants you to be for the picture, he just wants them. Nothing commercial ok. He's not weird or anything is he? No, he's a little bent in the body, something wrong with his legs. No one wanted to. Please, look I promised him, listen I even said no price this time, it's a favour, see he did a few things for me. You gonna be around Charlie? No I can't he doesn't want me to. Two of them left the room saying they were going back to sleep. Listen he's got a good job, he really does photograph ships and things, stuff for brochures. He's very good, he's not a cop, the idea coming into his mind that second as a possible fear of theirs. He's a kind man. Nobody wanted Bellocq and more went away. I'll give you a free knock anytime Charlie but not this. They went then and Nora shrugged sorry across the room. It's morning Charlie, they were all up late last night at Anderson's. All I could do was get them here. And they were watching the two of you arrive. He looked like something squashed or run over by a horse from up here.

Listen Nora you have to do this for me. Let him take some pictures of you. Just this once to show the others it's ok, I promise you it'll be ok. She had moved into the kitchenette and was looking for a match to light the gas. He came over, dug one out of his pocket and lit the row of hissing till they popped up blue, something invisible finding a form. He let her fill the kettle and put it on. Then he put himself against her back and leaned his face into her shoulder. His nose against the shoulder strap of her dress. Come out with me into the hall and meet him. Give him some of this tea. He's a harmless man. He put his head up a bit and watched the blue flame gripping the kettle. He was exhausted. He couldn't hustle for others, he didn't know the needs of others. He was fond of them and wanted them happy and was willing to make them happy and was willing to hear their problems but no more. He didn't know how people like Bellocq thought. He didn't know how to put the pieces of him together. He was too shy to ask Bellocq *why* he wanted these pictures or what kind they would be. Three floors up on North Basin Street he was nuzzling this lady. That's all he knew. His mind went blank against the flesh next to him.

What's he got on you? Nothing. He separated himself from her, picked up a knife and tapped against the small window of the kitchen, looking out. It was cold out, there was steam over the river. He had tried to get Bellocq to wear a coat when he had picked him up, but they had gone on, Bellocq cold and so trying to walk fast. He placed his palm against the glass and left the surface of his nerve pattern there. Rubbed it out. Turning he walked past her quickly through the door into the hall. As he was opening the door she said OK very fast. He turned and saw her leaning in the kitchen doorway with a cup in her hand. Then he opened the door to the stairs.

And then running down the stairs fast, almost crying, down two flights before he saw the figure in the main hall standing against the wallpaper looking up at him — the face pale and embarrassed. He must have heard them laughing in there, must have sat there for ten minutes and taken more than five minutes to walk down.

Yes or no, whatever it is, I'm not walking those stairs again.

I'll carry you up then. So decide. Shouting as he ran down.

Bugger you fuck you shit those voices carry you know.

I know. But it's ok. Nora will do it. He stood on the first stair looking at Bellocq, at Bellocq's sweating face. It's alright, she said she's gonna do it ok? She'll pose.

I heard them Buddy I *heard* them.

They didn't understand man, it's ok now come on. Come on.

Then he lifted the thin body of his friend and carried him up the three flights of stairs. Going slowly for he did not want to damage the camera or hurt the thin bones in the light body he was carrying. Still, he was tired and shaking and exhausted when he put him down on the top step.

She didn't speak to him about Bellocq. Not till this last night. He asked her about Bellocq and she told him what Webb had said, that Bellocq was dead. Died in a fire. This was about an hour after she found him sleeping in his red shirt with the children.

I only did that for you cos you know why?

No. Why?

Because you didn't know what to say, you didn't know how to argue me into it.

She threw in a taunt.

Tom Pickett could have hustled anyone to do what you asked in a minute.

No shit.

The last remark had flowed under him, he was thinking about Bellocq, crushed and scurrying to the front door that morning while the others had watched from the windows.

You didn't feel sorry for him?

I hated him Buddy.

But *why*? He was so harmless. He was just a lonely man. You know he even talked to his photographs he was that lonely. Why do you hate him? You never even saw his pictures, they were beautiful. They were gentle. Why do you hate him?

She turned to face him.

Look at you. Look at what he did to you. Look at you. Look at you. Goddamit. Look at you.

The next morning his daughter saying, I had this awful dream. Mum made some food for us out of onions and hair and orange peels and we hated it and she said eat up it's good for you.

Coming down Iberville, warm past Marais Street, then she moves free of the crowd and travels at our speed between us and the crowd. My new red undershirt and my new white shiny shirt bright under the cornet. New shoes. Back in town.

Warning slide over to her and hug and squawk over her and shoulder her into the crowd. *Roar.* Between Marais and Liberty I just hit notes every 15 seconds or so Henry Allen worrying me eyeing me about keeping the number going and every now and then my note like a bird flying out of the shit and hanging loud and long. *Roar.* Crisscross Iberville like a spaniel strutting in front of the band and as I hit each boundary of crowd — *roar.* Parade of ego, cakewalk, strut, every fucking dance and walk I remember working up through the air to get it ready for the note sharp as a rat mouth under Allen's soft march tune.

But where the bitch came from I don't know. She moves out to us again, moving along with us, gravy bones. Thin body and long hair and joined by someone half bald and a beautiful dancer too so I turn from the bank of people and aim at them and pull them on a string to me, the roar at the back of my ears. Watch them through the sun balancing off the horn till they see what is happening and I speed Henry Allen's number till most of them drop off and just march behind, the notes more often now, every five secor ls. Eyes going dark in the hot bleached street. Get there before it ends, but it's nearly over nearly over, approach Liberty. She and he keeping up like storm weeds crashing against each other. Squawk beats going descant high the hair spinning against his face and back to the whip of her head. She's

Robin, Nora, Crawley's girl's tongue.

March is slowing to a stop and as it floats down slow to a thump I take off and wail long notes jerking the squawk into the end of them to form a new beat, have to trust them all as I close my eyes, know the others are silent, throw the notes off the walls of people, the iron lines, so pure and sure bringing the howl down to the floor and letting in the light and the girl is alone now mirroring my throat in her lonely tired dance, the street silent but for us her tired breath I can hear for she's near me as I go round and round in the centre of the Liberty-Iberville connect. Then silent. For something's fallen in my body and I can't hear the music as I play it. The notes more often now. She hitting each note with her body before it is even out so I know what I do through her. God this is what I wanted to play for, if no one else I always guessed there would be this, this mirror somewhere, she closer to me now and her eyes over mine tough and young and come from god knows where. Never seen her before but testing me taunting me to make it past her, old hero, old ego tested against one as cold and pure as himself, this tall bitch breasts jumping loose under the light shirt she wears that's wet from energy and me fixing them with the aimed horn tracing up to the throat. Half dead, can't take more, hardly hit the squawks anymore but when I do my body flicks at them as if I'm the dancer till the music is out there. *Roar.* It comes back now, so I can hear only in waves now and then, god the heat in the air, she is sliding round and round her thin hands snake up through her hair and do their own dance and she is seven foot tall with them and I aim at them to bring them down to my body and the music gets caught in her hair, this is what I wanted, always, loss of privacy in the playing, leaving the stage, the rectangle of band on the street, this hearer who can throw me in the direction and the speed she wishes like an angry shadow. Fluff and groan in my throat, roll of a bad throat as we begin to slow. Tired. She still covers my eyes with hers and sees it slow and allows the slowness for me her breasts black under the wet light shirt, sound and pain in my heart sure as death. All my body moves to my throat and I speed again and she speeds tired again, a river of sweat to her waist her head and hair back bending back to me, all the desire in me is cramp and hard, cocaine on my cock, eternal, for my heart is at my throat hitting slow pure notes into the shimmy dance of victory, hair toss victory, a local strut, eyes meeting sweat down her chin arms out in final exercise pain, take on the last long squawk and letting it cough and climb to spear her all those watching like a javelin through the brain and down into the stomach, feel the blood that is real move up bringing fresh energy in its suitcase, it comes up flooding past my heart in a mad parade, it is coming through my teeth, it is into the cornet, god can't stop god can't stop it can't stop the air the red force coming up can't remove it from my mouth, no intake gasp, so deep blooming it up god I can't choke it the music still pouring in a roughness I've never hit, watch it *listen* it *listen* it, can't see I CAN'T SEE. Air floating through the blood to the girl red hitting the blind spot I can feel others turning, the silence of the crowd, can't see

Willy Cornish catching him as he fell outward, covering him, seeing the red on the white shirt thinking it is torn and the red undershirt is showing and then lifting the horn sees the blood spill out from it as he finally lifts the metal from the hard kiss of the mouth.

What I wanted.

Born 1876 ? A Baptist. Name is not French or Spanish.

He was never legally married.
Nora Bass had a daughter, Bernadine, by Bolden.
Hattie ———————— had a son, Charles Bolden jnr, by him.

Hattie lived near Louis Jones' neighbourhood. (Jones born Sept 12, 1872, a close friend of Bolden).

Manuel Hall lived with Bolden's mum and taught him cornet. Hall played by note.

Other teachers were possibly Happy Galloway, Bud Scott, and Mutt Carey.

Mother lived on 2328 Phillip Street.

Bolden worked at Joseph's Shaving Parlor.

He played at Masonic Hall on Perdido and Rampart, at the Globe downtown on St Peter and Claude, and Jackson Hall.

April 1907   Bolden (thirty-one years old) goes mad while playing with Henry Allen's Brass Band.

He lived at 2527 First Street.

Taken to House of Detention, 'House of D', near Chinatown. Broken blood vessels in neck operated on.

June 1, 1907   Judge T.C.W. Ellis of the Civil District Court issued a writ of interdiction to Civil Sheriffs H.B. McMurray and T. Jones to bring Bolden to the insane asylum, just north of Baton Rouge. A 100 mile train ride on the edge of the Mississippi.

Taken to pre-Civil War asylum buildings by horse and wagon for the last fifteen miles.

Admitted to asylum June 5, 1907. 'Dementia Praecox. Paranoid Type.'

East Louisiana State Hospital, Jackson, Louisiana 70748.

Died 1931.

❖

The sunlight comes down flat and white on Gravier, on Phillip Street, on Liberty. The paint on the wood walls has crumpled under the heat, you can brush it off with your hand. This is where he lived seventy years ago, where his mind on the pinnacle of something collapsed, was arrested, put in the House of D, shipped by train to Baton Rouge, then taken north by cart to a hospital for the insane. The career beginning in this street of the paintless wood to where he gave his brains away. The place of his music is totally silent. There is so little noise that I easily hear the click of my camera as I take fast bad photographs into the sun aiming at the barber shop he probably worked in.

The street is fifteen yards wide. I walk around watched by three men further up the street under a Coca Cola sign. They have not heard of him here. Though one has for a man came a year ago with a tape recorder and offered him money for information, saying Bolden was a 'famous musician'. The sun has bleached everything. The Coke signs almost pink. The paint that remains the colour of old grass. 2 pm daylight. There is the complete absence of him – even his skeleton has softened, disintegrated, and been lost in the water under the earth of Holtz Cemetery. When he went mad he was the same age as I am now.

The photograph moves and becomes a mirror. When I read he stood in front of mirrors and attacked himself, there was the shock of memory. For I had done that. Stood, and with a razorblade cut into cheeks and forehead, shaved hair. Defiling people we did not wish to be. He comes into the room, kneels in front of the mirror and sits on his heels. Begins to talk. Holds a blade between his first two fingers and cuts high onto the cheek. At first not having the nerve to cut deeper than scratches. When they eventually go deeper they look innocent because of the thinness of the blade. This way he brings his enemy to the surface of the skin. The slow trace of the razor almost painless because the brain's hate is so much. And then turning to his hair which he removes in lumps.

The thin sheaf of information. Why did my senses stop at you? There was the sentence, 'Buddy Bolden who became a legend when he went berserk in a parade ...' What was there in that, before I knew your nation your colour your age, that made me push my arm forward and spill it through the front of your mirror and clutch myself? Did not want to pose in your accent but think in your brain and body, and you like a weatherbird arcing round in the middle of your life to exact opposites and burning your brains out so that from June 5, 1907 till 1931 you were dropped into amber in the East Louisiana State Hospital. Some saying you went mad trying to play the devil's music and hymns at the same time, and Armstrong telling historians that you went mad by playing too hard and too often drunk too wild too crazy. The excesses cloud up the page. There was the climax of the parade and then you removed yourself from the 20th century game of fame, the rest of your life a desert of facts. Cut them open and spread them out like garbage.

They used to bury dogs on First Street. Holes in the road made that easy. While in Holtz Cemetery the high water table conveniently takes the flesh away in six months and others may be buried in the same place within a year. So for us you are here, not in Holtz with the plastic flowers in Maxwell House coffee tins or four inch plastic Christs stuck in cement or crosses so full of names they seem like ledgers of a whole generation.

The sun has swallowed the colour of the street. It is a black and white photograph, part of a history book.

*

House of Detention. Three needles lost in me. Move me over and in the fat of my hip they slip in the killer of the pain. And open my eyes and the nurse is there, her smiling rope face and rope neck. Awake Bolden? Nod. Look at each other and then she is off. No conversation. I can't sing through my neck. Every three hours I walk to the door for then she will come in carrying the needle in her sweet palm like an egg. Roll and dip and lose it in the bum. Go to sleep now. Nod. 7 am. I am given a bath. I sit up and she comes over unbuttons me at the back, pulls it over my shoulders. You see I can't use my arms. She pours the cold soap onto my chest and rubs hard across the nipple and hair. Smiling. Good? Nod. And then pulling my white dress further down and more cold soap in the circle of my crotch. As she leans against me there is the red morning on her face. Everyone who touches me must be beautiful.

Bolden's hand going up into the air
in agony.
His brain driving it up into the
path of the circling fan.

This last movement happens forever and ever in his memory

Interview with Lionel Gremillion at East Louisiana State Hospital.

Bolden's mother, Alice Bolden, wrote twice a month. Called him 'Charles'.

He died November 4, 1931 at the hospital.

His sister Cora Bolden Reed was notified when he died.

Geddes and Moss, Undertaking and Embalming Co. of New Orleans, took care of the body. Nov. 4, his sister sent telegram — 'PLEASE DELIVER REMAINS OF CHARLES BOLDEN TO J.D. GILBERT UNDERTAKING CO. BATON ROUGE TO BE PREPARED FOR BURIAL'.

Buried in unmarked grave at Holtz Cemetery after being brought from the Asylum through Slaughter, Vachery, Sunshine, back to New Orleans.

Reverend Sede Bradham, Protestant Chaplain at the Hospital, worked at the hospital in his youth. He had seen Bolden play in N.O. 'Hyperactive individual. When he blew his horn he kept walking around on the bandstand ... had tendency to go to a window to play to outside world.'

Dr Robard: 'He acted as a patient barber. Didn't publically proclaim himself as a jazz originator.'

Wasn't much communication between whites and blacks and so much information is difficult to find out. No black employees here.

Gremillion theorizing: 'He was a big frog, he had a following. Had a strong ego, his behaviour was eventually too erratic. Extroverted and then a pendulum swing to withdrawal. Suspiciousness. Paranoia. Possibly "an endocrine problem".'

Patients sometimes brought up by boat along Mississippi to St Francisville.

Typical Day:

Rose early. Summer 4.30 am. Winter 5 am.
If a person was in a closed ward he was returned there after breakfast.
Bolden was probably in open and closed wards. If open ward he was
given duties. His assigned duty was to cut hair. Lunch 11.30.

Recreational facilities: volleyball, softball. Dances twice a week.

Cold packs for the overactive. Place was noisy.

4.30 – 5 pm. Supper.
In bed by 8 pm.

Some isolation blocks. 'Untidy Wards' for old patients who couldn't
control bowels. 'Closed Wards' for escapees, deteriorated
psychopaths. 'Violent Wards' for unmanageables.

＊

Am walked out of the House of D and put on a north train by
H.B. McMurray and Jones. Outside a river can't get out of the
rain. Passing wet chicory that lies in the field like the sky. The
trees rocks brown ditches falling off the side as we go past. The
train in a wet coat. Blue necklace holding my hands together.
Going to a pound. My beautiful snout is hit by McMurray for
laughing at the rain. My neck is warm is wet and it feels like a
shoe stuck in there. T. Jones next to me, the window next to me,
McMurray in front of me. His hand came up like magic and got
me for laughing as loud as the train. Strangers sitting next to the
horizon. Wet in my neck. Teasel in my neck. You see I had an
operation on my throat. You see I had a salvation on my throat.
A goat put his horn in me and pulled. Let me tell ya, it went
winter in there and then it fell apart like mud and they stuck it
together with needles and they held me together with clothes.

Am going to the pound. McMurray and Jones holding my
hands. Breastless woman in blue pyjamas will be there. Muscles
in the arms will be there. Tie. Belt. Boots.

They make me love them. They are the arms looking after me.
On the second day they came into my room and took off all my
clothes and bent me over a table and broke my anus. They gave
me a white dress. They know I am a barber and I didn't tell them
I'm a barber. Won't. Can't. Boot in my throat, the food has to
climb over it and then go down and meet with all their pals in the
stomach. Hi sausage. Hi cabbage. Did yuh see that fuckin boot.
Yeah I nearly turned round 'n went back on the plate. Who is
this guy we're in anyway?

The sun comes every day. Save the string. I put it in lines across the room. I watched him creep his body through the grilled windows. When the sun touches the first string wham it is 10 o clock. It is 2 o clock when he touches the second. When the shadow of the first string is under the second string it is 4 o clock. When it reaches the door it will soon be dark.

Laughing in my room. As you try to explain me I will spit you, yellow, out of my mouth.

✢

In the summer they were up each day at 4.30. They washed and moved among themselves for an hour and then by 6 they filed in and took forks off the table, ate. At 7 they held the forks above their heads so they could be collected. Meals silent in the mornings and noisy at lunch. That was their only character.

On Monday mornings he cut hair for them. He was never much of a barber but the forms said he was one. So he shaved and cut in a corner of the dining room with an old man who was better than him but who died two years after Bolden arrived. He was asked to train someone new, he didn't react, but a couple of them learned by watching him. One of the patients, Bertram Lord, came every week and tried to get the scissors off him and each day as the shift ended Bolden held up his arm with the scissors and razor and they were collected and locked away.

Lord, who knew of Bolden's reputation, was always trying to persuade him to escape. The noise of Lord so constant it was like wallpaper and Bolden could blot himself against it without even having to turn away the meaning of the words, using the noise as a bark around himself.

Till the day of the escape he had never seen Lord do anything more than talk, so that when Lord saw his chance and without hesitation jumped, Bolden was for the first time impressed. Though not having listened to the shadow who had been using his silence as an oracle, he had no idea what Bertram Lord was up to.

Everyone was jumping on the tables to look. It had begun with Antrim who was getting his weekly needle so he would detour his fits, forget to express them. He had begun to argue with Dr Vernon, some ridiculous reason. The doctors had alternated arms with Antrim who was certain that this week it was supposed to be his left arm and Vernon had begun rolling up the right sleeve. Vernon had put down the needle to calm the furious patient when Lord passing the open room had leapt in scooped up the needle and thrown his other arm around the doctor's neck.

He dragged the doctor down the hall with the needle held inches from the eye, he forced the guards to open the doors. The two guards hesitated and Lord, nervous, tightened his fist round the glass syringe so much the glass tubing was crushed. Still he held onto the needle, gently now, like a dart, and the guard seeing it not even waver from the doctor's eye, opened the doors. Lord then called out for others to follow, he called out Bolden's name again and again but his friend was now sitting on the barber chair watching it all, waiting for the next customer who was somewhere on a table leaping up and down. So Lord went out. He was away for two days loose in the town of Jackson and then was brought back and beaten. He had a limp, said he almost broke his ankle going over a fence. But that wasn't the cause. In his time out he had separated precisely the bottom circle from a bottle of Coca-Cola. He had ground it into a sharp disc and he kept it hidden under the instep of his left foot. He had it there in his tight shoe. He had his weapon and he'd come back for Bolden.

Selections from *A Brief History of East Louisiana State Hospital*
by Lionel Gremillion

Hospital was opened in the year 1848. 87 patients transferred from the Charity Hospital in New Orleans.

1853. A minority report from a special committee stated patients in direst poverty and lacked sufficient food. Dinner consisted of a tin cupful of soup, meat about the size of a hen's egg, and a small piece of bread. Breakfast was bread and coffee. Supper was bread and tea. Women patients not properly clothed. Cells had no heat.

1857. J.D. Barkdull made Superintendent. First time the institution was under the control of a medical man.

1861. Hospital included thirty-six girls, mostly under twelve years of age.

1855. Dysentery swept crowded wards and it was stated that 'the diseased patients fell like grass before the scythe.'

1859. Some of the causes of insanity were listed as: ill health, loss of property, excessive use of tobacco, dissipation, domestic affliction, epilepsy, masturbation, home-sickness, injury of the head. The largest category was 'unknown'.

1864. Supt. Barkdull was shot and killed in the streets of Jackson by a yankee soldier.

During the Civil War it was almost impossible to get food or water supplies to the hospital.

1882. Introduction of occupational therapy. Patients assigned to make moss mattresses.

1902-1904.	1397 patients. 490 were black. The Hospital purchased iron lavatories and toilets. A 20' fountain was constructed on the lawn in front of the female building and stocked with gold and silver fish.
1910-1912.	1496 patients. The death rate was 11% per year. A moving picture machine was purchased for the amusement of the patients. A hearse was made at the hospital. A motor car was purchased to convey seven to eight passengers to and from the station.
1912-1914.	The Hospital Band played every afternoon on the hospital lawn from 2 pm till 4 pm. 1650 patients. Wasserman tests were taken for the first time from 1924 onwards. Bolden given test. Negative.
1924 onwards.	Dr T. J. Perkins made Superintendent. 2100 patients.
	1931. Buddy Bolden dies.
	1948. The Medcraft Shock Machine was purchased. Still in use today.

*

Willy Cornish

Then everyone was becoming famous. Jazz was now history. The library people were doing recordings and interviews. They didn't care who it was that talked they just got them talking. Like Amacker, Woodman, Porteous, anybody. They didn't ask what happened to his wife, his children, and no one knew about the Brewitts. All I had of Buddy was the picture here. Webb gave that to me. I never wanted to talk about him.

Didn't know what to say. He had all that talent and wisdom he stole and learnt from people and then smashed it, smashed it like ice coming onto the highway off a truck. What did he see with all that? What good is all that if we can't learn or know? I think Bellocq corrupted him with that mean silence so Buddy went and Bellocq stayed here shocked by his going and Buddy gone for two years then coming back and gentle with us till he had to go ... crazy in front of children and Nora and everyone.

Then jesus that, *jesus* that hospital and the company there which he slid through like a pin in the blood. With all his friends outside like they were on a grandstand watching him and when they began to realize he would never come out then all the people he hardly knew, all the fools, beginning to talk about him ...

*

In the room there is the air
                    and there is the corner
and there is the corner and there is the corner
and there is the corner.

If you don't shake, don't get no cake.

Bella Davenport married Willy Cornish in 1922.
Cornish 6′ 3″ – 297 lbs.
'When I married him he was healthy as a pig'

Cornish had his first stroke on Rampart and
Julien while playing. Arm paralysed.
Bella questioned about those Cornish
had played with –

'He and Buddy were just like that'
&
'All of them mostly lost their minds'

*

When protests began over guard rapes, bad plumbing, labour, lack of heat, the patients organised a strike. This did nothing. They then cut their tendons. Not Bolden, who sublime took rapes from what he thought were ladies in blue pyjamas. And work as his duty to the sun. Bertram Lord walked down the hall and slid the coke bottom under each door to the patients. They took the sharpened glass, cut their tendon, and passed it back. Bolden who saw the foreign weapon enter his room left his window where he was waiting for morning, heard the whispered order on the other side of the wood, peered at it, touched it with his foot and pushed it back slowly to Lord who eventually covered 28 doors.

In the morning men were found heels bandaged in their nightshirts and naked when the doors opened. The sun fell on Bolden's waiting face, he smiled, walked out spry and was almost alone at breakfast where he met his visitor again, this morning as a brilliant lush bar of light that lay in an oblong stretch nearly touching his plate. So bright it showed him the textures of the old fork-scarred table. He almost didn't want to eat today. He kept putting down his spoon in the tin bowl and placing his hand over the warm yellow of his friend and his friend magically managed to put his light over Bolden's hand simultaneously, so that it was kept warm. Later in the day he moved following his path. He washed his face in the travelling spokes of light, bathing and drying his mouth nose forehead and cheeks in the heat. All day. Blessed by the visit of his friend.

❖

Webb in town years later, 1924, talked to Bella Davenport, Willy Cornish's wife then, Bella Cornish then, in the corner of a loud party. Talking and eventually sliding onto the subject of Bolden. Webb said he had been an old friend of his. This was the year Tom Pickett was shot and killed on Poydras Street. The party was on Napoleon, everybody crowded into two floors and stairs and on the steps outside. Webb back here after many years, standing beside Bella Davenport and not too interested until she said she was Bella Cornish rattling her white china pearls, and Webb looking at her and recognizing they were all growing old, the lines deep and thin and dark on their faces.

So it must have been over Pickett's death that they got onto Bolden. He and Willy were just like that, she said. Sitting with her on the bend of the stairs he said that Buddy's death had surprised him, he'd always expected Bolden to jump out of his silence when he got bored, shit I was sure he was just hiding you know hiding from us all and that he'd put on a red shirt and come back, yeah, Nora's letter surprised me alright, I'd been going in every few months to visit though he said nothing and then she writes not to bother anymore because Buddy died, how things get to you huh. Looking up then because the rattling of pearls had stopped and Bella Cornish was not moving. *But he's not dead*, whispered. He's still at the hospital, the state hospital, he's still there, heaven. When did Nora write you?

Eight years ago.

He's still there, eighteen years now. Willy saw him a year ago. He does nothing, nothing at all. Never speaks, goes around touching things. One of the doctors told Willy who had to pretend to be his brother. Willy sat in the hall all day to talk to the doctor and Willy just getting over his stroke, heaven, they told him Buddy touches things, there are about twenty things he will touch and he goes from one to the next, that's all. Won't talk, do you know they even have a band but he has nothing to do with it, was cutting hair but that stopped a while back. Now this touching thing. Willy nursing his soft hand goes all the way to the hospital and stays in places like Vachery overnight to get there and Buddy don't say a thing to him. And he and Willy were just like *that*. Don't even pretend to know who he is. The doctor says that most of the patients don't know who their visitors are but they pretend they do so they have company but Buddy won't. Willy walked round with him while he went about, like doing a tour or inspection of the place, the taps on the bath, the door frame, benches, things like that.

She talked on and on repeating herself and her descriptions, going back to things she'd mentioned and retelling them in greater detail for Webb. Who could not talk just strained his body and head against the wall behind him as if he were trying to escape the smell of her words as if the air from her talking came into his mouth and filled it puffed it up with poison so the brain was put to sleep and he could do nothing with it only react in his flesh. She talked on not knowing he had brought Buddy home, instead, seeing the effect of her words, she whispered on bending nearer to him like a lover surrounded by the loud moving of the party against them telling him again and again *he touches things,* like taps first the hot water one and then the cold, which was not true for there were only cold water taps at the East Louisiana State Hospital, but she continued to describe – as fascinated by that strange act as if it was the luxurious itch under a scab. While he arched away his body stiff and hard trying to break through the wall every nerve on the outside as if Bella's mouth was crawling over him, and his unknown flesh had taken over, and crashed fast down the stairs stepping on hands and glasses almost running over the bodies on the crowded stairs smiling and excusing himself out loud I gotta throw up 'scuse me 'scuse me, but knowing there was nothing to come up at all.

Bella watched the flapping body on its way down the stairs and noticing now the damp mark on her right where his sweat had in those few minutes gone through his skin his shirt his java jacket and driven itself onto the wall.

＊

Frank Amacker Interviews. Transcript Digest. Tulane Library. Also present William Russell, Allan and Sandra Jaffe, Richard B. Allen.

Reel I. June 21, 1965

Plays (almost immediately) old rag with wide arm spread. He cannot remember the name of the rag. He discusses his prowess in playing with hands far apart. He'd like to bet that nobody can beat him at that. He now says that he made up the last song.

He then talks about this wide arm spread being the natural way of playing the piano. He then talks about the public acceptance of pianists who can't play as well as he. Asked how old he is, he replies that he was seventy-five years old on March 22, 1965. AJ asks for 'My Josephine'. FA plays 'Moonlight on the Ganges'. He says he and Jelly Roll Morton hung around the BIG 25 together. He was playing there on the night of the Billy Phillips killing at the 101 Ranch. Gyp the Blood killed Billy Phillips right in front of his own bar at 4.20 am on Easter Monday and then went across the street and killed Harry Parker. The salary was $1.00 to $1.50 a night, plus tips. Money was worth a lot more then. He explains the meaning of 'Lagniappe'. He explains the term 'can rusher'.
END OF REEL ONE

Reel 2.

There follows a discussion of waltzes. He says he can play 'The Sweetheart of Sigma Chi' and 'Schubert's Serenade'. WR asks for the latter, and FA plays 'Drigo's Serenade'. He became quite wealthy he says, but lost all of it. At one time he owned five places. At one time he had a bar and a restaurant. The welfare department has all the records of his former wealth.

END OF REEL TWO.

Reel 3.

He plays 'The House Got Ready'. He plays the Amos 'n' Andy theme song. Next a slow rag with wide arm spread again. (Some of his rags have obscene titles. He would not give them in front of SJ or RBA.) FA says he used to play thousands of rags. He doesn't know how to play Jelly Roll Morton's 'The Pearls'. Then he plays and sings 'I'll see you in my dreams'. Asks for a little shot.

END OF REEL THREE

Reel 1. Digest Retype. July 1, 1960

Frank Amacker born in New Orleans, March 22, 1890. He began playing music when he was sixteen, playing in the District. His first instrument was piano, he later took up guitar. RBA asks if FA ever played (Tony Jackson's) 'The Naked Dance'. FA says he played many naked dances, but the piano player was just supposed to play, keeping his eyes on the keyboard and not looking at the whores. FA then says that it is God's will that he looks as young as he is today, that it must be that he is being saved for something special by God.

He says he knows he could play most of the things he hears on television, that all he needs is a chance.

END OF REEL ONE.

Reel 2.

[No interesting information]

Reel 3.

FA says a really good singer, like Perry Como, should be able to take the song he now plays, which he composed, and make a hit out of it. FA then says that A.J. Piron heard him playing the song, years ago, and told him it was the most beautiful song he ever heard, that he would write it down and make him famous. The name of the song is 'All the boys got to love me, that's all'. Johnny St Cyr wrote the words and Piron wrote it down. All the people in the District praised the song. It was the most unusual blues you ever heard. It was so sad. It's about a man who takes his girl to a dance. The girl starts flirting with another man. He doesn't start a fight, but takes her home and sings this song. (FA plays and sings). The lyrics are full of regret, he tells her he is sorry he met her, among other things, and finishes by saying he is going to take her into the woods and shoot her. He kills her but he still loves her and he tells the undertaker to be very careful with his beautiful baby.

END OF REEL THREE

Reel 4.

FA answers questions about good trumpet players by saying that Buddy Bolden was the loudest. Freddy Keppard was a master, and so was Manuel Perez, but the most masterful master of all was James McNeil who was college trained. In contrast Bolden played this 'old lowdown music'. FA says he remembers 'Funky Butt' (also known as 'Buddy Bolden's Blues'). FA does not remember August Russell. He says Johnny Delpit was a good violinist. He says Frank DeLandry (or D.Landry or Delandro?) was the greatest guitarist he ever heard. He says all the guitars were buried when DeLandry died.

END OF REEL FOUR

＊

T. Jones

'The train he was on – sorry, let me start again. The train journey took up the first 100 miles. Nobody knew who he was so there was no problem. The surgery round his throat done in the House of D covered with bandage. Above it his emotionless face looking straight ahead – they all do that, as if showing how they can control themselves. Black coat, open shirt. And all day the river at our side, Mississippi, like a friend travelling with him, like an audience watching Huck Finn going by train to hell. Oh sure I read too you know. I can see the joke. I know he was important, but he was also sick and crazy...

At Baton Rouge the bandage was full of red though he had hardly moved. I gave him a cloth to cover it. Whole trip went well. No trouble. He must have been tired from the operation the day before. From Baton Rouge we took the wagon up through Sunshine, Vachery, and Slaughter. Forty-eight miles. Again he was very calm. North of Slaughter McMurray and I wanted to swim. It was hot. We stopped and found a small river. We got him down off the wagon and took him the 100 yards to the water and he just stood on the bank. He watched while we took turns swimming. That was the fifth of June, so he was admitted late that day. We never saw him after that. We put him in the chair in the Superintendent's office, got the papers signed and left him with them.'

They had gone through the country that Audubon drew. Twenty miles from the green marshes where he waited for birds to fly onto and bend the branch right in front of his eyes. Mr Audubon drew until lunchtime, sitting with his assistant who frequently travelled with him. The meal was consumed around a hamper, a bottle of wine was opened with as little noise as possible in order not to scare the wildlife away.

*

I sit with this room. With the grey walls that darken into corner. And one window with teeth in it. Sit so still you can hear your hair rustle in your shirt. Look away from the window when clouds and other things go by. Thirty-one years old. There are no prizes.

Credits

Dude Botley's monologue appears in Martin William's *Jazz Masters of New Orleans* and appears with permission of the Macmillan Publishing Company.

The picture of the dolphins' sonograph with explanatory note is reprinted by permission of Charles Scribner's Sons from *Mind in the Waters*, Joan MacIntyre, editor. Copyright © 1974 Project Jonah.

Louis Jones interview, John Joseph interview, Bella Cornish interview and Frank Amacker tape digest used with permission of the William Ransom Hogan Jazz Archive, Tulane University Library.

Sections from 'A Brief History of East Louisiana State Hospital' used with the kind permission of Lionel Gremillion.

The photograph of Bolden's band originally belonged to Willy Cornish, is now in the Ramsey Archive, and is reprinted with permission from Frederic Ramsey jnr.

Acknowledgements

Many points of historical information were found in 'New Orleans Music' by William Russell and Stephen Smith, from *Jazzmen,* edited by Frederic Ramsey jnr and Charles Smith (Harcourt Brace, 1939). And in Martin Williams' *Jazz Masters of New Orleans,* (Macmillan, 1967).

Al Rose's *Storyville, New Orleans* (University of Alabama Press) also contained interesting social and historical information.

E.J. Bellocq's photographs in *Storyville Portraits* (Museum of Modern Art), edited by John Szarkowski, were an inspiration of mood and character. Private and fictional magnets drew him and Bolden together.

I would like to thank all those at the Jazz Archives at Tulane, especially Richard Allen who helped me a great deal when I was there. The original work done on the tape digests at Tulane was by Paul R. Crawford.

I would also like to thank Lionel Gremillion, Superintendent of the East Louisiana State Hospital, who was of much help to me, showing me files and letting me read his history of the hospital.

There were, for me, the important landscapes of Holtz Cemetery, First Street, and Baton Rouge to Jackson.

Of interest is a rare 10″ LP, 'This is Bunk Johnson Talking...', issued by William Russell's American Music Label, which has Bunk Johnson whistling the way he remembers Bolden playing.

While I have used real names and characters and historical situations I have also used more personal pieces of friends and fathers. There have been some date changes, some characters brought together, and some facts have been expanded or polished to suit the truth of fiction.

—M.O.

For Quintin and Griffin. For Stephen, Skyler, Tory and North.

And in memory of John Thompson.

F O R

COMPUTER BUFFS

& Other
Technological Types

Second Edition

Marjorie Eberts
Margaret Gisler

with the assistance of
Maria Olson
Rachel Kelsey

VGM Career Horizons
NTC/Contemporary Publishing Group

Library of Congress Cataloging-in-Publication Data

Eberts, Marjorie.
  Careers for computer buffs & other technological types / Marjorie
Eberts and Margaret Gisler with Maria Olson and Rachel Kelsey. — 2nd ed.
    p.   cm. — (VGM careers for you series)
  ISBN 0-8442-4707-3 (cloth). — ISBN 0-8442-4708-1 (pbk.)
    1. Computer Science—Vocational guidance. 2. Electronic data
processing—Vocational guidance.   I. Gisler, Margaret. II. Title.
III. Series.
QA76.25.E23   1998
004'.023'73—dc21
                                                          98–30218
                                                             CIP

Published by VGM Career Horizons
A division of NTC/Contemporary Publishing Group, Inc.
4255 West Touhy Avenue, Lincolnwood (Chicago), Illinois 60646-1975 U.S.A.
Copyright © 1999 by NTC/Contemporary Publishing Group, Inc.
Printed in the United States of America
International Standard Book Number: 0-8442-4707-3 (cloth)
                                    0-8442-4708-1 (paper)
18   17   16   15   14   13   12   11   10   9   8   7   6   5   4   3   2   1

To our computer-buff
husbands—Marvin, Les,
Larry, and Matt—who truly
savor their time on
the computer at work
and at home.

Contents

Acknowledgments

N o industry changes faster than the computer industry, with its rapid technological innovations. The Internet is ushering in a new age in communications. We sincerely appreciate the work Rachel Kelsey has done in creating a new chapter on careers associated with the Internet. And we are grateful for the revisions Maria Olson made to the chapters on systems analysts, computer operators, information systems management, and using computers on the job. Their contributions to this book are substantial.

CHAPTER ONE

Careers for Computer Buffs

Endless Opportunities

"If the auto industry had moved at the same speed as our [computer] industry, your car today would cruise comfortably at a million miles an hour and probably get a half a million miles per gallon of gasoline. But it would be cheaper to throw your Rolls Royce away than to park it downtown for an evening." GORDON MOORE, INTEL CORPORATION

T he computer industry is fast moving and exciting, and it is rapidly changing the way we do business. Just thirty years ago, computers were enormous, exotic machines found only at large companies. By the turn of the century, there will be more than one computer for every two people in the United States, and personal computers (PCs) will then be more powerful than the supercomputers of 1995. The days ahead in the computer industry are going to be increasingly challenging because of the Internet. This international network has started a communications revolution that is moving so rapidly that the Net, as the Internet is often called, is different every few months. This revolution will be long lasting and widespread and will ultimately change the ways in which people communicate with each other.

Many visionary and colorful people have played important roles in the developing computer industry. Most are young, and many are millionaires—a few are billionaires. Computer buffs are well aware of Steve Jobs and Steve Wozniak, who created the Apple computer in a garage, and of Bill Gates and Paul Allen, who founded Microsoft while Bill was still in his teens. Then there is

1

David Filo, who doesn't wear shoes and sleeps on the carpet in his cramped office with his head jammed under his desk about once a week. He and Jerry Yang founded Yahoo!, one of the two most popular Internet search engines, while they were graduate students at Stanford University. Yahoo! began as an idea, grew into a hobby, and then turned into a wildly successful company. Perhaps one of the readers of this book will have the insight to join these computer-industry pioneers in creating a company based on a revolutionary new idea.

The Birth and Growth of the Computer

Before you begin to explore the intriguing careers available to you today in the computer industry, you need to become acquainted with its history and its pioneers. Looking at the past to recognize trends can help you predict some elements of the future.

The computer's parents were the mathematicians and scientists who desired a machine that would reduce the time required to do complex mathematical calculations. Their first efforts resulted in the invention of the abacus approximately five thousand years ago. The ancient Babylonians, Egyptians, Chinese, Greeks, and Romans all used devices with movable counters to improve the speed and accuracy of their calculations. It was not until the 1600s, however, that the first mechanical calculating machines were built. One of the more notable machines was built in 1642 by Blaise Pascal, a French mathematician and scientist, to help handle his father's business accounts. Pascal's machine used rotating wheels with teeth to add and subtract numbers of up to eight digits. The name "Pascal" is remembered today by computer buffs every time they use the computer language that bears his name. Just a few years later, in 1673, Gottfried Leibniz developed a more complex calculating device that also had the capability of multiplying, dividing, and finding square roots.

The Father of the Computer

Early calculating machines were not reliable, and all had problems carrying over numbers in addition. Mathematicians, scientists, engineers, navigators, and others who needed to do more than very simple calculations were forced to rely on printed mathematical tables that were riddled with errors. Disconcerted by the enormous effort required to make calculation tables, Charles Babbage, an English mathematician, developed the idea of an automatic calculating device called the "difference engine." Financial and technical difficulties precluded the building of the complete machine; however, the section of the machine that was completed is regarded as the first automatic calculator. Nevertheless, Babbage is not primarily remembered for the difference engine but for his design of a machine that he called the "analytical engine." This machine, which was designed to perform complicated calculations, contained the basic elements of modern electronic computers. Babbage's machine separated memory and storage and was programmable. Babbage kept developing and refining the design of this machine until his death, but the problems that had beset him in attempting to build the difference engine discouraged him from making a concerted effort to build the analytical engine.

Interest waned in the development of automatic calculation machines after Babbage's death. Progress was made, however, in developing calculators. By the end of the 1800s, reliable calculating machines were readily available. In addition, data processing became automated through Herman Hollerith's development of an automatic punch-card tabulating machine. He had been commissioned by the United States Census Bureau to resolve the crisis the bureau faced in handling the 1890 census data. Millions of immigrants had turned the process of analyzing the 1880 census data into an almost eight-year task. With the nation growing so rapidly, the Census Bureau feared that the 1890 census data would never be analyzed before the next census was taken. Herman Hollerith's data processing device saved the day, permitting the data to be analyzed in just two and one-half years. Hollerith had developed a code that used a pattern of punched holes to represent data. His machine recognized whether or not a hole was covered, and electricity passed through the holes to activate motors that moved counters, which gave out totals. Number-crunching industries such as accounting, banking, and insurance enthusiastically embraced the use of perforated cards to handle data. In fact, punched card equipment was used in data processing until the late 1950s. Even today some elements of Hollerith's code still are being used in computers to read input and format output. The Tabulating Machine Company that Hollerith organized to sell equipment for commercial use went on to become one of the companies that merged together to form IBM in 1911.

The Modern Computer Age Begins

After Hollerith constructed his tabulating machine, several computing devices were developed. These computers were never well publicized. ENIAC (Electronic Numerical Integrator Analyzer and Computer), however, gained instant worldwide attention when it was introduced at a press conference in 1946. ENIAC was a gigantic machine—over one hundred feet long and eight feet deep and weighing eighty tons—developed by J. Presper Eckert and John W. Mauchly, two engineers at the University of Pennsylvania. ENIAC, the first fully electronic digital computer, worked approximately one thousand times faster than previous machines. It could perform five thousand arithmetic operations in a second. ENIAC proved that large electronic systems were technically possible. Unfortunately, ENIAC had a serious flaw. It was very time consuming to program because switches had to be set and boards had to be wired by hand. It took days to set up programs that took only seconds to run. In spite of its flaws, ENIAC inaugurated the modern computer age.

John von Neumann solved ENIAC's flaws by introducing the idea that programs could be coded as numbers and stored with data in a computer's memory. His idea was used in building EDVAC (Electronic Discrete Variable Automatic Computer), which was the first stored-program digital computer.

By 1945, the Census Bureau was again drowning in a sea of paper. Eckert and Mauchly signed a contract to develop a new computer to solve the bureau's problems. They also contracted to build computers for three other clients: Northrop Aircraft Corporation, Prudential Life Insurance, and the A. C. Nielsen Company. Eckert and Mauchly developed a more advanced electronic digital computer for their customers, which they called UNIVAC I (Universal Automatic Computer). Unfortunately, their financial skills did not match their computer expertise, and they were forced to sell the company to Remington Rand in 1950. UNIVAC achieved fame in 1952 when it was introduced to television to predict the results of the presidential election. UNIVAC predicted that Eisenhower would win in a landslide, but the people at CBS did not agree with the prediction. The next day everyone learned that the computer had been correct and the humans incorrect.

Remington Rand's success with UNIVAC inspired Thomas Watson Jr. to have IBM enter the fledgling computer business. Within a few years, IBM secured a dominant position in the industry with its moderately priced computers, which tied easily into existing punch-card installations.

The Inventions That Revolutionized Computers

ENIAC and UNIVAC I used vacuum tubes for arithmetic and memory-switching functions. These tubes were very expensive, used considerable power, and gave off an enormous amount of heat. In 1948, the transistor was invented at Bell Telephone Laboratories, spelling the end of the vacuum tube. By using this new technology, second-generation computers became much smaller than earlier computers, had increased storage capacity, and were able to process data much faster.

The invention of the integrated circuit in 1958 by Jack Kilby of Texas Instruments signaled the start of another new era in computing. Previously, individual components had to be wired together; now it was possible to print the wiring and the components together on silicon circuit chips. By 1974, continuous technological progress through large-scale integration (LSI) made it possible to pack thousands of transistors and related electronic elements on a single chip, and the personal computer (PC) revolution began. Since 1965, the number of components per integrated circuit has doubled about every year, and this trend shows no sign of slowing. With each technological advance, computers continue to become faster, cheaper, and smaller. Furthermore, as integrated circuits permitted the design of computers with ever more memory capacity, the need for reliable software generated the birth of the software industry.

A Quick Look at Computer Buffs

Everyone today needs to be computer literate to some extent to survive. Computer buffs, however, are a special breed. They try to spend as much of their waking time as they can working—or playing—on their computers. The magnetic pull of the computer dictates almost everything they do. Today, much of their time is spent surfing the Net or chatting and playing games on-line. Most have forsaken pen and paper correspondence for E-mail. Computer buffs spend hours browsing through computer stores, studying computer magazines, and researching on-line to make sure that they know about the latest hardware and software. Contemplating how they can upgrade their computers is another favored pastime, as is devising new programs to meet their needs. The computer invades virtually every aspect of a computer buff's everyday life. You will even find confirmed computer buffs playing solitaire on their computers.

Computer buffs do not have to limit their interest in computers to the role of a hobby. They can readily find satisfying careers that will let them spend their working hours in jobs devoted entirely to the computer. The computer revolution is here, and new and exciting jobs in the industry are emerging at an astonishing speed. Today there is scarcely a business or industry that does not utilize the computer in some way. From agriculture to aerospace, there are many exciting careers for computer buffs. The computer was *Time* magazine's Man of the Year in 1982. Working with a computer will be the job of the twenty-first century, and computer buffs will be our heroes because they are creating and using technology to make positive things happen.

An Overview of Today's Careers for Computer Buffs

This book is dedicated to helping all computer buffs realize their dreams of finding jobs that allow them to work with computers on company time. Here is a bird's-eye view of some of the careers you will read about in this book.

Working with Hardware

People with vision are employed to create computers—from personal computers (PCs) to supercomputers—as well as the peripheral devices essential to their operation. Jobs are not limited to research and development, as computers need to be manufactured, sold, and serviced. What's more, no machine can be sold without the manufacturer both documenting how the machine is to be used and training the user to operate it, if necessary. Some computers are so complex that customers require ongoing technical and support service.

Working with Software

Without software, the computer is just a box. It is software that tells a computer what to do. Developing software is very labor intensive. Programmers are needed to write the system software every computer requires to manage its operation. Programmers also create the programs that tell the computer how to perform specific tasks, from word processing to surfing the Net. Besides developing software programs, computer buffs are needed to sell the programs and provide documentation and training for program users.

Providing Computer Services

As the number of computers in the world approaches 550 million units, more and more people are needed to provide a variety of services to computer users. A growing employment area exists for those who can plan, design, and implement computer systems and networks. Furthermore, with so many companies drowning in paperwork, transaction-processing services need employees to process all kinds of transactions from payroll to medical records. The current explosion of information also has led to the creation of information service providers who use computers to collect, manipulate, and disseminate information (usually over the Internet) about all kinds of topics from stock market quotations to statistics on school enrollment.

Solving Users' Problems

Systems analysts do not just burrow their noses in computers. They are professional problem solvers who listen to computer users in order to meet their needs and solve their problems. Systems analysts improve existing systems and may even design new systems. All of their work is designed to give users the computer resources they need. Systems analysts are the "people persons" in the computer profession, and they are also among the most sought-after employees in the industry.

Operating Computer Systems

Computer systems must be kept running, whether they are operated by airlines, catalog stores, or the Internal Revenue Service. For many organizations this means round-the-clock jobs for computer systems operators. The computers and all their related machines must operate smoothly. When the systems are down, the operations staff must get them on-line again as quickly as possible. Running the computer also involves entering data and instructions into the computer and handling the computer's output. Furthermore, librarians are needed in some organizations to catalog, file, and check out magnetic tapes and disks.

Managing Information Systems

Computers no longer are used just to handle everyday business tasks such as billing and payroll. Now computers are providing all types of information to help management make decisions about products, sales, marketing, and almost every aspect of a company's business. Computers have the capacity to spew out so much information that managers are now required to manage databases of stored corporate information and direct what new material should be developed. Besides handling these new tasks, managers of information systems purchase equipment and software and supervise all the other data-processing tasks.

Using the Computer in Special Areas

Computer buffs can use the computer to express their creativity, whether it is in design, manufacturing, animation, music, or entertainment. One of the fastest-growing areas of computer use is CAD (computer-aided design). These are the jobs that let computer buffs design and plan automobiles, houses, clothing, and such computer staples as microchips and integrated circuits. CAM (computer-aided manufacturing) lets people be involved with the fabrication of products under computer control. If you have an artistic flair, you can find jobs that combine this talent with your interest in the computer. For example, in the music arena you can use the computer to create compositions and play a variety of instruments. You also can use the amazing graphics capacity of computers to create commercial artwork and all types of special effects seen in TV shows and movies.

Finding Internet Jobs

The Internet is the new kid on the block in the computer world, and it is having a terrific impact. In 1996, more than one million new jobs were created in just this one area of the computer industry. Companies are begging for savvy technical types who can help them get on-line, create new hardware, and develop software for the Net as well as for those who have the new skills of a Webmaster or Web graphics designer. There is also a demand for people who can advertise, market, and sell products and services on the Internet.

Using Computers on the Job

Banks, insurance companies, retailers, hospitals, and manufacturers all have computers playing essential roles in the operation of their businesses. Airlines, supermarkets, and newspapers depend heavily on computers. No matter what occupation you choose from A to Z, whether it is an airline pilot, a doctor, a librarian, or a zookeeper, you will most likely find yourself using the computer in your job.

Exploring Future Computer Careers

The range of job options for computer buffs will continue to widen as we enter the twenty-first century. Completely new jobs will emerge as computers become more skilled at making decisions, more capable of reading handwriting and understanding the human voice, and better able to communicate with other computers—in short, "smarter." Even more new careers will appear as wireless communication increases and Hollywood and the computer become more closely linked. At the same time, emerging technology will change the nature of many jobs, and some of today's jobs will disappear.

A Computer Buff's Dream—Finding a Career with the Machine

The inventors of the first computers had no idea of the numerous ways computers would be used. Today computer buffs can find jobs with the machine in almost every workplace. And job opportunities abound as technology companies and companies that use information technology are actively searching for qualified employees. Evidence suggests that job growth in information technology now exceeds the production of talent. There is an especially competitive market for high-tech professionals (computer scientists and engineers, systems analysts, computer programmers, and database administrators) who are being lured to jobs with performance bonuses, stock options, excellent salaries, and other perks.

The Job Search

Traditionally, job searches have been conducted by reading want ads and contacting companies by mail or phone. This picture is rapidly changing as more and more companies, especially information technology companies, are using the Internet to recruit employees. Aboard the Internet, computer buffs will be able to find huge databases of job listings, such as Monster Board (http://www.monsterboard.com). And they will be able to chat with career counselors, practice their interview skills, and go to a

Web site to learn more about a company and see what job opportunities may be available—all without leaving the home computer.

One of the very best resources on the Internet for learning about employment opportunities and job resources is *The Riley Guide*, http://www.jobtrak.com/jobguide. It will tell you how to incorporate the Internet in your job search, find Net career planning services, prepare your resume for the Net, and find the best research sources for your job search. It will also tell you how to find salary information. An excellent print resource is *The Guide to Internet Job Searching* by Margaret Riley, Frances Roehm, and Steve Oserman. Just a glance at the following listings from the Internet will give you an idea of what an excellent resource it is for discovering job opportunities:

Associate Web Developer

Responsibilities: Building and maintaining HTML Web pages and ensuring our pages meet the highest standard of technical quality.

Qualifications: Experience building and managing a commercial Web site, comprehensive technical understanding of HTML and the Internet, knowledge of JAVA, ActiveX, and CGI scripting a plus.

Technical Support Representative

The primary duty is to assist customers via the telephone and E-mail with connectivity problems. We also provide first-level support for the use of various Internet-related products contained on our Web page.

Typical duties and responsibilities:

- Provide excellent customer service

- Assist in resolving technical issues via telephone and E-mail

- Provide a high level of professional and competent support to all customers

- Ensure that individual and department goals of problem resolution and call duration are met

- Act in a mature and professional manner towards customers, vendors, and other company employees at all times

Required Abilities:

- Flexibility to work staggered hours

- Excellent customer service skills

- Strong aptitude for problem solving

- Previous Internet experience desired

- Experience which demonstrates the ability to effectively communicate with customers over the phone

- Experience with computers and operating systems preferred

Hours: All shifts; training to be done during normal business hours. Part- and full-time positions available.

Junior Programmer in the Technology Department

Education requirement: Bachelor's degree

Professional experience: All experience levels

Job description: Entry-level programmer trained in C and UNIX. Maintain legacy ordering systems written in PL1 on Stratus. Assist in porting such systems to C and UNIX. Fluent in C and UNIX; good problem-solving skills.

Order Entry Clerk

You will be responsible for coordinating, reviewing, and inputting advertising insertion orders into a database. The job requires a high school diploma, or equivalent, and two or more years of order-input experience. You must have excellent data-entry skills and proficiency with Excel. Requires good organizational and phone skills and ability to follow through with pending issues. General database experience required, preferably with Microsoft Access.

Job Qualifications

Computer buffs seem to be welded to their machines. The unbreakable bonds they forge with their computers may lead them to gain such expertise that no special training will be required for them to begin their careers in the computer industry. Computer buffs with the appropriate know-how may be employed with little training as computer service technicians, salespeople, telecommunications technicians, and computer operators. Today, more and more applicants for professional-level jobs in the computer industry have college degrees. Some computer buffs (Bill Gates of Microsoft Corporation and Steven Jobs of Apple and NeXT) have been extremely successful without completing college. Nevertheless, as the computer industry matures, more and more firms are requiring successful applicants for professional-level positions to have college degrees. Although majors in computer science did not exist thirty years ago, companies are increasingly expecting those who are interested in the technical or systems side of computers to have this degree from a quality program. In the Appendix, you will find a list of accredited programs in computer engineering and science. Since computers are used in so many different arenas, job applicants have an advantage if they combine computer study with another area such as engineering, mathematics, logic, economics, business, science, art, or music.

As is true in most occupations today, successful applicants for computer positions will have logged many hours in part-time jobs, in internships, or in cooperative education programs in the computer field before applying for full-time positions.

Where the Jobs Are

Have you ever heard the song "Do You Know the Way to San Jose?" The city is in Silicon Valley, which has the reputation for being the center of the computer world. If you are interested in a career in the computer industry, this could be your career destination. In Silicon Valley, much of today's valuable computer technology has been created and is still being created. It is a close-knit community where everyone knows everyone else, works a mind-boggling number of hours, and lets off stress playing such games as Ultimate Frisbee.

Other states that have a large number of computer companies creating both hardware and software are Massachusetts, Illinois, New York, and Texas. And of course, Washington is the home of Microsoft. Computer jobs are no longer limited to computer companies. There are opportunities with every organization that uses computer technology, from the government to the smallest firms.

Learning Even More About Computer Careers

Computer buffs know that the computer industry is changing so rapidly that books can be outdated even before they make it to the library shelf. Being aware of what is going on in the computer industry is absolutely essential for finding the perfect job. Going on-line as well as reading current issues of such computer periodicals as *PC Magazine*, *PC Computing*, *PC World*, *MacWorld*, *Windows Magazine*, *Computer Life* and *the net* are the best ways to keep abreast of what is happening in the world of computers. Computer buffs interested in the latest statistics on all aspects of computing should look at a copy of the *Computer Industry Almanac*, which is available in libraries. This almanac will give you information on salaries, employment trends, education, computer organizations and users groups, and almost everything you could possibly want to know about the computer industry. You also can learn more about computer careers and the computer industry by contacting the many professional organizations associated with the industry.

CHAPTER TWO

Working with Hardware

Computers and Peripheral Equipment

A computer is a programmable electronic device that can store, retrieve, and process data. It is composed of software programs that make the computer work; peripheral devices that are used to input, output, and store data; and the computer processor, which is the actual computer in charge of everything that happens. All of the computer chips, circuit boards, and peripheral devices (keyboards, mice, joysticks, monitors, printers, disks, tapes, and communication devices) are referred to as *hardware*. If you can see it, it's hardware.

The individuals who are actively involved in the design and building of hardware are usually computer or electrical engineers. Of course, assemblers, inspectors, technicians, production staff, product managers, quality control experts, sales and marketing people, education specialists, technical writers, and maintenance people also play key roles in bringing computers to individuals and organizations.

If you want to work with hardware, you will typically be employed at a computer or computer component vendor from Apple to IBM to Dell to thousands of other companies. You may be involved with computers, parts used in computers, or peripherals. No longer are jobs concentrated at computer manufacturers; now it is highly possible that you will work at a company that manufactures chips, disk drives, or other components that can be used with different computers. You may find a job within a large, well-established company such as Hewlett-Packard, Intel, Compaq, or a newly established company. But you are more likely to work in California than anywhere else as the majority of the computer companies are located there.

If you are seriously thinking about a career in the computer industry, you must keep track of current trends to make solid career decisions. For example, the distinction between mainframes, minicomputers, and microcomputers has blurred. A cutting-edge microcomputer may be more powerful than a mainframe of just ten years' vintage, and some powerful microcomputers that are equipped with remote terminals have been changed into minicomputers. Furthermore, competition is so fierce in the computer industry that giant firms can stumble and newcomers can rapidly appear and disappear.

Computer Engineering

Whenever you see a finished computer product, whether it is a personal computer or a printer, an engineer had to play a big role in its creation. These engineers, who frequently work in teams, must have considerable technical prowess to design, develop, test, and oversee the manufacture of computers and peripheral equipment. A minimum of a bachelor's degree in electrical or computer engineering is essential, and graduate course work is often needed. Many engineers hold advanced degrees in complementary fields. Thus an engineer with a bachelor's degree in electrical engineering might have a master's degree in computer engineering. At the same time, engineers wanting to hold managerial positions may get advanced degrees in business. Because technological advances come so rapidly in the computer field, continuous study is necessary to keep skills up-to-date. Continuing education courses are offered by employers, hardware vendors, colleges, and private training institutions.

As far as advancement goes, engineers enjoying hands-on experience can choose to stay on the technical side, climbing the career path from junior engineer to such positions as senior engineer, engineer, principle engineer, or project leader. Others can elect to become managers or supervisors, roles in which most of their time is devoted to managerial responsibilities and only a limited time is spent on engineering.

A Look at Salaries

In 1994, there were 345,000 computer engineers and scientists. By 2005, this number is expected to grow by 90 percent to 655,000. Competition for skilled computer engineers has contributed to substantial salary increases. The following chart gives an excellent idea of the median salaries of computer engineers at different career levels in semiconductor design and manufacturing.

Computer Engineers' Salaries		
Title	Semiconductor Design	Manufacturing
Junior Engineer	$44,000	$37,000
Engineer	$49,000	$42,000
Senior Engineer	$58,000	$46,000
Principle Engineer	$65,000	$56,000
Staff/Project Leader	$76,000	$69,000

Source: Excerpted with permission from Source Engineering. Copyright 1996, Source Engineering, P.O. Box 809032, Dallas, TX 75380.

Developing a Microprocessor

A microprocessor is an integrated circuit on a silicon chip. Equip it with primary and secondary storage and input and output devices and you have a microcomputer. Much of the engineering work in hardware occurs at the chip level. Just out of college with a degree in electrical engineering, Curtis Shrote wanted to design chips. Those positions, however, were filled on the microprocessor team he joined at Motorola. Nevertheless, Curtis chose this job because he liked the idea of being on a team assigned to develop a general-purpose microprocessor that had 1.3 million devices on it and would run the software for an operating system. The microprocessor was being designed for the workstation market and would go into a computer the size of a pizza box.

When Curtis first came to Motorola, the design team had already talked to customers and decided what they wanted on the chip. The original team ranged from fifty to one hundred members, mostly electrical engineers. The project was headed by three first-line managers who dealt with the team members on a daily basis. One was a senior design engineer whose job was to see that everything was done correctly and to oversee the junior engineers and less-experienced engineers like Curtis. There were also subteams, and Curtis was assigned to the cache team. (A *cache* is a storage area that keeps frequently accessed data or program instructions readily available.) His subteam of five core people—which consisted of three engineers with master's degrees, one with a bachelor's degree and prior design experience, and Curtis—clearly illustrated the level of expertise hardware engineers must have.

This subteam was responsible for logic design, data cache control, and instruction cache control. Curtis was given the responsibility of debugging (locating and correcting errors on) the cache control unit on the chip. This involved designing an external simulation environment and writing test cases for all cache areas on the chip. Once the chip was in real silicon, he checked in actual tests what could not be simulated earlier.

Projects at Motorola typically take from six months to four years to complete. Curtis's project took four years. Toward the end of the project, his subteam was downsized, and Curtis started doing some design work as he corrected errors. Curtis also started working on a new project, which was to produce multiple products from a M.Core™ microprocessor. He became the team manager of simulation verification. This did not involve hardware design but the development of software tools.

Now that he is more experienced, Curtis has begun to advance along the career path toward being a senior engineer, a position that requires considerable work experience. Right now he hopes to follow both technical and managerial paths. During his current project, Curtis began working on his master's degree in computer engineering, a move that Motorola strongly supports. After several years, he earned his degree from National Technological University by taking ABET (Accreditation Board for Engineering and Technology) courses on site and on company time. The courses are live or pretaped presentations of courses approved by ABET that have been taught and recorded at their actual schools. Curtis was able to phone and talk to the instructors of these courses. It is quite important for individuals wishing to have a solid background in hardware engineering to be graduates of a school with an accredited computer science or engineering program. A list of these schools can be found in the Appendix.

As a child Curtis was thoroughly intrigued by the computers at his father's workplace. Furthermore, his father, an information systems manager, would talk to his family all the time about the business side of computers. By junior high, Curtis had decided that he wanted a career in the computer industry. After investigating a number of schools, Curtis elected to attend Purdue University and obtain a dual degree accredited in both electrical and computer engineering. Although initially he was not interested in taking part in the school's co-op program, interviews with companies participating in the program made him change his mind. Cooperative education programs let students alternate studying at college with an off-campus job. Students are able to earn all or a great part of the cost of college. The Purdue program required five semesters of work to obtain a cooperative education certificate. Curtis actually worked off-campus in the computer industry for six semesters.

Students must interview with companies and be selected by them in order to participate in the co-op program. Curtis had several choices, and he decided on a co-op program at the IBM facility in Kingston, New York. There he was assigned to work in facilities engineering, updating building floor plans. Although Curtis had his heart set on being in chip design, he knew it was not realistic to get such a position for a first assignment. Nevertheless, he was quite pleased to be working for a major computer firm as co-op experiences often lead to job offers in the future. Like all co-op students, Curtis had to interview for each subsequent off-campus job. Since IBM lets you change departments, he moved to the interconnect products group after his first co-op experience and stayed with this department, working on a variety of projects for the rest of his time off-campus. The department built network boxes that interconnect mainframes and connect mainframes with peripherals. Although he wasn't able to do design work, he had the advantage of working with an actual design, saw a long-term project evolve from simulation to actual system integration, and observed the turnover in management and employees. Curtis believes that working at IBM in the cooperative education program gave him a better idea of the courses he needed at school plus the obvious benefit of experience in the computer industry. In the semester before graduation, Curtis interviewed with five companies and was offered a job by every one.

Working in Research and Development

A job in research and development is the dream of many computer buffs who are eager to be involved in the front end of developing a product. For Loyal Mealer, this dream became a reality when he started his career in the computer industry as an engineer (entry-level position) in research and development in the Scientific Instruments Division at Hewlett-Packard. He was able to dive immediately into working on the design of an analog/digital board for a research-grade mass spectrometer—work that was done almost entirely on a computer. Loyal was able to design immediately because of his hobby and work experience and because many schools are now giving their students experience in designing. He holds a bachelor's degree in electrical engineering/computer science. Without design experience at college, he would have needed a master's degree to handle this job.

Career Path

After one year, Loyal became a hardware design engineer. For the next few years, he designed many circuit boards and was even the sole designer for one product (all boards), which was fun and immensely satisfying work. Loyal became a hardware technical lead and then a project manager doing the hardware design for an array processor board. Twelve years after starting with Hewlett-Packard, he became a section manager for research-grade mass spectrometers in the research and development department. In this position, he directly managed ten engineers and two project managers. This involved evaluating their work and managing their career paths. He also managed some projects directly. Although he sometimes offered engineers design help, Loyal says that the higher you climb in management, the harder it is to return to the technical side. For individuals in this position, the next career step is into a research and development lab manager position or some type of marketing or manufacturing management position. He moved into a position in manufacturing where he managed forty engineers and technical specialists. Today, Loyal has left the hardware side of computing to manage a software project.

Advice

Loyal points out that as growth has accelerated in the computer industry, it is now easier for college graduates to find entry-level positions in design. Loyal advises graduates with this goal to start in manufacturing so they can learn how to solve design problems as a stepping-stone to a job in research and development.

Microchip Applications Engineering

The design of any complex machine or system—be it an automobile or a microchip—is always broken down into several specialized areas. For an automobile, you will find designers in charge of designing engines, transmissions, radiators, and safety door locks. For a microchip, there are physicists who know how to implant the right kind of impurity to make the silicon the right kind of semiconductor and to interconnect circuits with the right kind of metal. There are also circuit designers who know how to pack transistors as tightly as possible, and there are logic designers who can implement any desired logic function at the highest speed using the smallest possible number of components.

Designers start with a requirement to develop a specific microchip. They bring to their individual areas of design a perspective on such things as producibility, reliability, functionality, power consumption, operating speed, and cost efficiency. On the other side are the purchasers (users) of microchips who are concerned with the whole chip—how it will fit into their systems and what portion of a given task the microchip will do. These are the people who are using microchips in medical equipment, computers, printers, cellular telephones, gas pumps, and so forth.

At Xilinx, a maker of microchips, the views of the designers and users are brought together so that the company makes a chip that users want. Peter Alfke, director of applications engineering, tells the designers what the users want and communicates to the users what Xilinx chips can do. This is not a simple task, as it requires good communication skills plus a solid technical background. Peter meets these requirements handily. He holds a master's degree in electrical engineering, has worked as a design engineer and design team manager for ten years, and has been in applications engineering for thirty years, either working alone or with up to one hundred people reporting to him. Besides finding out what users want in new chips, Peter consults with users on any problems they are having using the company's existing microchips. His job is not a traditional engineering job as he spends so much of his time writing and talking about his company's products and users. Nevertheless, without his engineering background, he would not be able to bring the different perspectives of designers and users together, and his company would not be making the chips Xilinx customers want.

Providing Technical Help and Support to Computer Users

Computer users have always needed help when problems occur. Their problems are frequently solved by customer service calls or actual visits from technical support specialists. For computer buffs who are intrigued by the challenge of analyzing and solving users' problems, jobs as customer and technical support specialists can be quite satisfying. You usually need to have a strong background in computer science coupled with an ability to devise creative solutions to diverse problems in order to handle these jobs. Support specialists will typically work for computer and computer component manufacturers or large user organizations. Your career path may lead to positions in management, or you may elect to remain a troubleshooter.

A Technical Support Representative

Ashley Dunham worked for Hayes Microcomputer Products as a technical support representative. She spent her workdays answering users' questions about the company's data communications products as well as general communications questions. Most of her time was spent on the phone helping users with problems, but she also answered letters from customers as well as E-mail queries. Although Ashley had a computer science degree as well as several years experience working in the college computer science center as a user assistant, she still needed on-the-job training at Hayes to learn about users' problems and how to help them work through these problems.

Ashley became so fascinated with computers in high school that her father actually gave her a computer. She also had the opportunity to spend half of her school day at a science center where she had classes two hours each day in computer science. In college, she specialized in programming and data communications, and her goal is to incorporate the two in her work. Ashley was very pleased with her job as a technical support representative as she genuinely enjoys helping people and working in the computer industry. Demand for support specialists is strong and should continue to grow.

Selling and Servicing Computers in Retail Stores

According to the *Computer Industry Almanac*, 35 percent of the households in the United States have a computer at home, and more than 50 percent of all workers now use a PC on the job. Furthermore, in many organizations, employees have desktop PCs for office use and laptop or notebook computers for use on the road. And the number of computers is expected to grow even more dramatically in the next ten years. The amazing growth in PCs has resulted in an equally amazing growth in the number and type of stores selling PCs. But this is not all these stores sell; they also sell peripheral devices from printers to mice. You will find them selling an astounding number of accessories to help computers run smoothly as well as supplies such as paper, ribbons, and printer cartridges. Many stores also rent, lease, and repair computers. Some offer training and consultations. Computer buffs can find a variety of jobs in computer stores and superstores, department stores, discount and warehouse stores, and mail-order and catalog firms. The opportunities for employment are good in this area, as there are more than 45,000 stores and businesses selling computer products in the United States, according to the *Computer Industry Almanac*.

Owning and Operating a Computer Store

Seventeen years ago, Alfonso Li went to a computer show and saw a booth that was labeled "franchising." Shortly thereafter, he was the owner of a MicroAge computer store. After some initial training, he opened his store and worked in both sales and repair with only two employees to help him. His business expanded into a larger store with twenty-five employees. This business took a lot of his time—it was decidedly not a nine-to-five job.

Every day since Alfonso opened his MicroAge store, he has spent time learning more about computers. He reads, goes to seminars and schools, and talks to manufacturers. Technology is advancing so rapidly that Alfonso says everything would be changed if he took a six-month vacation and then returned to the computer business.

Alfonso was able to respond well to the changes in the computer retail business because of his strong business background. Besides having an M.B.A., he also worked as a corporate controller for seven years. The focus of his store changed as computers became so much cheaper and computer users so much more knowledgeable. With profits disappearing from the sale of PCs, Alfonso shifted more into selling high-end and expensive computers. He also greatly expanded services to customers in setting up and getting their computers running, including programming. His store also sold software and peripherals. Because he could not find good technicians, Alfonso set up a school for technicians at his store several years ago. Successful store owners cannot just be computer buffs; they also must have a solid understanding of business and be prepared to work long hours.

Working in a Computer Store

Behind every computer sold in a computer store there is usually a salesperson. The more computers salespeople sell, the more they are likely to earn from commissions. They need to be willing to work long hours to make those commissions. Although no formal course of study is required for these positions, salespeople need to be knowledgeable about the computers and equipment they sell. Store owners like Alfonso Li also look for skilled technicians who have completed a community college or training school program in repair work.

Repairing Computers

As the amount of computer equipment increases, so does the demand for people to install, maintain, and repair this equipment. The majority of repairers find jobs with wholesaling divisions of equipment manufacturers and with firms that provide maintenance services for a fee. As computers become more complicated, employers are increasingly looking for employees who have formal training in electronics. Newly hired repairers, even those with training, usually receive more training on-the-job. It could be self-instruction from manuals, videos, or programmed computer software. After four years of work experience, repairers can take an examination and receive certification as a Certified Electronic Technician. Such certification can lead to jobs as specialists or troubleshooters or as maintenance supervisors or even to jobs in sales. Salaries for top-notch repairers can exceed $900 a week.

Employment Trends

The computer industry is maturing. While growth is no longer as dramatic, and downturns do occur, this industry is still expanding, and many segments actually grow from 50 to 100 percent a year. Where jobs for hardware professionals were once concentrated at mainframe manufacturers, they now are distributed among companies that make computer components. Demand should remain high for professionals in networking and communications as technology is changing so rapidly in these areas. And because products are becoming so complicated, an increased need exists for sales and marketing professionals and technical support specialists with computer expertise.

CHAPTER THREE

Working with Software
Programs That Make Computers Run

S oftware brings hardware to life. Whether you use your computer to play video games, write a report, or create graphics, it is software that makes what you are doing possible. It is also software that lets you use E-mail, send faxes, or browse the Web because software tells your computer what to do to perform these tasks.

Many individuals are involved in developing software and delivering it to retail stores, businesses, and other organizations. There are careers in software for developers, salespeople, marketing experts, advertisers, teachers, trainers, technical writers, managers, and researchers, to name just a few areas. Nevertheless, the central figure in the development of software is the programmer.

Computer Programming

Computers can do only what they have been told to do, and the people who tell them what to do are typically called programmers. They write the programs (lists of instructions) that make computers act in a certain way, test the programs, debug the programs (correct errors), maintain and update the programs, and may even write the documentation (instructions on how to use a program or computer system effectively).

On the job, programmers may work alone or be part of a group. They may be responsible for creating an entire program or just a segment of a program. It may take just a few minutes to write a program, or it may take years.

In the past, systems analysts designed software programs to meet specific needs, and programmers had the task of writing programs to fill those needs. Today there is a blurring of these responsibilities and job titles, and many individuals are performing both tasks, especially in smaller firms.

Training

Professional programmers often have bachelor's or master's degrees in computer science. Nevertheless, many excellent programmers have little or no formal instruction in programming. For example, many computer buffs regularly enjoy writing programs for their own computers. To gain professional expertise, they will have to learn how computer circuits are structured and should have a strong background in several programming languages. These languages have a fixed vocabulary and a set of rules that allow programmers to create instructions for a computer to follow. There are numerous programming languages, and no one language meets the needs of all programmers.

Certification

While certification is not mandatory, it may give a job seeker a competitive advantage. The Institute for Certification of Computing Professionals gives individuals who have at least four years of experience or a college degree and two years of experience the designation Certified Computing Professional. To qualify, it is necessary to pass several examinations. More information about certification is available by contacting the Institute at 2200 East Devon Avenue, Suite 268, Des Plaines, Illinois 60018.

Skills

Being a programmer requires an ability to pay extraordinary attention to detail. For example, just omitting a comma in an instruction can cause a system to fail. Programmers also must be able to think logically and concentrate on a task for long periods. In addition, they need to have stamina. It is not unusual for programmers to work eighty-hour weeks and go for days without much sleep when they are trying to meet deadlines. Creativity is also an asset for programmers who must find unusual solutions to resolve difficult problems. And, of course, programmers must stay current on programming languages as well as the continual changes in technology.

Salaries

A continuing shortage of programmers has pushed salaries up significantly. Even if shortages ease and upward pressure on salaries is reduced, programmers have traditionally received high wages. A superstar programmer might earn as much as $150,000 a year.

Programmer Salaries, 1998

Title	Large Installations[a]	Small Installations[b]
Programmer/Analyst	$40,000–$52,500	$35,000–$45,000
Programmer	$34,000–$40,750	$30,000–$40,000

[a]Large installations generally have staffs of more than fifty and use larger mainframes or multiple minis in stand-alone and/or cluster configurations. PC utilization commonly involves LANS or PC-to-server-to-host communications, tying multiple sites together using telecommunications networks.
[b] Small installations usually have fewer than fifty staff members.

Source: Excerpted with permission from Robert Half International Inc., P.O. Box 33597, Kansas City, MO 64120.

Areas of Specialty

Most computer professionals begin their careers as programmers. You can divide programmers into two basic groups: systems programmers and applications programmers. Some might want to add other groups for those who work in very specialized programming areas.

Working as a Systems Programmer

Systems programmers design and develop all the software used to operate a computer system. They also are involved in installing, debugging, and maintaining systems software once it is installed. You will find most systems programmers working on mainframes for computer vendors, from giants such as IBM to small start-up companies. The trend toward standardization of operating systems has now made it possible for systems programmers to move more easily from working with one vendor to another. Formerly, most vendors tended to have their own operating systems, making it essential for programmers to learn a new system when they switched jobs. A few systems programmers work at end-user organizations where they support applications programming, make evaluations of hardware and software, and modify existing software. They also develop programming standards.

CAREER PATH Most systems programmers begin as junior or trainee programmers and receive considerable direction from project managers or team leaders. They typically advance to programmers, who receive less supervision, and then to senior systems programmers, who work independently. They can advance to project leader in charge of heading a team of programmers and to manager of operating systems with the responsibility for directing all activities of the department. The number of levels on the career path of a systems programmer depends on the size of the organization. Systems programmers do have a variety of career choices. Some elect to go into management, some choose to remain in programming, and others may prefer to move into systems analysis.

EDUCATION   Systems programmers usually have degrees in computer science. They also need to have a good knowledge of C and C++, computer languages used in operating-systems programs. In addition, they should understand computer architecture, which is the overall design by which the individual hardware components of a computer system are interrelated.

Working as an Applications Programmer

Applications programmers write programs that tell computers how to perform specific tasks, from billing customers to sending the shuttle into space. They turn design specifications into computer code, which means putting the steps necessary to execute a program in a programmable language. At the present time, the hot languages are C and C++. Applications programmers also debug and test programs and may write documentation. All of their work is user oriented rather than system oriented, like the work of systems programmers. They write programs that can be used on computers, from PCs to mainframes, and you will find them at work in a variety of places. They may be creating software at Microsoft, Netscape, a grocery chain, banks, universities, research centers, or NASA; or they may be working by themselves at a mountaintop retreat.

Wherever they are, applications programmers will frequently be working as part of a team made up of sales and marketing, documentation, training, and quality control people to create a product. You also will find them in tense, pressure-packed situations trying to meet deadlines to finish a program on time.

Formerly, applications programmers would develop systems from the designs of systems analysts. Now they work more closely with the users of their programs and often take over the design function as well. Thus, they may more appropriately be called programmer/analysts or software engineers.

CAREER PATH   Applications programmers work in two distinct areas: business applications and scientific or engineering applications. The career path in either area is similar to that of systems programmers. Applications programmers also begin as junior or trainee programmers, then advance to programmer, to senior programmer, to project leader, and on to manager of applications programmers. As for systems programmers, the number of intermediate steps in their career paths depends on the size of the organization for which they work. Applications programmers may change career direction and become systems programmers or systems analysts. Because applications programming is often the first job for those who are interested in information systems, many applications programmers will ultimately take managerial positions.

EDUCATION   Applications programmers do not always have college degrees. There are high school students working as programmers. However, most applications programmers are college graduates, and for some jobs graduate degrees are required. Those specializing in scientific or engineering applications need to have strong backgrounds in those subject areas, while those working for businesses may need courses in management information systems and business. Applications programmers also need to be proficient in a high-level programming language such as C++.

Developing the Programs You Use— a Programmer's Story

When Fred Parsons sits down at a computer to program, he sees himself as an artist with the monitor his canvas and the keyboard his brush. Fred's first job as a programmer was at Timeworks, which produced education and productivity software. The company was one of the top one hundred producers of software in the United States and had won awards for several programs.

As an undergraduate, Fred took only one computer course, a course in FORTRAN, and really enjoyed the programming part of the course. After graduating from college, he did not become a programmer but was a high school teacher for four years. The increasing number of layoffs occurring in teaching at the time convinced Fred to go back to college and work for a master's degree in computer science. Halfway through the degree program, he started looking for work and found a job as a programmer/analyst at Timeworks. His first job was to write demos of programs the company was selling so customers could see the actual screens from these programs in smaller software stores. It was a compiled BASIC program. Fred was pleased with this assignment. The project manager would tell Fred what he would like to see and whether the job was going according to specifications. He also helped Fred with programming problems.

Career Path

By his next assignment, Fred had begun to climb up the programmer career ladder. He was the only programmer on a team that included a writer, a packager, and people from marketing and advertising. All worked together under the direction of a project manager to produce a database program. The company told Fred what type of program he was to create and left some things to his discretion. He had learned about databases in his graduate school courses in computer science but had to teach himself the programming language he used to create the database program. Logic and discipline from his undergraduate programming course and five or six graduate-level programming courses helped make this endeavor easier. Fred's experience clearly shows how helpful computer science courses can be to programmers in their work.

On the database project, Fred worked on the coding part alone and even did some of the design work. Coding involves writing down every single instruction the computer is to perform in a given computer language. For example, if a computer were to ask a question, it might take from one to one thousand instructions to make it ask the question in a user-friendly fashion. In coding, you write down certain key words or variables and mathematical equations; then a compiler turns your language into actual instructions for the computer in a language the computer can understand.

Once Fred's company saw that he could come up with ideas (programmers must be creative) and specifications, he advanced to the position of project manager and reported to the director of research and development. At one time, he was supervising four projects at once. Fortunately, the deadlines for the programs were staggered.

A New Job

After several years at Timeworks and a short stint as a consultant, Fred elected to go to work at Comdisco, a technology services company that handles the design, acquisition, management, and protection of corporations' entire technology infrastructuresz. He is now working with six other programmers on an asset management and procurement program for PCs. According to Fred, programs have become more sophisticated so more programmers need to work together on them. One advantage of his current job is that his hours are shorter now since he is working at a larger company that is not as dependent on the programmers to get the software out. Nevertheless, he is always working under a deadline.

The Future

As far as his future goes, Fred says that programming is habit-forming—you get hooked on it—so he likes the idea of continuing to program. He also likes the idea of being in management as he is able to express his opinion more as well as work with people. In any case, Fred says he never gets bored working in programming as the possibilities are endless, and there is always new technology to learn. For example, he learned the high-level language C++, which he is using in his current project, by simply buying a book and going on from there. Fred strongly believes that there will always be a need for programmers. He is especially glad to have a job creating software for a software company rather than working for an organization where he might only be modifying old programs.

Debugging Programs to Make Them Work

Being a computer buff may run in some families. Rob Needham's father and grandfather worked with computers most of their lives, and he seems to be following in their footsteps. While Rob was attending college and working as a volunteer at a supplemental food program, a program secretary asked him to look at a computer program that was giving her trouble. He looked at the program, saw where it failed, and contacted the program's developer at a local firm. After many conversations with the owner of the small company, CK Computer Consultants, Rob was offered a part-time job doing data-entry work. This led to a position as a quality control specialist. The company specialized in software applications in the medical field and was a very small firm with just four employees.

Rob's basic job was to make the company's programs bulletproof. Anytime a modification was made in one of the firm's programs, he had to check that program in a variety of ways to make sure that it still worked properly and didn't fail. When a new program was developed, he tried to "destroy" it (make it fail), and many times he succeeded. For example, in one program, patients were identified by their social security numbers or machine-generated numbers. Rob discovered that the same number could be given to more than one patient, which would have quickly corrupted the data. After he found this flaw, he described how he caused it and offered a solution. The owner, who designed all the programs, corrected the flaw, and Rob then retested the solution in several other ways. He also tried to recreate errors by going through a different path. The process continued until Rob could no longer find any errors. In an eight-hour day, his error sheet might list as many as fifty or sixty errors to be corrected. Rob discovered far more errors in new programs than in existing programs that were being modified for new customers.

Because the company was small, Rob also did general office work and data-entry work for the company or the purchasers of the company's programs. When he worked outside the office doing data-entry work, he introduced the workplace staff to his company's program. At the same time, he also might find errors in the program. Rob says that he could test a program seven ways only to discover that the customers were using it in an eighth way. For example, he found out that individuals switching from typewriters to computer keyboards often retain the habit of leaving their hand on the space bar, which can generate errors all over the place. The company's program had to be corrected so that more than three hits of the space bar would not be acknowledged.

Rob is largely a self-taught computer buff, although he has had courses in writing programs in BASIC and FORTRAN plus a course in WordPerfect. He is fascinated by computers and would like to continue debugging programs, as well as get into programming directly.

Technical Writers in the Computer Industry

When you want to know how to compute averages on your software spreadsheet program, you can easily find the answer by consulting your user manual. Programmers at end-user organizations use technical manuals when they are customizing programs to interface with their system. Installers use manuals when they are implementing a system. All of these manuals are written by skilled technical writers who have a solid knowledge of computers and how they work. They also have the ability to talk to technical specialists about a product and then translate this information into language that nonspecialists can easily understand.

Education

Most technical writers have a college degree. Often, employers want them to have a degree in communications, journalism, or English. While a knowledge of computers is desirable, people with good writing skills can often pick up the specialized knowledge they need on the job, especially if they are computer buffs.

Salaries

Experience is very important in determining the amount of money that technical writers earn, as this chart illustrates.

Technical Writers Salaries, 1998

Years of Experience	20th percentile	Median	80th percentile
Less than 2 years	$36,000	$37,100	$41,900
2 to 3 years	$38,300	$40,400	$42,800
4 to 6 years	$41,000	$43,500	$46,500
More than 6 years	$48,000	$49,800	$52,000
Staff/Project Leader	$54,400	$59,400	$63,600

Source: Excerpted with permission from Source Engineering. Copyright 1998, Source Engineering, P.O. Box 809032, Dallas, TX 75380.

Working as a Technical Writer

Although Betsy Morris graduated from college with a major in psychology, she has spent most of her career writing about how to use computers and training others to use them. In her first job with a start-up electronics company, she worked in production control buying parts and making sure they would arrive when needed. She then moved to a much larger company, where she continued to work in production control. That company brought in a new software system to organize production, and Betsy turned into a computer buff. She became quite expert at using the mainframe production software and soon was putting together manuals on using the computer and holding training classes. This led to a full-time job as an engineering support specialist, which also entailed preparing materials for computer courses and writing a newsletter on the implementation of the new computer software.

After moving to a new town, Betsy answered a newspaper ad seeking someone to do technical writing and user support and was immediately hired for this position at a heavy-construction company. The company had several programmers who developed programs geared to the needs of the engineers and office staff in the firm. Betsy wrote manuals for the users and trained them to use the applications programs. She also was involved in selecting software and computers.

After a move across the country, Betsy made a decision to concentrate on technical writing in her next job. Although she liked to do support work, she felt it was difficult to be good in both areas as there were so many new technological developments to learn. Once more she found a job through a newspaper ad, this time as a technical writer for a software house producing very complex programs in the financial area. The programs were sold to large institutions such as banks and insurance companies. The learning curve was very steep at this job because Betsy had to learn not only about how each new program worked but also about the companies for whom she wrote the manuals.

On the Job

As a technical writer, Betsy is usually working on manuals for two or more software programs at one time. The point at which she gets involved with a project depends on the project manager and her other commitments. If she is rushing to meet a deadline or has two or three manuals going at once, she cannot get involved in anything new until her schedule clears. Ideally she is brought in during the design phase and asked for input, but she often joins a project when this phase is completed. Because documentation has to be delivered a few days after the new software program, Betsy is always busy writing the user manual as the programmers are creating the program. She has to work closely with the programmers to get the information she needs for the manuals.

Demand for good technical writers is increasing. Today, there are more than the typical user, technical, and installation manuals to write. Technical writers produce security manuals, training manuals, and whatever the needs of the client and the complexity of the program dictate. On one project, Betsy wrote all nine manuals. On others, she has shared the writing task with others. Also, the job of technical writer now extends to writing and putting material on the Web. In Betsy's case, this even includes doing the graphics. Plus, in her job she often writes proposals and marketing materials.

Betsy wants to remain a technical writer because she truly enjoys the challenge of this work. She describes a good technical writer as an individual who is an excellent writer first and who also understands what he or she is writing about. Betsy sees no lessening in the demand for technical writers, but she does see a tendency in many firms to use contract writers when they need them rather than having a large staff of in-house writers.

Software Products Management

Companies that make computers also make or buy systems software. Mike Tognoli is one of Hewlett-Packard's many product managers. Once he is assigned a new software product, a team is

put together and a business plan is developed. His team will negotiate with a number of different groups in Hewlett-Packard. For
example, Mike must make sure that the new software is compatible with the systems on which it is designed to run. He also works
with the group signing contracts with customers. The product
must be marketed, which includes pricing and packaging. And, of
course, it must be shipped to customers. In addition Mike is concerned about service and maintenance of the product. This area
is rather like a new car warranty, as the company will fix problems
with the software. Mike also spends time updating customers on
the product.

Positions as product managers are usually held by individuals
who have some business background. Mike says that managers
tend to have or are working towards their M.B.A. degrees. Besides
having his M.B.A., Mike has work experience as a financial analyst, a marketing manager, and an integrated circuit buyer. The
next step up the career ladder for product managers is to fully
manage a larger group, rather than individual products.

Training People to Use
Software Programs

When Ellen Leeb went to work at NeXT, she was not a computer
buff but a college graduate with a journalism major looking for a
job. She took a job as a receptionist, promising herself to stay at
that position only for a year as she looked for other job possibilities in the company. By networking with employees, she discovered an opening for a publications assistant in the software
department and was hired for this position, proving that taking an
entry-level job can lead to future job opportunities.

As a publications assistant, Ellen oversaw the production of
three user and eight technical documentation books. Her job was
to coordinate the work of technical writers and graphic artists in
producing the books. She also worked on having the books local-

ized, which means translating them into different languages in such a way that they fit appropriately into the culture and business strategies of other countries. After SW Publications acquired NeXT's training department, Ellen became involved with the production of training manuals as well as all the arrangements for training sessions for users and outside developers. Then she was promoted to a position in training where, in addition to overseeing the production of training manuals, she also managed groups of trainers.

In creating and producing software as well as hardware, many people are needed to handle administrative tasks. Ellen truly enjoyed being involved in the training of users and developers and appreciated the special atmosphere of the NeXT corporation, which respected everyone's individual work ethic. The company had no set hours and operated on a "just-get-the-job-done" philosophy, which made for a very dedicated staff that really worked hard. Today, NeXT is part of Apple Computer.

Selling Software

Just a few years ago, software was largely sold to consumers in retail stores, which included small stores and chain stores devoted to software as well as bookstores and computer stores. It was also possible to order software by mail. Today, the number of small software stores is greatly reduced, and retail chains devoted to selling just software have largely disappeared. Instead, most software is now being purchased at computer superstores, huge office supply stores, mail-order companies—and from the new kid on the block, the Internet. Each of these venues has a need for knowledgeable salespeople who can assist customers in the selection of the appropriate software to meet their needs. Computer buffs who are software gurus can get sales jobs without a college degree. In fact, it is even possible to work in sales part-time while you are still in school.

Software sales jobs certainly aren't limited to retail stores. Both small and large software companies must have salespeople. At the business level, this typically means selling a system that involves both hardware and software. While companies will train their salespeople, they also expect to hire people with considerable computer expertise and often want employees who have degrees in computer science.

Customer Support

The rapid spread of computers and computer-based technologies has raised a need for consumers and small businesses to get personal help with software problems. Since many of them do not have access to expert computing advice, they call software companies for this help. Working in customer support can mean talking to people on the phone or answering questions that have been sent to the software company by fax or the Net. You will find customer support jobs at giant software companies such as Microsoft, Symantec, Borland International, and Intuit, or with companies that sell only a few software programs—or just one program.

Seeing the need for providing help with software programs, Intel launched a service called Intel AnswerExpress Support Suite in 1998. The service promises to respond within ten minutes to questions that customers ask over the Internet. The service will offer help on using and troubleshooting more than one hundred programs. While customer support people are typically trained on the job, computer literacy is definitely a prerequisite for this job. And at most companies, employees will be required to have a bachelor's degree.

Salaries

The median salary for individuals working in customer support with less than two years of experience is $41,200, while those who have worked in the field for four to six years will earn $50,000, according to Source Services Corporation.

Employment Trends

Programmers will be in the driver's seat in 1998 and 1999. Companies are clamoring for these skilled workers to handle all of the Year 2000 conversion work. This problem has emerged because important computer software used in industry and government may not recognize a change to the new century and thus could generate erroneous data. Nevertheless, at some point after the turn of the century, the Year 2000 problem will be largely resolved and the tremendous demand for programmers will abate. Then the number of computer programmer positions will grow at a slower rate. Part of the reason is that systems analysts may assume more programming responsibilities, aided by the introduction of a variety of programming software that simplifies the programming process. Also, the increased overseas outsourcing of computer programming and the increased reliance by organizations on prepackaged software will slow the demand for programmers.

Overall, as the number of computers grows, so will the demand for more and more software to handle an ever-increasing number of tasks. This translates into a bright future for those of you who wish to be involved in the creation and distribution of software products. This includes product developers, programmers, technical writers, quality control people, end-user support persons, and the many individuals involved in the sale of software in both business and technical positions. Many new jobs for programmers and others involved with software will be associated with the Internet—the latest major growth area in the computer world (see Chapter 9).

CHAPTER FOUR

Providing Computer Services

A Growth Area

The United States has led the world into the Information Age. Today, there are few businesses, manufacturers, or individuals in this country that do not rely on the computer in some way. This has fostered the development of a computer services industry that provides professional services such as helping customers design, operate, and maintain computer systems. This segment of the computer industry also processes large volumes of data for businesses and provides individuals, businesses, and organizations access to large information databases.

There are jobs for programmers, systems analysts, systems integrators, database experts, information systems managers, word processors, data-entry clerks, project managers, and computer operators within the computer services segment of the computer industry.

Professional Services

Large organizations have information systems departments that oversee the operation of their computer systems. Nevertheless, most organizations will probably use outside professional services at times. They may need help in such things as selecting new equipment, networking existing equipment, setting up a disaster recovery program, or creating a new program. Organizations with a small staff of computer professionals will use outside professional services for designing and implementing systems, customizing software, training staff, and maintaining equipment. There is also a trend at present for organizations, large and small, to have service companies handle all or a great part of their information systems work. This is called *outsourcing*.

Service companies vary in the number of services they offer. The most important service today is systems integration. This involves planning, designing, and implementing computer systems and networks. While some service companies are quite large, there are also a great number of individuals providing these services—many only working part-time.

A Systems Integrator

Jim Horio works part-time as a systems integrator at TJ and K Incorporated, the company he owns with his partner, Carl Lindke. When the two established the company, Jim knew a lot about accounting and Carl was an expert programmer who had work experience as a systems engineer with IBM. Jim swiftly learned how to program with help from Carl by working on the S/32 computer in his apartment. Many of their company's clients come from referrals by people they know who work at CPA firms. Their clients (small to midsize companies) are looking for new computer systems or to upgrade their current systems. Jim and Carl will analyze a client's needs, determine hardware and software needed, and put the system together so it works. They also write software programs, if needed.

Jim and Carl are telecommunications specialists, a skill which is in high demand today. Much of their current work involves putting in telephone switches. They provide custom programming services to integrate telephone technology into computer applications programming. The two write programs that allow telephones to talk to computers. In addition, they sell Manac Development Company software solutions to legal firms. Then they do custom programming to adapt the software to individual firms and integrate legal applications with telephony. Jim and Carl also have written their own application program, called JD Calltrack, which Manac Development Company is marketing for them.

When they first started their firm, both Jim and Carl worked full-time at it. Then the emergence of the PC changed the nature of their work, and both took other jobs and did TJ and K work in the evenings and on weekends. Because both are confirmed computer buffs willing to spend most of their free time doing company work, they have been successful.

Processing Services

Today's organizations have to process vast numbers of transactions and considerable data. They must handle payrolls, insurance claims, inventory, and numerous tax forms as well as perform many record-keeping functions. Some of these chores are routine while others are large-volume, one-time projects. Even companies with large information systems departments are now having much of their large-volume transaction and data work done by processing services. Typically these services will use their own hardware and software. Processing services offer computer buffs such jobs as programmers, project managers, systems analysts, computer operators, and data-entry clerks. They also employ numerous managers and salespeople.

A Data Processing and Accounting Services Company

DPAS started out as a small data-entry shop in 1931. It has grown into a large data processing and accounting services firm with a main office in San Francisco and three branch offices. Recently, the firm was acquired by FYI Incorporated, a nationwide consolidator of document and information management companies. DPAS has from 175 to 500 employees depending on processing needs. Many of these individuals are actively working with the company's client server networks linked to IBM AS400s. The company provides a wide variety of services; smaller companies might only handle one type of service. By looking at some of the many services that DPAS provides, you can get a better idea of exactly what processing services these companies offer as well as the types of positions available for computer buffs.

- *Database Design and Management.* DPAS consults with clients regarding their needs and designs databases that contain critical information used in conducting analytical reports and supporting marketing campaigns.

- *Tax Reporting.* The federal government requires companies issuing more than 50 1099s or 250 W-2s to report them on magnetic tape. DPAS puts tax information on magnetic tape and provides firms with a duplicate tape as well as a printout of the contents.

- *Inventory.* DPAS does customized inventory processing using custom programming to give retailers the output they need.

- *Data Entry.* DPAS uses on-site programmers to customize each data-entry project. The company has over 190 key stations for fast, accurate data entry and quick turnaround.

- *Processing Services.* DPAS processing services include transactional batch processing for large banks; large-volume, one-time projects; surveys; payment processing; and product registration, plus many other services.

- *Order Processing and Fulfillment.* DPAS handles the mail and telephone order business of firms. Every order from arrival through delivery is tracked by computer.

- *Direct Marketing Support Services.* DPAS supports customers' direct marketing programs through these services: data entry

of customer names, response documents, orders, and
registration forms; label production; list compilation and
maintenance; order processing; direct-mail letters; and
fulfillment services.

Information Services

Information services collect related information about a topic,
organize it in a useful manner, store it in large databases, and provide on-line or off-line access to the information. This information usually can be accessed by computer twenty-four hours a
day from wherever you are. The almost unquenchable thirst of
businesses as well as individuals for information ensures the continued growth of this sector of computer services.

Information services may provide information on hundreds of
topics or just a specialized topic. You can access information on
such common topics as:

business news and corporate profiles

current news stories

encyclopedia articles

market trends

movie reviews

sports updates

stock quotations

travel services

weather

In addition there are databases with information designed for
specific professions. Doctors now find out about new drugs and

treatments by accessing medical databases. And lawyers are more likely to research case law through a legal database service than traditional law books.

Computer buffs can find jobs in many areas in information services. There is a need for those interested in software and hardware to improve the technology in creating and distributing information. In addition, there are many jobs for customer service representatives and researchers. Individuals with database management skills especially will be needed as the demand for information continues to increase. They work with database software to reorganize and restructure data to meet customers' needs and are responsible for maintaining the efficiency of the databases and the security of the system and may aid in design implementation.

Salaries

According to Source Services Corporation, data center managers will earn a median salary of $64,700. Those who work in customer service have a median salary of $44,200.

A Small Information Service

Quite often when people think of information services, they think of industry giants such as LEXIS-NEXIS, Knight-Ridder Information, and Dow Jones. LEXIS-NEXIS is so large that it has stored more than one billion documents and employs sixty-seven hundred people worldwide. However, many smaller information services provide information for a particular customer niche. One of those services is the Indiana Career and Postsecondary Advancement Center (ICPAC). The mission of ICPAC, which was created by the state of Indiana, is to inform, encourage, and support the education and career development of the people of the state. During the school year, ICPAC mails eighteen communications to the homes of students in grades eight through twelve. In addition, ICPAC has a Web site that provides information about schools, majors, careers, financial aid, and other topics to help students plan their futures. Both the mailed communications and the Web site require the creation and management of databases.

Dr. Jack Schmit, the associate director of ICPAC, oversees the ICPAC databases with the help of a database services specialist, who has an assistant. The database management system originally was created by an outside consultant, who then adapted the system to meet ICPAC's needs. Jack's responsibilities include:

- deciding who will have access to the system

- setting up accounts for users, including the assignment of passwords

- monitoring the use of the system by individual accounts to ascertain whether an account needs access

- deciding what information should be in the database

- updating and maintaining information in the database

- creating new information for the database

- marketing the database

- being responsible for software development for the program

In managing the mailings database, Jack has to organize the records for about 320,000 high school students and their families. This involves obtaining the students' addresses and grade levels and entering the information in the system.

Jack has worked with ICPAC almost from the day it started. He is not formally trained in database management, but he has learned through doing. Jack, however, is very knowledgeable about education, as he holds a doctorate in this subject. Managing a database requires more than computer expertise; it also requires a solid knowledge of what information should be in the database.

Employment Trends

While the number of jobs associated with computers grows steadily each year, the location of jobs tends to change rapidly. For example, many jobs are now found with outsourcing service companies instead of in company or government computer facilities. No longer are many of the huge insurance companies, banks, and health-care organizations doing such back-office jobs as payroll; they have outsourced these jobs to processing services and so have many small firms. Because information has become so important in today's technology-based economy, computer buffs should be able to find more and more jobs with information service providers each year.

CHAPTER FIVE

Solving Users' Problems
Systems Analysts at Work

W ho are systems analysts? They are the key people around whom the computer systems of banks, insurance companies, consulting firms, financial services, manufacturers, government agencies, and computer companies revolve. They perform three different functions in their jobs. First of all, systems analysts are people-persons who work with users to find out what information the users expect the computer to generate. Systems analysts are also investigators who gather facts about existing systems and then analyze them to determine the effectiveness of current processing methods and procedures. This phase may also include preparing a cost-benefit analysis of the current system. Finally, they are architects who plan and design new systems, recommend changes to existing systems, and participate in implementing these changes. Being able to handle the three distinctly different roles of a systems analyst requires certain characteristics. If becoming a systems analyst interests you, take this quiz to see if you have most of the requisite traits.

- Are you self-motivated and creative?

- Can you work equally well with technical personnel and those with little or no computer background?

- Are you tenacious—able to stick with a problem until it is solved?

- Can you handle a number of tasks simultaneously?

- Do you have the ability to concentrate and pay close attention to detail?

- Are you able to think logically?

- Can you deal effectively with difficult people?

- Are you a team player?

- Are you a good listener?

- Are you interested in a wide range of subjects?

- Can you communicate effectively both orally and in writing?

- Do you possess the ability to coordinate activities among many levels in an organization?

- Do you have good organization skills?

- Do you have a broad knowledge of computer systems?

- Are you familiar with programming languages?

- Are you a college graduate?

- Do you have an analytical mind?

- Are you self-disciplined and self-directed?

- Are you able to work for long periods even if there are few tangible results?

- Do you enjoy attending meetings?

- Are you willing to write numerous reports—even when there has been little accomplishment?

- Can you manage time and resources effectively?

If you answered "yes" to most of these questions, you probably possess the personal qualities and skills to become a successful systems analyst. Your work will be with computer systems, which are made up of people, machines, programs, and procedures all organized to accomplish a certain task. Organizations have systems because a system is an orderly way to get things done. For example, colleges have systems to register students in the classes they want. These systems have such components as registration forms filled in by the students, lists of available classes, registration personnel, and computer programs.

How Systems Analysts Work

Whether your task as a systems analyst is to create a brand-new registration procedure for a college or to improve the system for regulating the air temperature inside the space shuttle, your project will usually have six phases. How many systems analysts will be involved in developing and implementing a new system and what their individual roles will be naturally depend on the complexity of the system as well as the analysts' expertise.

The preliminary investigation is simply a brief study of the problem to find out if it warrants further investigation. The systems analyst primarily handles this phase through personal interviews with end users who have knowledge of the problem as well as the system being studied. This phase is usually quite brief. At its conclusion, systems analysts usually give management a report of just a few pages telling what they found and giving their recommendations.

The systems analysis phase involves gathering and analyzing data. Systems analysts gather data from interviews, written documents, questionnaires, and personal observations. This phase takes a lot of legwork and time and can be quite expensive. Once all the data have been gathered, it is time to analyze them using such tools as organization charts, data-flow diagrams, grid charts, data dictionaries, and decision logic tables. The final step is to make a report to management that details what problems were found, gives possible solutions, and recommends what the next step should be.

The systems design phase involves the planning and development of the systems operation. Systems analysts begin this phase by finding out exactly what information must be produced by the system (output). Once they know what the desired output is, they have to determine what is required to produce it (input), how the data will be stored, and how the system will operate to produce the desired information. An important part of this phase is to develop system controls to ensure the data are input, processed, and output correctly. This phase concludes with a detailed presentation of the system to management and users and, perhaps, with approval to begin developing the system.

The systems development phase begins with the scheduling of all the activities that have to be performed. Then design specifications have to be prepared for all the programming that will be done including the selection of the programming language. After the programs have been written, the next step involves testing to see if all the programs work together satisfactorily. Finally, documentation is required to describe the programs for operations personnel and users of the system.

The systems implementation and evaluation phase indicates that the system is ready to operate. Systems analysts must evaluate whether everything is working as planned. The reliability of the system must be tested and necessary modifications made. In addition, the changeover from the old system to the new involves training personnel.

The systems maintenance phase begins when the development process is concluded. Changes have to be made to correct errors, give the system additional capability, or react to new needs of the users.

Working as a Systems Analyst

It helps to have a little bit of Sherlock Holmes in you in order to be a successful systems analyst. You must investigate until you find out exactly what an end user really needs and wants. This often takes some time as many end users are not able to express precisely their computer needs. You also must be a teacher willing to help reluctant users learn to feel comfortable with computers and computer technology. Furthermore, you must realize that you are changing a familiar system and may find some end users are reluctant or even antagonistic about these changes. Tact is absolutely essential in working with these people. Computer analysts must wear many hats as they work on devising new systems or modifying older ones. At times, they need to be a salesperson in order to sell new technology. Besides interacting with people, they must be skilled professionals who can choose the correct hardware and software and design systems that meet the needs of an organization and its end users.

A Systems Analyst at a Small Insurance Firm

Ann Steefer has always been interested in computers. When she was a little girl, her parents put basic spelling games and word games on their old Apple computer. While she enjoyed playing the games, she was continually thinking of ways to improve the screen graphics, layout, and performance of the game. When it came time for college, Ann went to Purdue University, where she obtained a B.S. degree in computer science.

Today, Ann is a systems analyst for small systems at the insurance firm where she started as a basic programmer and subsequently became a programmer/computer analyst before advancing to her current position. She oversees the development and support of a PC application that is used for placing orders over the entire nation. There are three programmers on her team.

In her job, Ann has continuous contact with the people in her firm who use the application in order to know what their needs are and how their needs are changing. There are also biannual meetings to determine what changes and improvements need to be implemented in the system. Ann prioritizes this work and delegates it to her team members. Depending on the complexity of a change, Ann may develop program architecture to assist the programmer or work on the code herself. Ann has always enjoyed working with the development of applications and does not want to let her technical skills go unused.

With technology continuously changing, Ann finds it difficult to keep abreast of all the newest technology. She takes classes offered through her company and local computer vendors on new applications and future products to keep her skills current. Ann also tries to read computer magazines.

A Systems Analyst at an Army Finance Center

David Charles is a true computer buff. He says, "The computer has great appeal to me—it enhances me." His interest in computers grew as he saw computers becoming so popular in the workplace and in homes. David truly enjoys spending his leisure time at home on the computer. He handles most of his correspondence using word processing and graphics packages on his PC. And during the bleak winter months, you will find him playing educational games on his computer.

David climbed the career ladder to his present position as a project manager for small systems by progressing though a series of jobs. He started as a basic programmer and subsequently became a programmer/analyst, a section leader, and a department leader. His current job consists primarily of managing a tax input system (PC-based, from external offices to a central-site mainframe). He writes procedures for system users, analyzes problems, and advises personnel at troubled sites. David also is a team chief responsible for nine systems analysts working in many subject areas within the military pay system.

David believes that as a systems analyst you are more marketable if you have management experience, which also can help you, in some instances, to negotiate a better salary. He likes the opportunities that are open for him in the future, which include either continuing to work for the government or moving to a large corporation. His advice for future systems analysts is to get a sound educational background and be careful not to become over-specialized in one area as technology is constantly changing.

A Systems Analyst at a Major Manufacturer

In high school, Denise Jatho not only expressed interest in the computer field to her counselor, business teacher, and math teacher, she also read books on computers and the computer field. Her math teacher, who served as a mentor, worked with the local college to enroll her in a computer course, as her school did not yet have computers. After taking the college course, Denise decided to attend the university to get a bachelor's degree in computer science. Since the computer industry is constantly changing, she continues to take an average of two weeks of training every year offered through the company where she works.

Today, Denise works as a team leader in the commercial systems and services department of corporate information services for a manufacturer of heavy equipment. Because the user base for the software Denise develops is distributed worldwide, her workday usually begins by answering any E-mail or telephone messages from company people in different time zones, from as far away as Switzerland and Singapore. Next, she checks her organizer for meetings throughout the day. Denise usually averages one meeting each day with users, her team, or special committees. People-interaction skills are essential to success in her position. It is very important for her to have a team that works and bonds as well as to have a good relationship with her manager.

Denise's primary job is to develop and support PC software for business unit users in her company. Throughout the day she will assign tasks to members of her team. She will also assist them with problems they have encountered or provide training required to complete an assigned task. She may also work on the development of new software and enhancements or changes to software. During the day, Denise receives approximately ten calls from users and other software developers in her company to discuss software support issues. As a team leader, she also has the responsibility of making sure her manager is up-to-date with what Denise's team is doing and any problems that have come up.

One of the main reasons Denise enjoys her job is because it is challenging. She has to be both creative and logical in her thinking. She finds it's like working with one big puzzle that is always changing; once she has successfully completed one piece of the puzzle, the next one is waiting. Because the field is in a constant state of change, there is always something new to learn, so she is never bored. Denise also gets the chance to teach and coach other people and see them progress and grow, which is extremely rewarding to her.

Career Advice

Denise advises future systems analysts to research this career through reading and talking to people in the computer field. She also suggests going to technical fairs, if possible. In addition, Denise believes it is important to find a mentor—someone you respect who can help you learn and grow.

Education Requirements for Systems Analysts

At present there is no course of study that will completely prepare an individual to become a systems analyst because employers have such different requirements. Not only are they seeking college graduates with degrees in some aspect of computer science, they also want their successful job candidates to have course work related either to business or to the area in which they will be working. For example, graduates who have an education background in physical sciences, applied mathematics, or engineering are preferred for work in scientifically oriented organizations. Furthermore, many systems analysts have M.B.A. degrees, which give them the additional expertise in business required for many analyst positions.

If you plan to enter this field, you need to realize that continuous study will be required as technology is advancing so rapidly. This can be accomplished through in-house training, vendor courses, classes, and seminars. It also will be important for you to obtain certification to reflect your professional experience. Certified systems professionals have five years of experience as an analyst and have passed a core examination and two additional tests in two specialty areas. You can find out more about certification by contacting the Institute for the Certification of Computer Professionals, 2200 East Devon Avenue, Suite 268, Des Plaines, Illinois 60018.

Climbing the Career Ladder

Almost all systems analysts begin their careers as programmers. After approximately two years, they advance to positions as programmer/computer analysts or senior programmers. This is where they gain customer-interaction and management skills before being promoted to systems analyst. At this point, they may decide their next step up the career ladder is to senior systems analyst, where they have more managerial responsibilities, or to technical support analyst, which involves more programming. The career route of many analysts leads to positions in information systems management or senior management.

Employment Trends and Salaries

In 1997, more than 550,000 people were employed as systems analysts. They worked for large organizations such as Fortune 500 companies, the federal government, and consulting firms. Some also worked independently as consultants. Most systems analysts, however, were found in manufacturing, processing, and financial organizations.

Demand is skyrocketing, with an estimated 928,000 systems analysts needed by the year 2005. This is due in part to advances in technology, which continue to lead to new applications for computers. Also, falling prices of both computer hardware and software are enticing smaller organizations to expand the computerization of their operations. In addition, as end users become more aware of the computer's potential, the need for systems analysts will increase. This will be especially true in the areas of office and factory automation, telecommunications technology, and scientific research. Attrition in the field of systems analysis is very small. Individuals leaving this occupation usually transfer to jobs in management or administration.

Because systems analysts typically have several years of work experience before reaching this position, their pay scale is high. The chart on the next page shows the current range of salaries for systems analysts at different levels of an analyst's career path.

Systems Analysts' Salaries

Title	Large Installations[a]	Small Installations[b]
Senior Project Manager	$62,000–$79,000	
Project Manager	$56,000–$72,000	$47,000–$60,000
Senior Project Leader	$53,000–$67,000	
Project Leader	$49,500–$62,500	$44,000–$53,500
Systems Analyst	$47,000–$60,000	$38,000–$50,000

[a]Large installations generally have staff of more than fifty and use larger mainframes or multiple minis in stand-alone and/or cluster configurations. PC utilization commonly involves LANS or PC-to-server-to-host communications, tying multiple sites together using telecommunications networks.
[b]Small installations usually have fewer than fifty staff members.

Source: Excerpted with permission from Robert Half International, Inc., P.O. Box 33597, Kansas City, MO 64120.

CHAPTER SIX

Operating Computer Systems

Hands-On Work with Computers

*I*t was not too long ago that large staffs were required to operate the mainframe computers companies were using. They had to input the information through punched cards, mount and remove magnetic tapes, and handle the printed output from the computer. At that time, preventive maintenance was performed almost daily by computer engineers sent by the manufacturers. As computers have become more powerful and sophisticated, entering and storing data are much easier tasks. In fact, it has become so easy to input data that end users are handling most of this work rather than data-entry personnel.

While computer operations staffs have now become smaller at most facilities, many individuals are still needed to keep computer systems running. Within computer operations, you will find such positions as shift supervisors, computer operators, peripheral computer operators, hardware technicians, data-entry staff, and librarians. There are also careers related to computer operating for those involved in setting up the computer software and hardware environments that allow the systems to run smoothly, especially in the area of networking.

Computer buffs can find entry-level jobs within computer operations in which few technical skills are required. However, many jobs require specialized training in computer hardware and software technology. Furthermore, with the constant changes in technology, individuals who work in operations must be willing to learn new skills because today's equipment is likely to be tomorrow's dinosaur.

One interesting aspect about operations is the possibility of working in shifts or on weekends or even part-time. Since computers at many organizations run twenty-four hours a day seven days a week, there is frequently a need for the operations staff to work around the clock.

As organizations have come to rely more and more on the information generated by their computers, the importance of the smooth and reliable operation of computer systems has increased. It is easy to understand why the Internal Revenue Service, nuclear power plants, transportation systems, airline reservations systems, and many other organizations need solid performance from their operations staffs.

Working as a Computer Operator

Who are the computer operators? They are the individuals responsible for the operation of computer systems. Computer operators work directly with computers. As the trend toward networking accelerates, more operators are working with personal computers and minicomputers, which serve as the center of local area networks (LANS) or multiuser systems. The tasks they perform on these computers are similar to those performed on larger computers. Operators typically have the following duties:

- Make sure the equipment is in running order.

- Load the equipment with tapes, disks, and paper as needed.

- Monitor the computer console.

- Execute procedures at the right time.

- Respond to computer generated messages.

- Print and distribute reports.

- Locate and solve problems or terminate a program.

- Assist end users with routine operational problems such as not being able to sign on.

- Help systems analysts and programmers test and debug new programs.

- Document key activities and all unusual events during a shift.

Much of their work is routine and involves following a run-sheet, which tells them what they should be doing each hour.

Training and Advancement

In the past, computer operators frequently got their training on the job. Today, more employers are looking for operators who have had formal training from vocational and technical schools, community colleges, the armed forces, or computer manufacturers. Constant learning to keep up with advancements in technology through reading and specialized courses is essential.

Peripheral equipment operators may advance to computer operator jobs. Computer operators can advance to supervisory jobs. Through on-the-job experience and additional formal education, some computer operators may advance to jobs in network operations or support.

Salaries

According to the salary guide of Robert Half International, console operators at large installations earn between $25,500 and $34,000, while operators at small installations earn between $23,000 and $30,000.

A Computer Operator at a Large Facility

Bryan Morrison starts his job as a computer operator at midnight when he is locked in a computer room about the size of a basketball court at a large army finance facility. He always finds the room's temperature between fifty-five and sixty-five degrees Fahrenheit in order to dissipate the heat generated by the computers and to control the humidity more easily. Bryan brings a solid background in computer skills to his job, as he graduated from college in computer technology. He also used a PC in his prior job with an advertising agency.

During the first ten minutes of Bryan's shift, he meets with the supervisor for a briefing and then has another briefing with the shift that is getting ready to leave. These briefings ensure that Bryan's graveyard shift will be able to handle anything that is going on during the turnover time between shifts. He finds out which jobs are running, which drives are down, and what problems might occur on his shift. In addition, Bryan is told which messages to watch out for on the computer screen.

There are thirteen people on Bryan's shift: a shift supervisor, a lead computer operator, five operators working on peripheral output, two operators on the AMDAHL system, three operators on the 22/600, and a floater. When Bryan works as an operator on the 22/600, which handles all pay, he has a variety of duties. First he needs to see what work has been started and then update daily retired pay, health professional pay, reserve pay, ROTC pay, and many other categories in the pay system. When a job is done, he puts the tapes on a cart so that they can be stored in the library. As an operator, Bryan's main responsibility is to get a job to run correctly. If there are any errors in the program, he must fix them, if possible. If he is unable to fix an error, he calls in a programmer.

Bryan really enjoys his job when he is able to help the system solve a problem. He finds this aspect of his job very challenging. However, when there are no problems and too much slack time, Bryan feels that he is not learning anything about computers. Because computer technology is advancing so rapidly, he says that operators must keep abreast of these changes. He plans to go back to school and learn more computer languages. Ultimately he would like to own a business in which the computer plays a major role.

Supporting Computer Operations

The PCs, printers, telecommunications devices, and other computer equipment found in organizations have to be serviced and maintained. Some organizations will have this work done by outside service organizations. However, many organizations have hardware technicians on their staffs to keep their computer systems up and running smoothly. As the use of computers continues to expand, so does the need for hardware technicians. Beginning technicians usually have some training in electronics or electrical engineering. They typically get their training from vocational and technical schools, junior colleges, the armed forces, or on-the-job experience. And as technicians climb their career ladders to more supervisory positions, they usually take specialized courses. The median salary for technicians in computer operations is $34,500.

Technicians need to have good manual dexterity and patience as well as the ability to communicate with computer users. Take the following quiz to see if you possess the skills needed to be a technician:

- Do you like to fix and install things?

- Are you a good listener?

- Can you ask questions to obtain information from others?

- Do you enjoy figuring out why something is not working?

- Do you have good powers of observation?

- Are you able to work under pressure?

- Do you enjoy working with tools?

- Are you able to handle working with people who are irate?

- Do you have an interest in computers?

- Are you willing to keep up-to-date on different systems?

- Are you physically strong enough to lift heavy equipment?

- Do you enjoy reading?

Having a career as a technician is definitely a hands-on job. You need to enjoy tinkering with equipment and have the persistence to locate and solve users' systems problems. You also will constantly be required to read manuals to update your knowledge.

Supporting the operation of computers also involves individuals who do the paperwork involved in purchasing, repairing, and maintaining computer systems. In addition, many technicians find themselves doing far more than maintaining and servicing computer equipment, as you will see in the following interviews.

Working as a Technical Analyst

Michael Holtz worked as a technical analyst at the Toledo Hospital. Michael felt good about his job because he was able to save the hospital money. He knew that they were getting his services cheaper than if they were to hire someone outside the hospital to repair computer equipment, as he did far more than computer repair work. Michael took the first step on his computer career path in 1983, when he applied for a scholarship to the Ohio Council of Private Colleges and Schools. He wanted to enter the computer hardware technology field. Michael received the scholarship and was granted full tuition in the ten-month program.

After graduation, Michael began working at Abacus II, a retail store that not only sells computers but provides technical support to customers. As a bench technician he had the responsibility of taking in CPUs (central processing units) and repairing them. After a year and a half in this slot, he went to a branch store, where he was the only person providing the needed support for the customers who purchased equipment from this store. He held this position for a year and then was promoted to head technician at the corporate store, where he supervised three technicians. Michael left this position to do on-site computer repair for large corporations that the company serviced. He stayed at this job until he began working at the Toledo Hospital.

Michael was the only technical analyst at the hospital. His duties included keeping the hardware running, repairing computers, keeping track of repair costs, purchasing necessary parts, doing paperwork for repairs and purchases, and providing assistance on the operating systems and the software programs. He assisted four systems analysts, which included giving them his recommendations on new systems they selected to purchase.

On the job, Michael was usually involved in a wide variety of activities. Here's what one of his days looked like: He did his weekly time sheets that showed where he had spent his time in the hospital. He installed a new printer and moved equipment. Michael also spent some time installing another hard drive in a system that needed more drive space. He then spent two hours with the systems analysts who brought to his attention the users who would be adding or upgrading programs.

After working for several years as a technical analyst, Michael became a network analyst and then a network server specialist at the hospital.

Working as a Computer Equipment Analyst

Within the operation of a large computer facility, it is essential to have staff involved in the selection of computer equipment and peripherals as well as repair and maintenance. This is Garrett Zawadsky's job as a computer equipment analyst at a large army finance facility. Systems analysts tell Garrett what type of new equipment or peripherals are needed. He then writes up the specifications. Before new equipment is purchased, he acts as a point of contact between the systems analysts, users, contractors, and commercial manufacturers. Once a contract is signed, he checks to make sure the equipment is received. And during all this process, he is constantly sitting and working on his PC to put it together. Another part of his job is going into the database to track computer repairs. He also does the paperwork for repairs.

Garrett became a computer buff shortly after his father gave him his first computer. Within two weeks, he was buying add-ons. Today, he has several computers and is constantly involved in upgrading each one. While reading computer magazines, one of his favorite avocations, he learns more about the latest computers and equipment, which is very helpful in his job, and at the same time dreams of future personal acquisitions.

Garrett did not work in the computer industry immediately after graduating from college. With his education degree, he did substitute teaching and then entered civil service, working first as a clerk/typist and then in army supply at the army finance facility where he now works. About the same time he got his first computer, he also took a job in the facility engineering department, where he started to use the computer at work. Although he was only entering data for a supply catalog, his aptitude for the computer was quickly recognized, and he was sent to a school to learn operator functions. In his next job, he was a computer operator working on a mainframe doing backups, taking care of input and output from the system, loading jobs, sending jobs to others, and making sure the computer was running. He held this job for one and one-half years before taking his current job. Many individuals who start as data-entry clerks as Garrett did quickly advance up the computer career ladder in operations.

Although unsure of where his career will take him, Garrett cannot imagine having a job where he is not using a computer. One area in which he would like to be involved is the software creation of multimedia type effects.

Working as a Network Administrator

As the role of computer operators changes due to new technology, the responsibilities of many operators has shifted to working with networks. Network administrators work with both the hardware and software of computer systems to ensure they run properly and are compatible. They may also work on designing new computing devices or computer-related equipment and software to make the end users' interaction with the input of data as error free as possible. Network administrators need to have many of the same personality traits and skills as computer operators.

Network administrators typically earn higher salaries than computer operators. According to the Robert Half International salary guide, salaries ranged from $37,000 to $58,000 in 1998.

A Network Administrator at a Major Manufacturer

Wade Bishop is a network administrator working in the computer operation department of a major manufacturer. He is part of a seven-person team that services the network computer needs for more than twenty-five hundred users locally and eight hundred other users throughout the world. His background includes taking computer courses in high school, working in the U.S. Air Force with computers, and studying computer science in college. While in school, he concentrated on the networking aspect of computing. This involved learning how everything fits together, both with hardware and software. Through courses in PC architecture, PC LAN technology, and systems analysis and design, he gained much of the networking skills he uses today. Wade has found that strong analytical skills for problem resolution and good interpersonal and communication skills are also prerequisites for success in his job. According to Wade, you have to like to learn if you work in networking because today's solutions to problems will be obsolete in eighteen months.

Daily Schedule

Upon arriving at work at 6:00 A.M., Wade first checks all of his messages via E-mail, voice audix, and cellular phone. Then it is time to start dealing with the problems reported by users to his area. Next, he checks back-up runs for completion and initiates any failed jobs after fixing all errors. Every day, Wade and his project leader try to sit down to discuss all current problems, fixes to problems, or new and upcoming projects. The remainder of his day is spent working on projects and resolving problems for users as they arise. Since Wade interacts with more than twenty users each day, he doesn't spend much time at his desk as he usually goes to the user's desk to look at the problem.

Working in Data Entry

Data-entry operators are the people who input data into computer systems. They key data into a terminal and see what they have typed on a computer monitor. Data-entry operators may work on a PC or be linked to a computer system. Information is keyed into the system to be stored on a hard disk, tape, or diskette. The basic criteria for obtaining a data-entry position are speed and accuracy on the keyboard. Clerical skills such as answering the phone, typing, and filing also may be essential. You can prepare for this position by taking high school or vocational school courses. Use the following quiz to determine if you have the necessary traits to be a successful data-entry operator.

- Can you easily follow directions?

- Do you mind sitting for an eight-hour day?

- Are you able to concentrate in a room with other workers?

- Are you able to work with little supervision?

- Do you like idea of inputting information into a terminal?

- Do you have good keyboarding skills?

- Are you able to cope with the pressure of deadlines?

- Can you handle working in front of a computer screen all day?

"Yes" answers to most of the questions indicate that you could probably handle working as a data-entry operator. You may begin as a trainee or as a data-entry operator. Advancement in this career path is limited to positions as supervisors who assign work to other data-entry operators and make sure the data-entry department is running smoothly. In the following interview, you will learn more about the tasks that data-entry operators do and discover that these operators are taking on many additional responsibilities.

Data-Entry Clerk at a Small Business

Kim Reed took only one computer class in high school, a basic programming course; however, her jobs have involved working exclusively on the computer. On her first computer job with the public defender's office, she spent five hours of her eight-hour day typing legal documents and correspondence. Her on-the-job training was in using Multimate, a word processing program. After two and one-half years in the public defender's office, Kim went to work as a data-entry clerk for a window and door company. The company has five outlet stores selling quality windows and doors and a main office where she works as the company's sole data-entry operator. Kim spends her day working on two different systems: the company system and the factory system.

Kim's workday begins when she receives a printout of all the files that she entered the day before on the factory system. She checks to make sure that the files have come back from the factory the way that she entered them. Kim then goes through all the orders that have been faxed in overnight and makes decisions about any changes that have occurred. At this point, Kim goes into the sales journal in the company file and logs in all jobs, construction types, sales representatives, and amounts of money.

The next step in Kim's job is to pull up customer files, make any necessary changes in individual files, and create customer files for new jobs. The next file that Kim works on is order maintenance, where she enters order headers and creates documents from the orders listing all products that have been purchased by the customers. After printing everything she has entered in the computer, she staples each printout to the order and gives it to the individual who will prepare the orders for the factory system. Kim's work for the morning is now completed.

After lunch, Kim spends the next few hours on the computer working on the factory system. She returns to the order maintenance file, creates order headers, and types in information for the orders needed from the factory. Before Kim leaves the factory system, she prints out all the order data that she has entered and sends the orders by modem to the factory. The final hour in her workday is spent doing additional data-entry work, making phone calls, answering questions, and printing copies of contracts. You can see that Kim's job description as a data-entry operator involves considerable decision making and is not just inputting data.

Kim says that her job has taught her about the importance of the computer to the operation of her company. She enjoys typing and having the same daily routine. Kim says she is good at what she does because she does it every day. Over the years, she has gained speed and accuracy because she knows not only the codes but also the system. Kim accepted a new job with the company in the order department because she wanted the additional mental stimulus of a more demanding job. Once again, the job of data-entry clerk was a stepping-stone to career advancement.

Working as a Computer Librarian

You probably think that you have heard of everything now! Yes, there really are computer librarians, and you will find them at large computer facilities and information centers. They have responsibility for classifying, cataloging, and maintaining files and programs that are stored on cards, tapes, CDs, disks, diskettes, and other media. And they also make sure that all this material is kept in good condition. Computer librarians store backup files, combine old files, and even supervise the cleaning of magnetic tapes and disks. Just like other librarians, computer librarians help people locate information, the difference being this information is retrieved from stored master computer files.

Education and Advancement

Computer buffs who want to work on computers do not necessarily need a college degree in computer science. This chapter has shown you a number of entry-level positions that will let you work with computers without spending four years in college. Most of these beginning jobs will offer you some on-the-job training. These jobs are not necessarily dead-end ones, as many can lead to your obtaining other positions working with computers, especially if you stay on top of new developments in technology.

CHAPTER SEVEN

Managing Information Systems

Technology and Management

*T*he history of information systems is a brief one, going back to the days when systems and procedures departments set up courses of action for the efficient use of paperwork and employees. Today's information systems departments revolve around using the computer to develop and provide information to the staff of organizations from the federal government to your local fast-food restaurant. When organizations first started using computers, they were usually placed in data processing departments and used to handle bookkeeping and inventory functions. These departments were typically run by data processing managers, who were considered technical experts by the senior managers, who really did not know much about computers or computer applications. At the same time, data processing managers were often inept in communicating to management the more sophisticated ways computers could be used in their organizations. The job of data processing manager was considered to be a dead-end job, not an avenue for advancement to the top management of an organization.

As computers became cheaper and more powerful and as a wide variety of software packages became available, companies started using computers for more than just mundane tasks. Computers were elevated to the realm of running the business of the organizations, and managers used them to order shipments, purchase inventory, and make decisions. The position of information systems manager evolved to coordinate the needs of management for computer information with the rapidly expanding capabilities of computers. And the term "information processing" came to be used for "data processing" in many organizations.

The Job of Information Systems Manager

The manager of information systems has the responsibility of efficiently and effectively directing the operation of the computer systems on which an organization depends, plus providing the employees with the information services they need. A typical information systems manager will have the following job responsibilities:

- keeping abreast of trends and advancements in hardware and software technology

- evaluating new technology for possible use in the organization

- making recommendations for systems improvements

- implementing appropriate backup and security measures

- making sure that the implementation of new systems is handled in a timely manner

- managing the staff of the information systems department

- training personnel in the information systems department

- creating a budget for the operation of the systems information department

- assessing the information processing needs of users

- providing specific help to users in operating equipment and obtaining needed information

- consulting with senior management on the organization's information needs

- developing a plan to meet the organization's information needs

- reporting on the status of all information systems operations to senior management

- staying in touch with the activities of the organization

- serving as a buffer between personnel in the information systems department and those outside the department

Where Information Systems Managers Report

Since most organizations introduced computers in the accounting area, it was quite common for managers of information systems to report to the controller or vice president of finance. In many businesses this is still true today. However, as the importance of information systems to organizations grew, the title of chief information officer (CIO) was created, and information systems managers became part of senior management, reporting to the executive vice president, president, or chief executive officer. When you think of the important role the information systems department plays in the success of such organizations as airlines, banks, insurance companies, and credit card companies, it is quite easy to understand why in many organizations the manager of this department is given senior management status. At the same time, in small companies the information systems department may have only one employee.

The Career Path to the Top

As long as computers were primarily used to handle basic processing applications, the manager of the computer department tended to have a technical background. Today, individuals who are selected to head information systems departments may come from either a technical or managerial background. In either case, managers of information systems departments must demonstrate communication skills that enable them to speak to users without overwhelming them with computerese. They also need to have a thorough knowledge of the organization for which they work. Typically, information systems managers have several years of experience working for an organization before they are selected to head an information systems department. A possible path to the top, which includes both technical and managerial experience, is as follows:

Programmer

Systems Analyst

Project Manager

First-Line Manager

Second-Line Manager

CIO or Top Manager

Leading the Information Systems Department of a Fortune 500 Company

International Multifoods, a Fortune 500 company, is a leading processor and distributor of food products to food service, industrial, agricultural, and retail customers in the United States, Canada, and Venezuela. Paul Taylor was the organization's first vice president of information services. Paul was very familiar with International Multifoods operations, as he had been responsible for the performance of one of the company's major operating divisions involving ten plants, one thousand employees, and $300 million annual sales. Although Paul had impressive managerial experience, he had absolutely no technical computer background. He did know, however, what he had wanted the corporate information services department to do for the division that he had recently headed. Furthermore, his division had been the company's largest user of the corporate data center resources.

Top management selected Paul for the position of vice president of information services because the company needed someone to turn around the computer operations. The department had not been meeting users' needs. Thus Paul became the company's first vice president of information services—a position that reported at first to the office of the chief executive and later to the chief financial officer. The corporate data processing department and all related operations were incorporated within the new information services department.

Paul's first task in his new position was to acquire the technical knowledge he needed, which he did by attending classes and seminars. During Paul's six and one-half years managing the information services department, he developed a coherent long-term strategy to ensure that the computer function of the department was meeting the needs of the users and that the corporation was making effective use of the available computer technology resources. Paul oversaw the building of a data center after recommending this major capital expenditure to the board of directors.

After the data center was built, a mainframe was installed. Later, the mainframe was shut down, and minicomputers and microcomputers were installed in corporate headquarters. The tasks formerly done by the mainframe were given to an outside service bureau. In addition, Paul decentralized computer operations so that the corporate headquarters' department did not have direct responsibility for the operation and maintenance of the computers of remote operating divisions. These divisions would just send in month-end consolidated financial information. The payroll operation, however, became centralized and was handled by the outside service bureau. By the time Paul left this position to work as an executive with a custom-printing service bureau, he had met the challenge of his assignment by making the computer operations responsive to corporate needs.

The Job of Second-Line Managers

The information systems departments of many organizations have large staffs composed of project managers, programmers, systems analysts, network operators, computer operators, database analysts, librarians, maintenance workers, and many other employees. Second-line managers are usually in charge of a specific function of the information systems department and the staff supporting that function. They report to the chief information officer and may advance within a few years to this position. Although organizations vary greatly in their number of second-line managers and the functions that they handle, the following chart illustrates some of the positions that you would commonly find at this level. Of course, job titles differ from organization to organization.

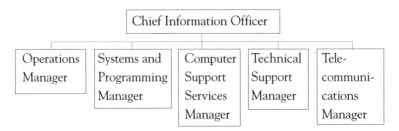

Education

While there is no universally accepted way to prepare for managerial positions, employers are increasingly preferring these individuals to have a bachelor's degree in computer science or engineering. For significant upward mobility, an M.B.A. or an M.S. in computer science is a definite asset.

Operations Manager at a Retail Chain

The job of operations manager is to direct and control the operation of all computer and peripheral equipment of an organization. The more essential the operation of computers is to the success of an organization, the more important the position of operations manager becomes. Just imagine the financial cost to an airline if the computers are down for more than a few minutes. Think of the dangerous situation that can occur if computers are not operating properly at nuclear power plants. Contemplate the confusion that occurs at banks, insurance companies, and brokerage houses when their computers are not working.

Bill Needham was the operations manager for the information systems department of an upscale retail chain with more than seventy outlets. One of the minimum requirements for being an operations manager is having a good knowledge of hardware, software, and operating systems. Bill amply met these requirements by having almost thirty years of work experience at IBM after graduating from college. His jobs at IBM ranged from education and marketing to systems engineering. While working as a systems engineer at IBM, Bill learned of the opening for an operations manager at the retail chain. He decided to take advantage of the early retirement program IBM was offering to become operations manager at the chain's headquarters.

In large organizations, operations managers may have many section managers and supervisors reporting to them. At the retail chain, Bill had four operators who were responsible for the operation of an IBM AS/400, a midrange computer. Throughout the day and evening, the point-of-sale equipment in the company's outlets sent records of all transactions to the AS/400, plus the time and attendance records of employees. The computer was used to keep track of sales and inventory and to generate a variety of reports for management.

Bill reported to the vice president of information systems and had responsibilities similar to those of most operations managers.

Because his department was small, and because of his personal interest in programming, he spent more hands-on time working on the operation of the computer system than do other managers. Nevertheless, looking at Bill's major responsibilities will give you a good idea of the type of work this position entails.

- reporting to management on the status of the system, including how close to capacity and speed it is operating

- ensuring adequate computing capacity is available to handle the work

- handling equipment breakdowns so that downtime is minimized

- keeping up-to-date on new technologies and how they apply to the company's system

- installing new software to update the system

- putting new equipment in retail outlets, which involves selecting, evaluating, testing, packing, and sending equipment to the stores

- negotiating some contracts with outside vendors for maintenance, supplies, and other services such as off-site microfiche storage

- staffing the operations department, which includes the hiring, firing, and training of operators

- checking operator logs to see if the operators are handling the problems of store personnel correctly

- working on disaster preparedness plans

Since the trend in many organizations is to decentralize computer operations and put personal computers on users' desks, the need for operations managers is not likely to increase significantly.

Still, this position remains important in systems management because downtime can be disastrous for many organizations. Bill, whose interest in computers goes back to his childhood when his father worked for IBM, believes opportunity for advancement in this position lies in becoming vice president of information systems or moving to a company with a larger operations staff.

Programming Manager at a Cruise Line

Jim Horio is a true computer buff who spends most of his time working with computers. During the day for the past fourteen years he has worked in the information systems departments of corporations, while at night and on weekends he works at home on projects for his own computer firm. You learned about Jim's company in Chapter 4. While working as a contract programmer several years ago, Jim saw a newspaper ad for a senior programmer with a major cruise line. Lured by the possibility of taking reduced-price cruises, Jim applied for and obtained the job. As a senior programmer, he designed, modified, and wrote new applications programs and worked on user programs for accounting, reservations, and purchasing on two S/38 computers. Within one year Jim was asked to become the programming manager, a second-line management position that reported to the manager of information systems. Besides programming, Jim now had the additional responsibilities of assigning work to the company's six junior and senior programmers, prioritizing assignments, and seeing all the work was done on time—typical responsibilities for a programming manager. Jim's rapid ascent up the information systems career ladder continued as he became a manager of information systems reporting to the vice president of finance one year later. When the cruise line moved its operations from California to Florida, Jim decided to leave the company. Nevertheless, he had fulfilled his original dream by taking cruises to Alaska, Japan, Europe, and the Caribbean, including a working vacation programming an S/34 computer aboard ship.

A New Job

Today, Jim is managing the information systems for a manufacturing firm that builds high-tech pumps for instruments. Reflect-
ing the trend to outsource work, all of the labor is contracted out.
The programmers and networking people whom he directs either
work at home or come to the firm; they are not company employees. Jim's job is an administrative one. He is dealing with the Year
2000 software problem, purchasing new software, and managing
the company's computer systems and networks. To handle a job at
this level, Jim says that you need management skills and knowledge of systems, applications, and networking.

Division Manager of Information Systems at a Very Large Corporation

Bill Fisher's father encouraged him to get a degree in business so
he would have the skills needed for a successful career. This has
proved to be solid advice as Bill has used the skills he learned getting a B.S. in marketing and an M.B.A. along with technical
training to swiftly climb the career ladder in information systems
at a large Fortune 500 corporation. After a two-year stint in the
U.S. Army, Bill became a trainee in information services at the
company where he is today a division manager of information
systems.

Career Path

Bill's technical training at the corporation began with an eight-
week course that covered all the fundamentals of systems. His first
assignment was on financial systems. After only four months, he
was moved to another product area where he supported and
developed marketing-related systems for two years. His next move
was to the information service training group, where he taught
technical courses and helped the company with recruiting for five
years. Then Bill was promoted to the position of senior analyst,

becoming part of a team developing systems to manage high-rise warehouses. After three years with the group, he became a project leader and one year later, a supervisor. As a supervisor, he left the technical area and returned to marketing, becoming responsible for a team that developed various marketing systems. His next step up the career ladder was a promotion to information services manager in Geneva, Switzerland, where he stayed for four years until returning to corporate headquarters and his present position.

On the Job

Bill has started a group that is responsible for all systems that support his company's ordering process. He finds that he is spending the majority of his time in meetings. He meets with his staff members regarding projects and personnel issues; with end users considering projects, visions, and changes; and with other personnel in information services concerning the information technology and product direction that should be pursued. A great deal of Bill's work revolves around the 110 people on his team who work in smaller teams to accomplish the tasks of his unit.

Career Advice

Bill believes that solid organizational skills are required to be a successful systems manager as so many demands are placed on your time. He also suggests developing your communication, technical, and decision-making skills.

More Second-Line Manager Positions

Technical Support Managers have the responsibility of finding new and better ways to use equipment and meet users' needs. In many organizations, the functions of this position are handled by the chief information systems officer or other second-line mangers.

Telecommunications Managers are in charge of the efficient transmission of information for organizations that are geographically dispersed. They also are responsible for the installation and administration of local-area networks (LANS).

Security Managers are increasingly being found at the second-level management. Their primary responsibility is to protect data so that unauthorized persons cannot examine, copy, or alter them.

Edp Managers are now moving away from their traditional location in the accounting area and into information systems. Their function is to supervise the evaluation of computer systems and operational procedures. They identify problem areas and suggest solutions.

Employment Trends and Salaries

Organizations are increasingly placing a greater value on information and expanding their information services. Demand is generally high for individuals to fill top-level positions in information systems management. Organizations are especially looking for managers who can communicate easily with information users and computer users. There is currently a trend in many organizations to decentralize computer operations, and this has resulted in the placement of many highly trained professionals (programmers and systems analysts) under the jurisdiction of department heads rather than top-level information systems managers. In addition, many organizations are "outsourcing," which is having service companies do information systems work formerly done in-house. Decentralization and outsourcing have resulted in many organizations looking for CIOs who can lead information systems departments through these profound changes. These changes also have led to reduced responsibility for some managers, less demand for middle-level managers, and the elimination of some second-level management positions. At the same time, many organizations are actively seeking second-level managers in telecommunications and security, two fast-growing areas in information systems.

Salaries continue to increase for top-level managers of information systems. Those employed at organizations earning the highest revenues tend to have the highest salaries. The following chart shows the current range of salaries for information systems managers:

Information Systems Salaries for Management

Title	Large Installations*
Vice President	$99,000–$147,500
Director	$83,000–$113,000
Senior Manager, Systems & Programming	$72,000–$ 92,000
Manager, Systems & Programming	$67,000–$ 82,000
Manager, Technical Services	$65,000–$ 83,000
Senior Manager, Operations	$54,000–$ 72,000
Manager, Telecommunications	$65,000–$ 80,000
Network Administrator	$37,000–$ 58,000

* Large installations generally have staffs of more than fifty and use larger mainframes or multiple minis in stand-alone and/or cluster configurations. PC utilization commonly involves LANS or PC-to-server-to-host communications, tying multiple sites together using telecommunications networks.

Source: Excerpted with permission from Robert Half International Inc., P.O. Box 33597, Kansas City, MO 64120.

CHAPTER EIGHT

Using the Computer in Special Areas

Design, Manufacturing, Animation, Music, and Entertainment

C omputers have absolutely revolutionized the way so much is done in the world. Things are so different now from what they were just ten years ago. The impressive special effects of movies such as *Titanic* and *Jurassic Park* owe their creation to what can be done on computers as do so many of the animated commercials that are seen every day on television. In music, musicians now create, record, and manipulate sound on the computer. It is not just the entertainment world the computer has changed. Everything—from bridges to stadiums to overcoats—is being designed on the computer. And in plants throughout the world, the computer is out on the floor helping in the manufacture of cars, tools, planes, and thousands of other items.

Designing with the Computer

The lower cost and increased power of computers plus the design of sophisticated software packages have led to the common use of computers by designers, whether they are architects, engineers, interior designers, or other design specialists. Today's homes, cars, planes, refrigerators, toasters, and furniture all are being designed on the computer. Computer-aided design (CAD) no longer is confined to large corporations such as Ford Motor Company and Boeing Aircraft; you now will find designers in small offices and homes creating designs on powerful PCs. CAD is swiftly replacing designers' drawing boards no matter what they are designing.

To use CAD, the designer can begin by scanning in a design, can use designs or elements of designs in a software-design program, or can use the computer to create a design. Throughout the design process, the designer makes changes by using the command functions of the CAD program. For example, lines can be shortened, lengthened, curved, erased, moved, and so on, and sections of the design can be moved around. The design even can be viewed in 3-D, and a part can be rotated to produce multiple views of it. When the design is finished, it can be stored for reuse or future modification. The design also can be reproduced with a printer or a plotter that uses special pens to draw the design.

Training

As CAD is used in so many different careers, the training requirements vary. Many individuals are self-taught while others have studied CAD at colleges and technical schools. On the job, most CAD users constantly update their skills by interacting with coworkers as well as learning new programs.

A Project Designer Uses CAD

After working for two commercial interior design firms, Dawn Jones started her own company, DJ Design. Her offices are in her home, where she has two computers set up on AutoCAD and a plotter to plot drawings. She subcontracts other designers who do CAD work to help out with drafting and space planning.

The primary focus of Dawn's company is facility management. One of her clients is a major consumer electronics company, where she works with the real estate and facilities operations department, coordinating requirements of growth with different departments and looking at the entire master planning for the campus of buildings. One of Dawn's primary tasks is to keep all the floor plans for these buildings up-to-date on CAD. Keeping track of approximately 650,000 square feet, just in Indianapolis alone, plus five plants/buildings in Juarez, Mexico, and El Paso, Texas, has proven to be more than a full-time job.

Dawn's company also does tenant space planning for developers of such facilities as medical offices, hospitals, and restaurants. Developers who lease space come to Dawn's firm requesting a space plan for tenants or prospective tenants. First Dawn meets with the tenant to ascertain what the tenant's needs are. Once she knows the tenant's space requirements, she does the actual design work on the computer. Her task is much simpler if the plan of the building is already on CAD. Then Dawn simply finds the plan and proceeds with her space design. If the building plan is not on the computer, she has to go out and measure the building, return to the office, and draw the shell on the computer before she begins her actual space plan. Her completed space plan is shown to the tenant. If the tenant likes her plan and the brokers and leasing agents come to an agreement, Dawn does the construction drawings. This involves such things as showing where walls, restrooms, and storage areas will go. She also does an electrical plan and a finish plan, which has details about wall coverings, carpets, and other finishing touches. All of her plans are done on the computer. After the design is approved by an architect and the necessary permits are obtained, Dawn supervises the construction.

Dawn gained her expertise in designing space while working for her degree in environmental design at Purdue University. Even though she had taught herself CAD in high school by doing the tutorial and reading the manual, she took three CAD courses in college. On the job, Dawn continues to learn more about CAD from her coworkers, who have different specialty areas in which they excel. Dawn would like to continue doing space design work. She sees an ongoing demand for individuals who can do this work, as so many developers want the plans for older buildings to be on CAD. Although the initial drawing of a building is not much quicker with a CAD program than with pencil and drawing board, the CAD plan is more accurate and can be revised quickly.

Civil Engineers Use CAD

Bob Stallard is an assistant project manager for Granite Construction Company. Although Bob primarily uses CAD for developing charts and graphs for presentations, the civil engineers who work for him use it for all their construction drawings of roads and bridges. Most of these engineers are self-taught because the CAD systems are so complicated. The engineers must do the tutorials and then learn all the options and possibilities by solving real problems.

Bob considers the computer a valuable aid that facilitates the production of drawings. It replaces the normal drafting tools such as pencils, compasses, protractors, and triangles. For example, to draw a circle, the engineer does not use a compass but instead keys in the radius and specific coordinates. By using the computer, the engineers in Bob's department are able to make precise—not just accurate—calculations and drawings. They also are more productive because drawings can be swiftly revised, a process that is both slow and expensive when done on the drawing board. Besides assisting engineers in their drawings, special CAD programs can be used to analyze their designs. CAD helps engineers answer questions: What is the maximum weight a bridge can hold? What is the most efficient design for a cloverleaf? And so forth.

Manufacturing with the Computer

The age of computer-aided manufacturing (CAM) is here. And robots are no longer just starring in movies; they are out in the factory doing innumerable tasks, from working in hazardous situations to performing the same job over and over until they are reprogrammed. The automation of factories continues to accelerate as does the demand for professionals who can design and implement these automated systems. Sophisticated CAD/CAM systems work together so that the design is developed on the computer and then sent to computer-aided manufacturing equipment.

An Engineer Works with CAD/CAM

Greg Lyon works at Aircom Metal Products, which manufactures products through sheet metal fabrication and plastic injection molding. Many of the parts produced by Aircom lend themselves to the use of CAD and CAM. Greg, who is an electrical engineer, spends considerable time designing parts using CAD. He learned how to use the company's system by reading manuals and observing an experienced CAD user.

Greg uses the customer's part drawings and specifications to develop and draw a tool design on the computer. Then a CAM expert, who is a machinist, will determine what aspects of the drawing can be machined by computer-controlled equipment. Because there are many different types of computer-controlled machines hooked directly to the CAD/CAM system, the CAM expert must choose the appropriate piece of equipment. After a machine is chosen, the CAM expert will use the computer-aided machining software to generate the program code, which is sent to the machine via serial cable. After minimal setup, a machinist can begin to produce the tooling designed to make parts according to the consumer's specifications.

Not only does Aircom's CAD/CAM system save considerable time and money, it also has increased quality through increased accuracy. In the years prior to CAD/CAM, these same tool designs would have had to be hand drawn and machined using calculations performed by the machinist. Today, with the computer's assistance, a piece can be drawn and machined accurately within four decimal places (.0001 inches), and the software is continually getting better. According to Greg, CAD/CAM is now the cornerstone of manufacturing, and companies must use it to be competitive.

Learning to Be a Graphic Designer

Sarah Craven is a talented artist who always took art courses in high school and college. After college, she attended a postgraduate school to learn graphic design with the ultimate career goal of becoming the art director of an advertising agency. Sarah did not spend her time at school learning how to draw layouts by hand. Instead, she constantly worked on the computer. In her classes, she learned how to use several graphics programs, all with different capabilities. Out of class, she worked on her own to master the programs. This involved working with a copywriter to create layouts and designs for print ads. Whatever she could visualize, she learned to do by manipulating images on her computer screen using a mouse or the keyboard. The only limitation she truly faced was having enough computer memory. Sarah has discovered that the more you know about computers, the more likely you are to be hired in today's job market. Since graduation, she has spent her days on the computer working as an art director on several national ad campaigns.

Animating with the Computer

Computers have changed the way animation is done. In fact, many movies could not have been created without the techniques that have been developed in computer animation. Although some animators are self-taught, many receive computer training at art or design colleges or schools. Before entering the job market, animators create portfolios that let prospective employers evaluate their work. Animators typically work for movie and television studios, advertising firms, and software companies.

A Computer Animator

Don Bajus is an animator who has made some imaginative commercials that you might have viewed on television. Today he has a new tool—the computer—to help him animate. Don can now animate in 3-D and light the characters and a scene as if they were real. The computer will know where the objects and the characters are as well as their dimensions and will be able to compute where the highlights fall and where to cast the shadows. If a client wants a different camera angle, it is no longer a task requiring weeks of work. Given the proper instructions, the computer will change the camera angle and the lighting automatically.

Don also can use the computer to move characters rather than draw every movement. The computer can make these changes easily compared to cel animation. In cel animation, every movement is a series of drawings made up of key position drawings and in-between drawings. It is the same process in computer animation, only the animator moves the character into key positions, such as in a walk sequence where the first key position could have the left leg on the ground and the right leg lifting. The next key position could have the right leg outstretched ready to come down, the left leg moved back, and the body leaning slightly forward. The animator creates all the key positions and then lets the computer do the in-between drawings. This is not an easier task than cel animation because of the difficulty of the dimensional concept. However, having the computer insert the in-between drawings can be timesaving if enough good key positions are done.

Now it is also very easy for animators to change colors. Cel animation art is finished on cels with inked/copied lines and paint. When the computer is used, colors are added through a paint program and are affected by the lighting of the scene. Colors in

computer animation can be adjusted quickly or changed completely, unlike traditional hand-painted cel animation. After
touching the cursor to the paint palette to pick a new color, the
animator then can move the cursor to the area and color to be
changed. By pressing the cursor button, every frame in that scene
will have the new color in the chosen area. In cel animation, this
kind of change would take weeks. In the new computer 2-D cel-
painting programs, which are replacing the old way of cel painting, the painting still takes a long time. Nevertheless, the benefits
include the capability of adding textures, having constant-density
shadows, and creating automatic drop shadows.

New software programs let Don either draw on paper and then
scan the drawing into the computer or draw directly on the
screen. From there he can paint the drawing. He also can swiftly
move characters in or out of a scene or from the foreground to the
background. The backgrounds, foregrounds, and characters are
on separate levels, and each level can be moved independently in
any direction. This allows for the multiplane effect, as in a zoom-
in where multiple levels of objects pick up speed as they move
closer to the viewer—something very complicated in cel animation. The more sophisticated animated commercials seen today
were most likely created by animators like Don using computers to
produce them.

Computer animation technology is advancing so rapidly that
programs are becoming more capable each year. Don, however,
feels that programs are still limited in being able to do things in
the ways most animators want, as you tend to feel more like a
computer technician than an artist when working with them. He
believes the main advantage to using computer animation is the
ultimate control it gives the animator over each and every item in
the scenes and sees very exciting days ahead for animators as the
computer programs become more user friendly. In the future, he
would like to film his own animated short stories using the emerging technology.

Learning to use a computer for animation can be quite frustrating, according to Don. "At first, the computer won't do anything you want," he says. "But as you gain skill, it will do almost whatever you want." Don is glad that he was an animator before he started to use the computer because he can think beyond the obvious things the computer can do to assist him in his work. Although there are schools teaching computer animation, Don believes that you should become an animator first so you will truly understand what animation is and will realize that the computer is just a tool—an expensive, powerful, and sometimes obstinate "pencil."

Computer Musicians and Technicians

The computer has invaded the music world. It is being used in composing, recording, and manipulating music and sound. One person with a computer can produce the sound of a symphony orchestra or a rock band. Musical computer buffs often work in the entertainment arena creating music for movies, games, CD-ROMS, videos, and other multimedia products. Some compose music while others work on the technical side, mixing and editing the sounds. Computer musicians often work for production studios, record companies, and music publishers, but many freelance.

Training

Formal training is not a prerequisite for a career making music on the computer. Many have learned the technical aspects of computer music through on-the-job experience and are self-taught musicians. Nevertheless, as more jobs in music involve computer technology, those with formal technical training will have an advantage in the job market.

Salaries

The salaries of computer musicians like, those of all musicians, vary widely. Starting salaries can be quite low. Experienced computer musicians, however, can earn as much as $70,000 annually.

Creating Music on the Computer

If Johann Sebastian Bach were alive today, he would probably be composing on the computer. Just as Bach wrote music to order for patrons, Doug Benge and Pete Schmutte, owners of Earmark Music Works, are creating music for clients, usually advertisers. The first step involves talking to the client to find out what the music is to accomplish—the desired mood or image. Then Doug or Pete will use a computer program as they compose a piece of music. The musical notation program transmits what they play on a keyboard to notes that they can see on the computer screen. They remove the floppy disk from the computer, go into their recording studio, put the disk into a computer, and assign their newly composed piece to different synthesizers using two software programs to create the music in a rough form. The client listens to the music, and any necessary changes are made before the final product is recorded. Just as Doug and Pete create music on the computer, so do other musicians throughout the world.

The Marriage of Entertainment and the Computer

Anyone who has seen movies recently is aware of the wide use of computer-generated special effects. In Hollywood, a great number of small firms are emerging to meet the demand of filmmakers who want to put the extra zing of special effects into their movies. Even the giant studios are setting up in-house departments to develop new film techniques. And these techniques can be used to save money. For example, the computer can turn a herd of ten charging bulls into one hundred and can eliminate the need to send actors to exotic locales for filming with just a little work from computer animators. The public's demand for ever more exciting special effects in films will lead to an increasing number of jobs for imaginative computer visual effects and software creators.

Games are not just appealing to children; adults spend hours playing them on computers and entertainment systems. After all, these games are fun. You can enjoy the challenge of Myst or try your hand at Final Fantasy VII. Besides playing video and computer games, computer buffs can find jobs creating the software for games as well as the hardware to operate them.

A number of small companies are emerging to produce not only interactive entertainment but also educational materials. In addition, Hollywood studios are entering this arena. Jobs in interactive media are available for computer buffs who are graphic designers, software programmers, and hardware creators as well as those interested in sales, marketing, and management positions.

Employment Trends

The computer is now an important tool in design, manufacturing, animation, music, and entertainment, and its importance will continue to grow. While the number of computer-related careers is expected to increase, there will be keen competition for these positions in the arts arena. This is one area, however, where computer buffs can combine their love of the computer with their special talents.

CHAPTER NINE

Finding Internet Jobs
New Opportunities

E ven though the Internet is very young, it is now a career destination that is offering computer buffs a wide array of new jobs because of the myriad ways in which it is being used. While the number-one use is E-mail, the Internet is also being used for its information resources, marketing, games, educational activities, and services ranging from checking a bank balance to planning a trip. Companies are begging for employees who are technically savvy and who can help them get on-line. There is also a demand for people who can adapt the traditional skills of advertising, marketing, consulting, researching, teaching, customer service, and sales to the demands of this new medium. As you read this chapter, learn more about Internet companies and employment opportunities by visiting Web sites that are given in the text.

Providing Access to the Internet

Providing access to the Internet is one of the fastest-growing areas in the computer industry. Both companies and individuals are clamoring for connection to the Net, and there is an intense competition among access providers to sign up new customers. From technicians to software engineers, from service representatives to marketing professionals, the demand for skilled computer buffs is high at companies providing access to the Internet.

Where the Jobs Are

Many different companies provide access to the Internet. You can find jobs with companies who maintain the Network Access Points (NAPs) such as the New York Network Access Point maintained by SprintLink, www.sprintlink.net, and the San Francisco Network Access Point hosted by Pacific Bell, www.pacbell.com/Products/NAP/. There are jobs with the national and regional backbone operators who run the high-speed lines and equipment that form the underlying structure or "backbone" of the Internet, such as UUNet/AlterNet, http://www.uunet.com, and BBN Planet, http://www.bbn.com. There are jobs with on-line service providers, which includes such giants as America Online, http://www.aol.com/corp/, and Microsoft, http://www.msn.com, as well as the smaller regional and local providers. Finally, many businesses need to create their own internal networks (Intranets) to provide secure business communications within companies as well as a connection to the resources of the Internet.

A Closer Look at an
Internet Service Provider

The majority of Internet Service Providers (ISPs) are local and regional companies that generally operate in just a few telephone area codes. Jim Deibele started Teleport in 1987 with one PC in a spare bedroom. Today, the company is the preeminent Internet provider in the Northwest, serving more than twenty thousand subscribers in Oregon and Southwest Washington. The company employs about seventy people in a community-oriented business that offers support and special discounts to teachers, librarians, and nonprofit organizations.

You can learn more about jobs at a regional Internet service provider by visiting the Teleport Web site at http://www.teleport.com. The two largest employee categories at the firm are customer service representative and technical service representative.

Other jobs associated with the Web include Web content developer and Web designer. And of course, as in every business, there are jobs in operations, accounting, and human resources.

Overview of Jobs

Jeff Shannon, in charge of outreach at Teleport, reports a trend among the rapidly growing ISPs to offer "24 by 7" or twenty-four-hour-a-day, seven-day-a-week technical support. This is the most labor-intensive position in most ISPs. Jeff calls the technical support staff "real bridge people" because of the connection they provide between the ISP and the consumer. He feels that it is a transferable skill in that a good tech can go anywhere and find a job. Jeff also sees continued demand for systems operators who can understand and manipulate the backbone and for creative services personnel who are versed in Web authoring languages such as CGI, HTML, JAVA, and PERL.

Outfitting Companies and Individuals with the Proper Hardware

The Internet is on a continuous cycle in which each advance in programs and services stimulates a demand for increased speed, and each advance in speed opens up a new area of possible services. The market for people to design and build Internet hardware will be strong for the foreseeable future, although just which line or piece of hardware will be the standard in the future is still to be determined.

Today's network is composed of equipment that is designed to work together regardless of the manufacturer, using the common standard TCP/IP (or Transmission-Control Protocol/Internet Protocol). This is called "open architecture" and is partly responsible for the proliferation of manufacturers as well as the rapid development of new technologies. When each part of a system will work with everyone else's part, then a new component of a system can be developed and integrated without having to rebuild the entire system. Small startup firms are able to get their products to a market that is no longer the exclusive province of the major firms.

If you are interested in helping to create the physical part of the Internet, you might work at one of the major equipment vendors such as Cisco Systems, http://www.cisco.com, or Bay Networks, http://www.baynetworks.com, or at a line provider such as Pacific Bell or Ameritech.

Developing Software for the Internet

Software developments are in large part responsible for the directions in which the Internet has grown. It has provided the protocols that let many different kinds of computers, ranging from PCs to mainframes, talk to each other. The popular E-mail services owe their existence to the evolution of software programs. The development of Web browsers has led to the great surge in popularity of Web surfing by providing a simple way to navigate the Web by clicking on links using the mouse. Two of the major browsers are Netscape's Navigator and Microsoft's Internet Explorer. Both companies are actively adding new personnel to support their rapid growth and to help them extend their range of services. Job offerings are listed on their Web pages at http://www. netscape.com and http://www.microsoft.com.

Search engines that use the Web browser interface have made it possible for Web users to find the information they seek, whether it is a place to buy a piano or the population of Tokyo. Popular commercial search engines include Yahoo!, http:// www.yahoo.com, and Lycos, http://www.lycos.com. As a computer buff, you could be the software guru who creates another way for the Internet to grow or who helps companies and individuals use the Net for entertainment or profit.

Helping Companies Get on the Net

As the use of the Internet in homes, offices, businesses, the government, and other organizations becomes more and more popular, companies are literally jumping aboard the Net for a variety of reasons. Some companies simply want their stockholders, customers, and employees to think that they are associated with the latest technology. An ever-increasing number want to advertise, market, or sell their products and services using this new medium. Others want to put information about their companies on-line to attract investors and customers and to describe employment opportunities. Whatever the reason, this avalanche of companies coming aboard the Net means jobs for computer buffs who can help the companies become active players on the Internet. There are jobs in marketing, advertising, sales, and consulting as well as jobs in more technical areas such as software engineering and programming.

Working as a Webmaster

Once a company has decided to have an Internet presence, it needs someone to build and maintain its Web site. A successful Web site is often the result of efforts by a diverse group of people working as a team. The Webmaster is like the captain of a ship or the ringmaster of a circus—in charge of everything. A typical group might include a marketing director, a technical manager, a content manager, a public relations specialist, a graphics designer, and the Webmaster.

Duties of a Webmaster

- coordinate and evaluate Web development projects
- understand the company's goals
- work with marketing to be sure the Web site is directed toward the target audience
- have an understanding of design and be able to implement the work of graphic artists
- evaluate and implement Web tools and technology
- monitor Web traffic and determine bandwidth requirements
- maintain and monitor Web site security

Salary

Pay levels for Webmaster positions vary widely and depend somewhat on the size of the company offering the position as well as on the skill levels and responsibilities required. Average salary for an experienced Webmaster is about $55,000. Entry-level Webmasters can earn between $25,000 and $35,000, while a few top-level Webmasters earn more than $95,000.

The Webmaster's Guild

The Webmaster's Guild puts on events for members, runs on-line discussion groups so members can have an opportunity to communicate, and provides a reading list for Webmasters. It also offers seminars to train people to become Webmasters. See the guild's Web site at http://www.webmaster.org for more information.

Providing a Unique Service on the Internet

You don't have to be a technical whiz to work closely with the Internet. One reason the Internet is growing so fast is because it has so many practical uses. The number of unique services that you can find on the Internet is expanding in many imaginative ways. No longer do people have to visit a bank or brokerage firm; now they can turn their homes into branch banks and buy stocks and bonds using the Internet. Job hunting using the Internet has really taken off and is rapidly changing how professional, managerial, and technical people look for work. Webcasting has taken away the need to surf for news, sports, weather, and stock information by delivering the specially tailored information requested by customers directly to their desks. The millions of game players who have become accustomed to playing video games now have the opportunity to play games against or with multiple players on the Internet. On-line information services offer access to millions of documents. Students can now sit at home and take college courses on-line from approximately four hundred colleges and universities in the United States and Canada, with even more schools expected to come on-line soon.

All of these innovations offer a wide range of employment opportunities to match the skills and interests of computer buffs, whether they are technical types who want to work with databases, systems support, or software development, or those who want to be closely involved with the Internet as customer service representatives, marketing and sales team members, or researchers.

On-Line Banking—Wells Fargo Bank

Over one hundred years ago, Wells Fargo stage coaches traveled across the American West delivering mail and cash. Today the bank is one of the leaders in offering on-line banking services through the Internet, using ISPs such as America Online and Prodigy and software programs such as Quicken and Microsoft Money. Consumers can pay bills, view their account information, and transfer money between their Wells Fargo accounts. Furthermore, merchants can accept on-line payments for the goods and services they sell over the Internet with the help of Wells Fargo's secured Internet electronic payment service.

Wells Fargo has more than three hundred employees supporting their on-line business. There are approximately seventy-five professionals who handle marketing, systems development, channel management, and operational management. The other employees handle customer service of the on-line business. Computer buffs can go aboard the Net at http://wellsfargo.com to view employment opportunities for such positions as product manager, senior applications programmer/analyst, Web site manager, technical support supervisor, marketing manager, and many others.

On-Line Job Listing Service—JobTrak

When Ken Ramberg graduated from college in 1987, he saw first-hand the inefficiency in the way employers had to post job listings separately to different universities. Along with two partners, he started JobTrak in 1988 as a central data processing center. Today, most major university career centers have teamed up with JobTrak to process job listings and make them available to their job seekers both via the Web and in hard copy. In the future, Ken sees employers moving away from newspapers and onto the Internet to post job listings as they can include far more information for less cost.

When JobTrak started, the company had four employees. One was a programmer and the rest were out trying to get business. Today, JobTrak has more than eighty-five employees. In addition to top management and office and human resources managers, JobTrak has five full-time programmers who integrate the database with the Net. There are three trainers who work with the customer service employees who themselves need to have a broad knowledge of the Internet.

On-Line Gaming—TEN

In September 1996, TEN became the first commercial Internet entertainment network to offer nationwide high-speed multi-player gaming. In less than four months, more than twenty-two thousand paying subscribers registered to play TEN's hit action, strategy, simulation, and role-playing computer games. In just one year, the staff increased from 15 to 120.

Chris Lombardi is the editorial director at TEN, where he has three major responsibilities:

1. *Create editorial materials related to games on the ten service.* His team of six editors writes strategy and tips articles, news about games and events on TEN, and support materials such as "Help" and "ReadMe" files.

2. *Create and administer events on the game service.* His staff develops ideas for game tournaments and contests and then works with the marketing group to make these events happen.

3. *Evaluate new games for ten.* His team acts as the "gaming experts" for the company. Before a new game is brought onto TEN, the team makes sure it is a quality product and appropriate for on-line gaming.

In order to handle his responsibilities, Chris works between fifty-five and sixty-five hours a week. Throughout his workday, he goes onto the Web to do research, put up new editorial materials, get information from the company's Intranet, and see how things are going on the TEN site. He has continual contact with the artists and designers, the marketing team, the people who develop relationships with game companies and bring new games to TEN, and the various members of the technology staff, including programmers, HTML writers, and database managers.

Selling Products on the Internet

The excitement is high, and TV ads abound telling people how they can make big money selling a product on the Internet. While the opportunities are decidedly there for individuals to own successful Internet businesses, there are several reality checks that future Net entrepreneurs need to make. Sales on the Internet are not booming yet. There are more browsers than buyers in most on-line stores. Only a very few companies are now making a profit in cyberspace. It is not easy to establish a successful on-line business—knowledge, dedication, and hard work are the key ingredients. Do your homework before you try to start a business, learn your way around the Internet, and understand your competition.

Amazon.com—an Amazon-Sized Bookstore

Today, Amazon.com is considered a pioneer, and it has only been doing business since 1994. In keeping with its namesake river, this on-line bookstore has more than five times as many titles as you'll find at even the largest land-based chain superstores, and it is steadily growing. Visit the store at http://www.amazon.com to see the special features. Point and click on "Employment Opportunities" to discover the many positions available in such areas as programming, customer service, systems administration, Web design, finance, public relations, database architecture, copywriting, and advertising.

CarSmart—Driving Business to Car Dealers

CarSmart went on-line at http://www.carsmart.com in the third quarter of 1996 to assist consumers in locating, pricing, purchasing, and leasing new or used vehicles. Business really took off. One year later, the Web site was receiving twenty thousand requests a day from consumers wanting to find nearby dealers who had specific vehicles. And within one more year, the volume of requests had more than tripled and the staff required to handle the work had doubled.

Here's a brief look at some of the positions at CarSmart. The head programmer manages the programming department, which has four support programmers. They work with very sophisticated databases and are constantly adding new features as consumers and dealers request them. An advertising analyst spends the day surfing the Internet searching for sites where the company can establish links to get more customers. Six salespeople have the task of signing up more dealers. All have to be Internet savvy as they often show dealers how to get aboard the Net. Four dealer assistant coordinators who are able to get around in Windows process the inquiries and send them to the dealers. Four or more data-entry people are needed to update the car inventories. The president, Michael Gorun, who was one of the founders of the service, coordinates the entire process. This job, like those at any other start-up company, requires a tremendous amount of work. Twelve-hour days are common.

Keep Up with Changes on the Internet

Dedicated computer buffs, the Internet is the communications channel of the computer world. Use it to keep yourself informed about what is happening in the computer industry. Use it to chat with computer professionals and to find out about job openings and companies. Visit the home pages of Internet magazines and newspapers frequently to look for career and technology information. Check what is happening at companies like Microsoft and Netscape—leading players in the Internet world. As you become more and more knowledgeable about the Net, bookmark those sites that offer the solid career information you want. And have fun surfing!

CHAPTER TEN

Using Computers on the Job

An A-to-Z Look at Technology in the Workplace

T hirty years ago, only large corporations had computers. Now, more than 50 percent of all workers in the United States use a PC, and the number is steadily climbing upward. It is becoming quite difficult today to find a job that does not involve the use of a computer in some way. And some workers don't just have desktop computers, they also have laptops for use outside of the office. You'll find computers used in just about every job today. Police have them in their patrol cars, pilots use them to fly planes, engineers use them to design roads and bridges, and lawyers research legal issues on them. Indeed, this is the Information Age, with computers in firehouses, supermarkets, hotels, auto repair shops, restaurants, offices, factory floors, operating rooms, dairy barns, and just about every other workplace.

Computer-Related Jobs from A to Z

Much to the delight of computer buffs, almost every job in the twenty-first century will be involved in some way with the computer. This chapter explores the use of the computer in a wide variety of jobs from airline pilot to zoo manager.

A is for Accountant, Actuary— and Airline Pilot

Doug Allington is a senior pilot flying an MD-80 for Northwest Airlines. Almost everything he does as a pilot is related in some way to computers. When he bids for routes each month, the computer assigns him and the other pilots to routes by seniority. Upon arriving at the airport for a flight, a clerk punches his employee number into a computer, and the computer gives him a list of the flight crew. Then an hour before takeoff, he receives a computer printout from the flight planning computer listing such things as weather at takeoff, weather at destination, in-route weather, time of trip, routing, winds at cruise altitude, and fuel load. The computer also predicts the plane weight, winds, and temperature at takeoff and gives the optimal runway and takeoff speed. Just before the door closes, the computer provides him with the final weight. Once the plane is on the runway, Doug takes over and the computer doesn't have much to do. Of course, the computers in the control tower are busy tracking all the planes. A computer aboard the MD-80, which is taking in information from all over the plane, can land the plane in really bad weather. Doug puts information about the heading, course, and speed in this computer. An aircraft communications addressing and reporting computer sends information about arrival and departure times and delays to the airline computer system. This updates the arrival time you see on the screens at the airport. Doug also can use this computer to send in maintenance reports.

According to Doug, the MD-80 has only a first-generation computer system, while the airline's airbuses are the most computerized commercial planes. On the airbuses, the pilot watches six monitors instead of gauges, the plane is steered by a joystick instead of a wheel, and the computer monitors the pilot's actions and will not let pilots exceed the performance limit of the plane. Pilots flying these planes are acting like computer systems managers. Doug says that today's pilots must be computer-wise as computers play such an important role in all aspects of flying.

B is for Banker, Broker—and Beautician

Kenn Williams is a distinguished hairdresser and a computer buff who is very glad the computer age is here. Kenn would not like to run his salon without a computer. His previous salon was totally computerized, and he hopes his new one will be soon. Computers help Kenn with the business side of hairdressing in scheduling appointments, doing the payroll, keeping an inventory of all retail sales in the shop, and handling all his bookkeeping chores. The computer is a true time-saver for Kenn. For example, instead of taking six to eight hours to do the payroll every week, the computer lets him finish this task in minutes and even prints out the payroll checks. But beyond this, the computer is an aid in the artistic side of hairdressing. By just pushing a few keys on the computer keyboard, Kenn can find out the correct hair color for individual clients as well as the date of their last permanent. With computer imaging, clients will soon know what they will look like with a certain hairstyle and color. In the future, Kenn believes that clients will not have to wait until they arrive at a salon to get this visual image of themselves. Through direct computer linkups with salons, clients will be able to tell hairdressers what they want to look like for a special event even before they arrive for their appointments.

C is for Curator, Composer—and Copyeditor

L. T. Brown is one of several copyeditors at the *Indianapolis News*. Copyeditors review and edit the work of reporters so it is ready to be set in type. At the start of L.T.'s day, thirty or forty stories may be stored in the newspaper's computer system waiting to be edited. Reporters have written the stories and given them to their editors, who may have made some changes. The editors have also placed instructions on the stories detailing what kind of headlines are to be used and what the size of the story should be (column length and width). These stories are then sent to the copy chief—

the editor who parcels out assignments and makes sure that the copyeditors are working on what is needed. All this is done by computer on most newspapers.

L.T. pulls a story up on his computer monitor, and the copyediting process begins. As L.T. reads through the copy, he edits. At times, he must do considerable rewriting to meet space specifications that are sometimes so tight that he may substitute the word "try" for "attempt." By the press of a button on his computer, L.T. can tell whether the story is the correct length. When a story is the correct length, L.T. writes the headline and then sends it all to the copy chief, who glances through it for any errors L.T. has not caught and sends it to typesetting. The computer has truly replaced the copyeditor's pencil.

D is for Detective, Designer—and Doctor

Bob Cravens is a doctor who believes that the computer is becoming an intrinsic part of medicine. At present, the main application of the computer for him, besides handling the business of running his office, is for doing research. Bob originally used CD-ROMs for his research; however, he is now turning more to the World Wide Web for current information on new medical procedures. In fact, research has become so easy that he is now able to find years and years of medical research on a topic in a matter of seconds. Bob also carries a portable computer in his pocket, which he uses to keep appointment information, phone numbers, and his calendar of activities and meetings. As an orthopedic surgeon, Bob is looking forward to the day when he is doing hip replacement surgery with the aid of the computer. At present, it is very costly to use the computer for this procedure. However, using the computer in hip replacement surgery allows for a prosthesis that exactly fits the patient's hip to be constructed during surgery rather than having to trim the bone to fit the prosthesis.

E is for Editor, Engineer—and Educator

Rita Daniels is a public school teacher who is enthusiastic about computers. Rita is part of the HOTS (higher order thinking skills) program, which is designed to teach children through the use of computers. In order to work with the HOTS program, she participated in a summer training program. This computer program puts children in a specific situation. In the first fifteen minutes of class, the children learn the logical way of thinking about a problem through a teacher-led discussion. Then the children begin working with computers to explore and find the answers to open-ended questions. The children also use the electronic encyclopedia, which has an appealing multimedia approach that combines text, graphics, and sound. For example, the encyclopedia lets the children research President John F. Kennedy and actually hear important speeches in the president's own voice. It is not just her students who are using the computer. Rita uses a computer program to create lessons for her students. She can select pictures and put them directly into their computer lesson along with her own voiced comments.

Children in this two-year computer program, which usually starts in the fourth grade, show greater gains than children in other educational programs. Studies have shown that after third grade, repetition through drill and practice no longer motivates children. Not only does working with the computer motivate and stimulate students, other advantages to working with the computer include:

- reaching children with different learning styles

- helping children realize that no matter how many mistakes they make, the computer will wait for them to get it right before moving on

- forcing children to do correct work as the computer will not accept haphazard work

- improving children's hand-eye coordination skills

- permitting children to escape the embarrassment of turning in work with sloppy handwriting and poor spelling

The use of the computer is increasing each year in schools, with the goal of having all classrooms wired to the Internet in a few years.

F is for Farmer, Food Inspector—and Firefighter

David L. Klingler is the chief inspector of a fire prevention division. When he began working at the fire station in 1986, all files were manual and all reports were typewritten. David, who used his home computer for playing games, began taking the schedules home to put on his computer. The chief was so impressed with David's work that he purchased a computer for the firehouse. He admits to making every mistake in the book before learning how to use the computer, but David ultimately succeeded in giving the computer a vital role at his fire station.

Today, the fire alarm system is completely automated. The computer now gives the station ready access to information about all the buildings in the district. By pushing a few keys, David or any of the other fire fighters can find out the size of the building, the type of alarm system that the building has, and who occupies the building. The location of fire extinguishers also is stored on the computer as well as when they were last serviced. Furthermore, all the fire inspectors now carry hand-held computers instead of clipboards to inspection sites. They punch in record numbers and codes along with a 144-letter description to complete inspections. When the inspectors return to the station, the information can be uploaded quickly into the station's computer, and in less than one minute a printout of the inspection is available. The computer also has helped the firefighters cut 95 percent of all the writing involved in keeping track of hoses and hydrants. In addition, the station can get information and reports on fire responses and fatalities by linking its computer to one in Washington, D.C. The computer has truly become a firefighter at David's station.

G is for Geologist, Graphic Artist— and General Manager

Mark Goff studied music and business in school and is now the general manager of a music store. At his store, the employees cannot do their jobs without using the computer as everything they do is linked to it. All sales transactions and product information is entered into the computer. A record of the store's inventory and sales is kept on the computer. Customer correspondence and intra-office memorandums are done on the computer. The computer is even used to produce the company's bar codes. Here's an example of how the store uses its computer system: Mark just purchased two trombones. They were immediately entered into the computer as a purchase. Then bar code labels were printed to identify the instruments. The repair shop input the work history of each instrument. This allowed the music store to update an instrument's condition in the computer if it were to return to the store for resale or repair. Another task the computer has assumed is keeping track of the musical instruments the music store leases to over one hundred schools in the state. This involves billing over one thousand customers every month—a formidable job without the computer. Even though his store is completely computerized, Mark's background only includes one computer course, which was programming. He points out that most of the computer programs the store uses are very user friendly. Because the menu program is so good, most staff members can usually figure out at once how to use the computer for their tasks.

H is for Historian, Hotel Staffer— and Horse Farm Owner

At Glenmore Farm in Lexington, Kentucky, the owners Barbara, Clay, and Jeff Camp are using computers to help them run their 285-acre horse farm. An amazing amount of information has been stored on the computer for each of the approximately 175 horses on the farm at any one time. With this information, the Camps are able to know the exact location on the farm of each horse and what kind of horse it is, from a yearling to a racehorse. The computer also is used to keep track of breeding dates and when horses should foal. If anyone on the farm needs to have the health history of a horse, know when a horse needs a blacksmith, or when a horse will come in season, the answer is stored in the computer. Information about the arrival and departure of horses also can be found in the computer. Some mares from other states only visit the farm seasonally for breeding purposes. Information about what van company will be transporting a horse and what necessary health papers must go with it also can be found in the computer files.

When farm manager Jeff Camp goes on his daily visit to the barn, he does not bring pencil and paper but a laptop computer to note any actions he has taken with the horses. At the end of his daily rounds, he takes the laptop back to the office and uploads the data he has entered into the computer's master files.

The computer operates throughout the day at Glenmore Farm. All the billing and check writing for bills and payroll are done on the computer. Besides instantly providing information about the horses, the computer saves the farm money. When it is time to take the year's records to the accountant, everything is already itemized. Barbara believes that if the computer were not helping them run the farm, they would need to hire additional people. She also finds the computer invaluable in researching the background of horses. By using a computer data bank such as Jockey Club, she can check a horse's parentage, age, track earnings, and sales results. She can even register a horse by using the computer modem.

I is for Instructor, Investigator— and Indexer

An index is the alphabetical list of names and subjects together with the page numbers that tell where they appear in the text of a book. Indexers compile these lists, which are typically found in the back of books. Claire Bolton feels very lucky to have the computer help her with her work as an indexer. There are special programs that she uses to do this work. The computer has freed her from worrying so much about clerical details and allowed her to concentrate on the quality of what she is producing. The advent of the computer has cut the number of indexers required on the staffs of book companies. Many indexers, like Claire, are freelancers.

J is for Judge, Jeweler—and Jailer

Norman Bucker is assistant jail commander of a large metropolitan jail that houses fifteen hundred inmates. The computer system is up and running every day. It is a fantastic management tool that lets Norman and others on the jail staff know myriad details about the prisoners just by pressing a few buttons. The computer has information on where prisoners are located, movement of prisoners, rule violations prisoners have committed, past stays in prison, prison escapes, and what type of prisoner an individual is. Information is so detailed that the staff is able to find every car that is registered to a prisoner's family.

At this large jail, everything is done on the computer, from visitations to library visits for inmates to employee attendance records. The computer system makes it possible to send memos and contact individuals such as prosecutors without having to spend hours playing phone tag. Jail policy can be created, adjusted, or even changed without too much difficulty. Using the computer has helped the jail staff cut down on paperwork, is cost effective, and has improved the overall management of the jail.

K is for Kindergarten Teacher— and Kennel Owner

Rick Smith is the owner of two kennels in Michigan. He realized that customers often made plans for the care of their pets over the phone and then changed their instructions when the pets were left at the kennel. In order to keep the pet owners happy and to provide the proper care for their pets, Rick developed the software program KennelSoft. The program is now being used by over three hundred different kennels throughout the country. Rick points out that so much of the successful operation of a kennel involves communication, and the computer helps to eliminate problems by storing information in such a way that everyone has access to it. For example, kennel care givers need to know the proper diet for each animal, and the computer stops workers from misreading another person's abbreviations or scribbles. The computer prints out a card that is put on each pet's run. The card tells the animal's name, breed, weight, color, and diet and lists any toys or other items that the animal has brought to the kennel. (Rick has had animals come with their own monogrammed Gucci luggage.) By looking at the computer-printed card, an employee quickly can see what care an animal requires and if the right animal is in a run.

Shawn Robertson, a manager at a kennel using KennelSoft, says the computer is the heart of their business. Shawn explains that every time a dog is checked in or out of the kennel, it is entered in the computer database. In addition, special notations on personality problems can be stored in the computer. Shawn adds that the computer also does inventory, keeping track of everything in the retail area. In addition, the computer is used to determine how many animals can be accommodated at the kennel. This is especially important during the busy holiday periods, when so many different animals are vying for a limited number of spaces.

The computer has been so helpful to Rick that he is able to run his Michigan kennels in the winter from his home in Florida. Every day by modem, Rick can find out how many different animals entered and left his kennels and the number of animals that were groomed. He is able to determine what the day's income was as well as check on the inventory at each kennel. The computer has enabled Rick to arrange his business so he can have other people actually see to the day-to-day operations.

Rick sees the computer as the catalyst for the development of chains of kennels. He believes that pet owners will get better care for their animals in these major operations because of the availability of professional advice on diet and animal health.

L is for Loan Officer, Legal Secretary— and Librarian

Suzanne Braun has been the librarian at the Indianapolis Zoo for the past five years. Suzanne, who has a master s degree in library science, points out that computer classes are mandatory for librarians as the computer has become such an important tool in libraries. Like that of all librarians, much of her workday involves using the computer.

The Indianapolis Zoo is part of the Indiana Department of Education's computer access network (IDEANET), which ties together schools and businesses in the state of Indiana to provide information to students and teachers. Using a modem and this free computer system, Suzanne spent one hour recently with a third grade class. During this live computer chat, students took turns typing in their questions about animals and received immediate input from Suzanne on their computer. She also spends many hours a day doing research on the computer system that links all public, academic, and special libraries across the country. This system enables her to track down books and articles through interlibrary loan and have a copy of the book or article sent to her. Suzanne is also one of a group of zoo and aquarium librarians in the United States who share information. For example, when she creates a bibliography on a certain animal, the information can be uploaded into another zoo librarian's system in another part of the country.

Suzanne spends additional time on the computer going through her E-mail messages and sending replies back to teachers and students wanting zoo-related information. She also uses E-mail to communicate with other zoo librarians. She sorts through her E-mail and keeps the information that will be helpful to zoo staff members. Because Suzanne works at a small specialized library, she uses a filing system for disks that works best for the zoo. She has her floppy disks stored topically and indexed. Due to the large capacity of her hard drive, considerable information can be stored right in the computer's memory. Suzanne considers the computer a necessity in order to do her job as a librarian efficiently.

M is for Mathematician, Mechanic— and Music Copyist

Music copyists transcribe each individual musical part from a score onto paper. For example, a copyist will go through a complete score and write out the entire part for the violin, making it much easier for the violinist to play his or her part. In the past, copying was done by hand with a special pen. Today, however, copyists can play on a keyboard directly into a computer. The information is then translated into printed notations.

Jeff Wiedenfeld and his wife, Julie, run Blue Note Engraving, a company that copies music. Their company is fully computerized, and the speed of the computer is very important in getting music to the clients on time. According to Jeff, the computer does it all. Publishing houses, music groups, and composers need copies quickly, and with the modem he can get copy to a publisher—even one in London—without much delay. Julie and Jeff do no copying by hand because they have instructed the computer to do it all. Although their business is based in the Midwest, they have clients throughout the world.

N is for Nurse, Nutritionist—and Newspaper Employee

Karen Braeckel is the manager of the educational services department of a major metropolitan newspaper. Her basic job is to encourage the reading of newspapers in the classroom. The Newspaper in Education program develops educational materials for teachers to use with students and gives workshops on using the newspaper in the classroom. Most of the work is done on the community relations department's four computers. Karen writes articles and memos on the computer to pass on to other newspaper employees. When one of the articles is ready to be printed in the newspaper, Karen sends it directly to the composing room. Karen is a true computer buff who says she could not possibly produce what she does today if she did not have access to a computer.

Karen Sprunger also works in educational services. She had never used a computer until she began working at a smaller newspaper seven years ago. She learned how to use the computer by simple trial and error. In her present job, Karen uses the computer for a variety of tasks including: writing letters, editing or compiling materials for teachers, designing student worksheets, formatting reports for committees, and creating special calendars and materials. What she likes best about the computer is the freedom it gives her to move text. Karen spends her workdays creating pages exactly the way she wants them to look. Karen enjoys using the computer in her job and is happy that she no longer has to spend as much time cutting and pasting layouts.

O is for Optometrist—and Officer in the Army

Dana Ball was issued a computer before her freshman year began at West Point, and when she graduated she took the computer with her to her first assignment. At West Point the computers were interfaced with Kermit—a network mail system that allowed cadets to log on to the system and communicate both with other cadets in the corps and with professors. She also was able to exchange information with any other school via E-mail and to transfer mail to the other academies. Dana used the computer for all her classes, from English to calculus. She also spent five to eight hours a day on it in her senior year, as she had selected the systems engineering track as her engineering area and all work was done on the computer.

Today, Dana is a second lieutenant and the executive officer for a two- to four-hundred-soldier advanced individual training company. Her main assignment is to relieve the administrative burden of her commander. She plans the training of the soldiers and uses the computer to create hard copy of the training schedule. In order to accomplish this mission, she spends time creating short-, medium-, and long-range calendars on the computer. Without the computer, it would take Dana countless hours to produce her weekly training schedules. By using the computer she is able to bring up previous schedules and keep all the items that remain the same each week such as wake-up and bed-check times. The computer is also an invaluable tool in handling her other duties. Dana uses the Harvard Graphics program to print awards for the soldiers. And she uses the computer to handle the paperwork for her other duties, which include serving as the local unit drug and alcohol testing officer, the moral welfare and recreation officer, and a member of the officer club and the arts and crafts councils.

P is for Postal Clerk, Paralegal— and Pharmacist

Rosie Perez is a pharmacist at a large chain drugstore. Call in a refill or hand her a prescription for a refill, and she will quickly pull the prescription up on her computer. Then the computer will print the label. Rosie fills the prescription from the label. If you have a new prescription, she will enter it into the computer, which will then print the label. The first time customers visit her drugstore to fill a prescription, they also complete a form giving information about allergies, health conditions, and prescription insurance plans. Rosie enters all of this information in the computer. If a customer's new prescription does not go with other medications or is contraindicated because of allergies or health conditions, the computer will alert Rosie to this fact. In addition, the computer will print insurance forms for customers needing them. It also will bill insurance companies directly for some customers. Besides serving as a pharmacist's helper and bookkeeper, the computer also keeps inventory of all the drugs that are sold and updates the inventory on a weekly basis. The inventory list goes by computer to company headquarters so that drugs can be replenished automatically when the weekly supply truck arrives. Rosie considers the computer to be a valuable aid in completing her work.

Q is for Quilter—and Quality-Control Technician

Engineers design the printers manufactured by the Silicon Valley company where Mary Lai works as a quality-control technician. Her job is to make sure the production model meets the engineers' design standards. Before the advent of computerized testing, most quality-control work was done by selecting a sample of the factory's products and then measuring or testing the product to see if it worked as it was designed to. In some cases this actually involved tearing products apart to see that they were made correctly. Using this approach meant that not every product could be tested. In Mary's company every printer is tested to ensure it meets the design parameters. This is possible because the company uses a computer-based system with special sensors that quickly tell if the printer is meeting acceptable limits. The computer is actually making 100 percent quality control possible.

R is for Realtor, Reporter— and Reservation Clerk

Carol Love is a reservation sales representative for an international airline. During her eight-and-one-half-hour workday, she spends approximately seven hours and forty minutes in front of a computer handling requests for reservations. She also can change or cancel reservations simply by modifying the record on the computer. Carol has to be knowledgeable about her company's policies and procedures as well as be aware of special promotions. When Carol first went to work for the airline in 1968, all her work was done by slides. Computers were introduced in 1969 and since then have been upgraded frequently to more efficient models that have much less downtime. Even though the computer makes Carol's job much easier, she still finds herself, at times, suffering from eyestrain at the end of her shift, even with special screens designed to reduce glare.

S is for Secretary, Sheriff— and Systems Accountant

Les Gisler works on a computer four or five hours a day as a systems accountant. He uses his terminal to interact with the mainframe to extract financial reports for end users who are usually staff accountants. He also uses the computer to solve accounting problems and improve the handling of information. Away from the computer, he trains accountant technicians in the use of hardware as well as the programs that he has designed. Les also has the task of coordinating major system changes between the programming staff and the accounting function.

The position of systems accountant requires a solid background in both computer science and accounting. Les was introduced to computers in the early 1970s, when he was in the army and took a data systems course that covered programming and included an introduction to hardware and systems analysis. After he left the service, Les completed his degree in accounting. Several years later his growing interest in the data processing side of accounting compelled him to return to school to earn an associate's degree in computer technology. This additional degree helped him obtain his present position as a systems accountant.

T is for Therapist, Ticket Seller— and Tennis Coach

P. A. Nilhagen is a tennis coach of professional and college players as well as junior players. During a match a tennis expert can key into a computer what is happening on the court. The computer can then produce charts giving coaches and players a statistical breakdown on such things as percentage of good first serves, the effectiveness of a player's serve in the deuce versus advantage court, a player's rate of success in going to the net, and the number of unforced errors committed. P.A. used the computer with former ATP tour player Todd Witsken and with several professional and college players. He finds that the computer-generated information about a match provides significant help, especially when he is unable to attend a player's match. P.A. also has discovered that most players are not pleased to read the printout of their matches and see the specific classification of their errors. According to P.A., what the computer cannot produce is a chart of the player's mental state during the match, which is critical in understanding when and why players make errors.

The computer is not just used in tennis to chart play during matches. P.A. considers it a very helpful tool in making draws for tournaments. For example, if a tournament is being held with a draw of sixty-four players, the draw would take hours to make on paper. With the computer the time can be reduced to eight seconds, once the necessary information has been keyed in. P.A. also finds using the computer at tournament check-in desks to be very helpful, especially in determining if players have current USTA (United States Tennis Association) numbers.

U is for Underwriter, Urban Planner— and Undergraduate

Before most college students enter the job market, they have started working with computers. Besides having science laboratories, colleges now have computer laboratories. And many colleges have elaborate networks that connect to every living group or even every student's room. Aaron Ball is a senior at a private university with a double major in Spanish and political science. Similar to most undergraduates, he took a computer class in high school and has taken two classes in college. Aaron has his own computer at college, and he also uses the computers on campus. He believes that word processing is critical to his academic success, since college professors expect all assignments to be word processed. He keeps all his work on disks so that revisions can be made easily. And he also uses the computer in managing his time as he keeps a running file on his current projects. In addition, as president of the university Political Science Association, he uses graphics programs extensively to print schedules and announcements of upcoming events and speakers. After graduation Aaron plans to enter law school, and his computer will be going right along with him.

V is for Veterinarian—and Volunteer

Volunteering has always been a part of the American culture and one of its greatest resources. In recent years the number of volunteers has swelled, and many of these volunteers are computer buffs who use the computer in their volunteer work. Steve Johnson has worked as a volunteer for the American Red Cross for the past five years. While the organization has been using computers for a wide variety of tasks, it only began linking all its computers together just a year ago. Steve says that this has allowed the Red Cross to transmit data quickly and easily to its regional headquarters. Previously, hard copy was printed and mailed to other locations, requiring considerable effort of staff and volunteers. The Red Cross also uses its computers to generate postcards reminding blood donors and others of appointments. With increased use of the computer, volunteers like Steve are able to help the Red Cross operate more efficiently as well as have more time for humanitarian efforts in place of paperwork.

W is for Writer, Ward Attendant— and Weather Forecaster

In 1982, Chuck Lofton became a full-time weather forecaster for a national television network and started spending most of his workday on the computer. He creates his own graphics for his weather segments on television; however, he also can get computer-generated graphics. Chuck accesses all his weather information via the computer from the national weather station. He can even get an update on the weather immediately before he goes on the air.

Chuck believes that advances in technology will bring higher resolution and cleaner pictures, more animation, and better presentations of the weather on television. RADAR NEXAR (next-generation radar) sites are being built throughout the United States. RADAR NEXAR will allow weather forecasters to analyze a storm in sixteen different ways. Weather forecasters literally will be able to see inside a storm, find out how high the winds are, and determine how much rain the storm will produce. This will be especially helpful when the weather forecaster is tracking severe weather. Using a computer is an absolute necessity for weather forecasters as it helps them forecast the weather more accurately.

X is for X-Ray Technologist

Constance Murray works in the x-ray department of a major metropolitan hospital. She points out that the application of computer technology has absolutely revolutionized the field of radiology. Computed tomographic (CT) scanning has employed computers since its inception. In CT scanning, three-dimensional reconstruction of two-dimensional images is possible with computers. These three-dimensional anatomic images can be rotated to visualize the structure in any plane. Orbital fractures and many facial reconstructive surgeries utilize these capabilities. Computer technology also is employed in digital radiography and fluoroscopy, which are becoming routine procedures in the clinical setting. Magnetic resonance imaging (MRI) also applies computer technology similar to CT. With MRI, images of patient anatomy are stored in the computer as bits of data, which can then be printed on film for hard copy and storage retrieval. Anatomical images digitized on a computer also allow manipulation of the image to highlight pathology or better demonstrate organs not otherwise seen well. According to Constance, the advances the computer has brought to radiology make her believe that *Star Trek*-quality medical care is not far away.

Y is for YMCA Employee

William Graham works as vice president/controller at YMCA headquarters in a midwestern city. The main computer is at headquarters and is linked to computers at the other YMCAs in the eight-county area. There also are several PCs in the headquarters office and in branches that help with maintaining correspondence, creating brochures, and monitoring program attendance. William says that the computer really helps him to do his job, as nonprofit organizations have to collect so much data for reports to the United Way and various units of government. The computer is used to keep track of revenues for the monthly reports and all financial work in the accounting and payroll departments. It also is used to keep track of all the members and the programs in which they participate.

Other YMCA employees are also turning to computers to help them do their jobs. Debi Roy works as director of aquatics at a small YMCA in Illinois. Just six months ago, she was given a computer and cannot remember what she did without it. The computer allows Debi to keep organized records of all the swim classes, teachers, and students. She has also put together a staff member database that lists the certifications and work experience of each of her staff members. This allows her to find vital information quickly. Being able to store all this information in a computer, rather than filing cabinets, has made Debi's desk area a lot cleaner.

Z is for Zoologist—and Zoo Manager

F. Kevin Gaza works in the business management office of the zoo. He says that the computer helps the zoo in business applications, animal management, and animal record keeping. ARKS is the database system used in keeping a detailed history of all animals. This is very important as it helps to avoid the interbreeding of vanishing wildlife. For example, there are not a lot of Siberian tigers in captivity, so finding a mate is not easy. However, by using the ARKS data base, the zookeeper can find every Siberian tiger in captivity and know what its gene makeup is. ISIS (International Species Information System) keeps such detailed information on its database that the exact breeding time of any animal can be swiftly ascertained for stud purposes. Zoo managers also use the World Wide Web to obtain information on animals. There are now more than one thousand sites available for this purpose. Some sites feature experts who can be contacted for more detailed questions.

CHAPTER ELEVEN

Exploring Future Computer Careers

Increasing Opportunities

The United States has led the world into the Information Age, a world in which there is a robust demand for workers who are highly skilled in the use of information technology. Although the explosive growth of the computer industry has slowed down due to its large size, it is still growing faster than most large industries. Some areas within the industry will explode and grow at absolutely fantastic rates in the future.

Future Trends

The U.S. Bureau of Labor Statistics recently listed the fastest-growing, highest-paying occupations for the next century. Of the top twenty-five careers listed, five are computer-related: systems analysts, database managers and computer support specialists, computer engineers, computer systems managers, and computer programmers. What the next hot job areas will be depends on emerging technology and applications. Computer buffs who stay abreast of what is happening in the industry will find exciting career opportunities. For example, in 1995 the Internet truly became a place for everyone to communicate, which led to the creation of one million Internet-related jobs just one year later.

Here are some of job areas that computer buffs may wish to explore in the future as many industry experts see promising career opportunities in these areas.

Communications

Sweeping changes are occurring in communications. More and more organizations are linking computers together in local- and wide-area networks so the users can share peripherals and files and exchange information. While fiber optics has greatly reduced the time required to transfer data, engineers are learning how to use satellite and cellular communications to transmit data even faster and more conveniently. These new types of transmitting signals allow computer users to access data from anywhere in the world— a sailboat on the ocean or a car on a freeway. For example, by taking advantage of the use of satellites for global positioning, drivers are able to receive real-time information on road construction, heavy traffic, and directions. The Internet can be used to distribute secure real-time information to computer users throughout the world. Videophones are becoming a reality for computer users. Soon, voice-over-data capabilities will be available to computer users, allowing them to send data and view and discuss it at the same time. Engineers with knowledge of fiber optics, satellites, and cellular communications are needed to implement these revolutionary changes in communication.

Security

Companies are rushing to set up secure Web sites limited to the use of their personnel on Intranets (internal Internets). The installation of firewalls ensures that nonauthorized users are denied access. Companies also want to have secure Web sites on the Internet. Security specialists who work in-house or as consultants are needed to provide this security.

Multimedia

Interest is steadily increasing in computer-based methods of presenting materials combining text, sound, and graphics that emphasize interactivity. Computer users can now create their own multimedia with the use of writable and rewritable CD-ROM drives and store removable data on CD-ROMs. Most new computers are equipped with internal stereo sound and 3-D graphic cards. These new graphic cards have opened up exciting design possibilities for designers, architects, engineers, photographers, and producers. For example, engineers now have the capability of using 3-D graphics to produce virtual images of the products they design, and computer game creators can produce mind-boggling special effects using these cards. The movie industry is changing as computer-generated effects become part of almost every movie that is being produced. Another use of multimedia connections just getting off the ground is access to the Internet through television sets. Hardware, software, and networking experts will be needed to make multimedia truly commercial.

Systems Integration

Organizations want to integrate different hardware, operating systems, and applications software so that they can share information with each other. As so many organizations have this need, both in-house staff and outside consultants are needed as system integrators.

Expert Systems

These systems are computer programs that contain much of the knowledge of an expert in a specific field. Most of these programs are available on CD-ROM or Internet Web sites. If you have questions about a certain topic, you simply type in a key search word or words, and the program provides the information you seek. For example, such systems are being used by doctors to suggest diagnoses. Organizations are actively seeking professionals, called knowledge engineers, who have the skills to design and develop expert systems.

Computer Careers in Other Job Areas

In the future, computer buffs can look forward to finding computers practically everywhere. No matter where you seek a job, a computer is likely to be involved in some way in your performance of that job. Your home life also will be greatly changed by what your home computer can do for you. Technological innovations in the use of computers have only begun to scratch the surface of their potential. Some researchers believe that the advances will be so great that it is very difficult to make predictions of how the computer will be used just twenty years from now.

Changes Are Coming

In the twenty-first century, computers may be used in some of the following ways, according to the computer buffs interviewed in this book. As a computer buff, you may be involved in making these things happen through your job working with computers.

1. Can you imagine home computers running robots? No longer will busy people have to waste their time looking for someone to come in and do their household chores. The robots will be cooking, cleaning, doing the wash, and even cutting the grass thanks to the technology that will be able to interface home computers to robots. To make it even more fantastic, your robot can be programmed to have the personality of Julia Roberts or Tom Cruise.

2. Have you ever been flustered by not being able to find your car keys? Have you ever run out of gas on the freeway? Your troubles will soon be over because even more computerized cars will soon be in the marketplace. In fact, some of the features that tomorrow's computerized cars will routinely have are already in some of today's cars. Cars are already using small computer chips in the keys as antitheft devices, and some cars have coded touch pads on the door to allow

you to unlock the car. On-board computers are able to figure how many miles worth of fuel remain in the tank and estimate arrival times for long trips. However, these features are only the beginning. In the future, you will be able to throw away your keys because the coded touch pads on the dashboard will allow you to start the car. Rear television monitors will replace your car's outside mirrors. You will be able to avoid hitting objects such as dogs, children, bikes, and other cars thanks to a sonar detection system. Using global positioning satellites, cars will one day be able to drive themselves. All you will need to know is your destination.

3. Because of 3-D interaction you will be able to have any kind of world your heart desires. You will have reached utopia, thanks to computer technology. By just going down the street to the virtual-reality store, you will be able to enjoy coffee in a cafe in Paris or be cruising down the Rhine in Germany. You will be able to visit a zoo and be in the cage with the gorillas or swim in the water with the dolphins.

4. Leading the way into the next generation of computers is something termed artificial intelligence (AI). It is fascinating to think that computers will be able to imitate human intelligence at levels including thinking, common sense, self-teaching, and even decision making. Even now, AI is being used in expert systems to help doctors pinpoint what disease a patient may have. Artificial intelligence also will make it possible for you to ask your computer a question and get an answer. This is beginning now with information retrieval from databases.

5. Voice recognition is being used today to help the handicapped communicate better by using typewriter-like machines. It is also being used to turn some appliances and equipment on and off. Soon, voice recognition technology will make it possible for us to dictate speeches and reports to the computer and receive a printed copy of the text.

6. Fast food today will be even faster tomorrow when a multiarmed robot is fixing and filling orders, collecting money, giving change, sweeping the floor, and even clearing tables. You may think that this only happens on television shows, but you are wrong. The robot will even be able to detect overcooked hamburgers and toss them in the trash. Furthermore, it will be able to go anywhere in the restaurant while its independently operating arms will be efficiently performing different tasks. And only one human engineer will be needed per shift to keep it running!

7. What a union! Computer technology will combine with telephone systems to create hybrid phones. These will not be ordinary phones. You not only will be able to send and retrieve your messages, you will use the phone to teach yourself a foreign language, and the phone will even remind you when it is time to send your relatives' birthday cards.

8. The computer in the future will help handicapped individuals who have no physical movement. This will be done through brain waves. For example, letters will be flashed on a screen, and as soon as a letter is recognized brain waves will change.

9. Computers will make prosthetic devices more realistic. These artificial devices will even be able to perform small-motor skills. Computers will also control artificial organs. Parts of tomorrow's computers will not just be mechanical like today's computers; they will have smaller parts that will be chemically and biologically controlled motors.

10. Eventually, the Internet will emulate all present-day communications functions. In the distribution of information, the Net will combine the capabilities of the telephone, radio, television, newspaper, and magazines.

Preparing for Your Future Career

Read as much as you can about the computer industry and go aboard the Internet often to find out where the jobs are and what the latest technology is. Explore the field by working part-time and in the summer or by participating in an internship or a cooperative education program. Employers value practical work experience. If you will be getting a degree in computer science, you can be certain the program is a quality one if it is certified by the Accreditation Board for Engineering and Technology (ABET) or the Computing Sciences Accreditation Board (CSAB). A list of these schools can be found in the Appendix.

Remember, too, that computer buffs can find satisfying careers in government, business, education, manufacturing, and anywhere computers are being used. If you will be going into business, be sure to get a well-rounded education. According to Max Messmer, chairman of Accountemps, while specialized skills are in growing demand in today's workplace, a general awareness of a broad range of disciplines will allow workers to better apply those skills within a company.

Accredited Programs in Computing

T he following list is of accredited computer science and computer engineering programs. The year of initial accreditation appears by the university name and degree. The list is reprinted with permission from the Computer Science Accreditation Commission (CSAC) of the Computing Sciences Accreditation Board (CSAB) and by the Engineering Accreditation Commission (EAC) of the Accreditation Board of Engineering and Technology (ABET).

*Program is accredited by the Engineering Accreditation Commission of the Accreditation Board for Engineering and Technology.
**Program is accredited by the Computer Science Accreditation Commission of the Computing Sciences Accreditation Board.
***Program is dually accredited by the Engineering Accreditation Commission of the Accreditation Board for Engineering and Technology and by the Computer Science Accreditation Commission of the Computing Sciences Accreditation Board.

Alabama

AUBURN UNIVERSITY

B.S. Computer Science**	1987
B.S. Computer Engineering (with or without Cooperative Education)*	1987

UNIVERSITY OF ALABAMA

B.S. Computer Science in the College of Engineering and College of Arts and Science**	1990

UNIVERSITY OF ALABAMA IN HUNTSVILLE

B.S. Computer Science**	1988
B.S. Computer Engineering (with or without Cooperative Education)*	1992

UNIVERSITY OF ALABAMA IN TUSCALOOSA
B.S. Computer Engineering   1996
(Option in Electrical Engineering)*
UNIVERSITY OF SOUTH ALABAMA
B.S. Computer and Information Science,   1988
Computer Science Specialization**

Alaska
UNIVERSITY OF ALASKA FAIRBANKS
B.S. Computer Science**   1991

Arizona
ARIZONA STATE UNIVERSITY
B.S. Computer Science**   1992
B.S.E. Computer Systems Engineering*   1980
NORTHERN ARIZONA UNIVERSITY
B.S. Computer Science and Engineering   1984
(with or without Cooperative Education)**
UNIVERSITY OF ARIZONA
B.S. Computer Engineering*   1987

Arkansas
ARKANSAS STATE UNIVERSITY
B.S. Computer Science**   1994
UNIVERSITY OF ARKANSAS AT FAYETTEVILLE
B.S. Computer Systems and Engineering*   1991
UNIVERSITY OF ARKANSAS AT LITTLE ROCK
B.S. Computer Science**   1990

California
CALIFORNIA STATE POLYTECHNIC UNIVERSITY, POMONA
B.S. Computer Science**   1994
CALIFORNIA STATE POLYTECHNIC UNIVERSITY, SAN LUIS
OBISPO
B.S. Computer Science**   1986
B.S. Computer Engineering*   1997

CALIFORNIA STATE UNIVERSITY, CHICO
B.S. Computer Science,   1987
General, Math/Science, and Systems Options**
B.S. Computer Engineering*   1989
CALIFORNIA STATE UNIVERSITY, DOMINGUEZ HILLS
B.S. Computer Science**   1996
CALIFORNIA STATE UNIVERSITY, FULLERTON
B.S. Computer Science**   1988
CALIFORNIA STATE UNIVERSITY, LONG BEACH
B.S. Computer Science
Option in Computer Engineering*   1974
Option in Computer Science**   1995
CALIFORNIA STATE UNIVERSITY, NORTHRIDGE
B.S. Computer Science**   1987
CALIFORNIA STATE UNIVERSITY, SACRAMENTO
B.S. Computer Science**   1986
B.S. Computer Engineering   1989
(with or without Cooperative Education)*
CALIFORNIA STATE UNIVERSITY, SAN BERNARDINO
B.S. Computer Science**   1990
CALIFORNIA STATE UNIVERSITY, STANISLAUS
B.S. Computer Science**   1986
SAN DIEGO STATE UNIVERSITY
B.S. Computer Science**   1994
SAN FRANCISCO STATE UNIVERSITY
B.S. Computer Science**   1993
SAN JOSE STATE UNIVERSITY
B.S. Computer Science**   1994
B.S. Computer Engineering*   1991
SANTA CLARA UNIVERSITY
B.S. Computer Engineering*   1987
UNIVERSITY OF CALIFORNIA, BERKELEY
B.S. Computer Science and Engineering***   1983
UNIVERSITY OF CALIFORNIA, DAVIS
B.S. Computer Engineering*   1995
B.S. Computer Science and Engineering***   1989
UNIVERSITY OF CALIFORNIA, IRVINE
B.S. Computer Engineering*   1996

UNIVERSITY OF CALIFORNIA, LOS ANGELES
  B.S. Computer Science**   1995
  B.S. Computer Science and Engineering***   1986
UNIVERSITY OF CALIFORNIA, SANTA BARBARA
  B.A. Computer Science**   1986
  B.S. Computer Science**   1986
UNIVERSITY OF CALIFORNIA, SANTA CRUZ
  B.S. Computer Engineering*   1989
UNIVERSITY OF THE PACIFIC
  B.S. Computer Science**   1990
  B.S. Computer Engineering (with or without   1983
  Cooperative Education)*

Colorado

UNITED STATES AIR FORCE ACADEMY
  B.S. Computer Science**   1986
UNIVERSITY OF COLORADO, BOULDER
  B.S. Electrical and Computer Engineering*   1982
UNIVERSITY OF COLORADO, COLORADO SPRINGS
  B.S. Computer Science**   1989

Connecticut

CENTRAL CONNECTICUT STATE UNIVERSITY
  B.S. Computer Science**   1990
SOUTHERN CONNECTICUT STATE UNIVERSITY
  B.S. Computer Science**   1992
UNIVERSITY OF BRIDGEPORT
  B.S. Computer Engineering*   1989
UNIVERSITY OF CONNECTICUT
  B.S. Computer Science and Engineering***   1972

District of Columbia

GEORGE WASHINGTON UNIVERSITY
  B.S. Computer Science**   1987
  B.S. Computer Engineering*   1984

HOWARD UNIVERSITY
B.S. Systems and Computer Science**   1988

Florida

FLORIDA ATLANTIC UNIVERSITY
B.S. Computer Engineering*   1997
B.S. Computer Science**   1991
FLORIDA INSTITUTE OF TECHNOLOGY
B.S. Computer Engineering*   1983
FLORIDA INTERNATIONAL UNIVERSITY
B.S. Computer Engineering*   1994
B.S. Computer Science**   1993
FLORIDA STATE UNIVERSITY
B.S. Computer and Information Sciences**   1987
UNIVERSITY OF CENTRAL FLORIDA
B.S. Computer Science**   1989
B.S. Computer Engineering*   1974
UNIVERSITY OF FLORIDA
B.S. Computer Engineering   1983
(with or without Cooperative Education)*
UNIVERSITY OF MIAMI
B.S. Computer Engineering*   1988
UNIVERSITY OF NORTH FLORIDA
B.S. Computer and Information Science   1987
Computer Science Specialization**
UNIVERSITY OF SOUTH FLORIDA
B.S. Computer Science**   1989
B.S. Computer Engineering*   1984

Georgia

ARMSTRONG ATLANTIC STATE COLLEGE
B.S. Computer Science**   1991
GEORGIA INSTITUTE OF TECHNOLOGY
B.S. Information and Computer Science**   1986
B.S. Computer Engineering (with or without   1991
Cooperative Education)*

GEORGIA SOUTHERN UNIVERSITY
  B.S. Computer Science**   1993

Idaho
BOISE STATE UNIVERSITY
  B.S. Computer Science**   1994
UNIVERSITY OF IDAHO
  B.S. Computer Engineering*   1996
  B.S. Computer Science**   1993

Illinois
ILLINOIS INSTITUTE OF TECHNOLOGY
  B.S. Computer Engineering*   1997
NORTHWESTERN UNIVERSITY
  B.S. Computer Engineering (with or   1997
  without Cooperative Education)*
UNIVERSITY OF ILLINOIS, CHICAGO
  B.S. Computer Engineering*   1976
  B.S. Computer Science**   1997
UNIVERSITY OF ILLINOIS, URBANA-CHAMPAIGN
  B.S. Computer Engineering (with or without   1978
  Cooperative Education)*

Indiana
PURDUE UNIVERSITY
  B.S. Computer and Electrical Engineering   1984
  (with or without Cooperative Education)*
ROSE-HULMAN INSTITUTE OF TECHNOLOGY
  B.S. Computer Engineering*   1995
UNIVERSITY OF EVANSVILLE
  B.S. Computer Engineering*   1997
UNIVERSITY OF NOTRE DAME
  B.S. Computer Engineering*   1994
VALPARAISO UNIVERSITY
  B.S. Computer Engineering (with or without   1990
  Cooperative Education)*

Iowa

IOWA STATE UNIVERSITY
    B.S. Computer Science**   1986
    B.S. Computer Engineering (with or without   1979
    Cooperative Education)*

Kansas

KANSAS STATE UNIVERSITY
    B.S. Computer Engineering*   1991
    B.S. Computer Science**   1992
UNIVERSITY OF KANSAS
    B.S. Computer Engineering*   1992
    B.S. Computer Science**   1995

Kentucky

EASTERN KENTUCKY UNIVERSITY
    B.S. Computer Science**   1991
UNIVERSITY OF LOUISVILLE
    B.S. Engineering Mathematics and   1996
    Computer Science**
WESTERN KENTUCKY UNIVERSITY
    B.S. Computer Science**   1993

Louisiana

GRAMBLING UNIVERSITY
    B.S. Computer Science**   1997
LOUISIANA STATE UNIVERSITY IN BATON ROUGE
    B.S. Computer Engineering*   1989
LOUISIANA STATE UNIVERSITY IN SHREVEPORT
    B.S. Computer Science**   1991
LOUISIANA TECHNICAL UNIVERSITY
    B.S. Computer Science**   1988
NICHOLLS STATE UNIVERSITY
    B.S. Computer Science**   1995
NORTHEAST LOUISIANA UNIVERSITY
    B.S. Computer Science**   1987

SOUTHERN UNIVERSITY AND A&M COLLEGE
  B.S. Computer Science,   1989
  Scientific Option**
TULANE UNIVERSITY
  B.S. Computer Science**   1990
UNIVERSITY OF NEW ORLEANS
  B.S. Computer Science**   1987
UNIVERSITY OF SOUTHWESTERN LOUISIANA
  B.S. Computer Science**   1987

Maine

UNIVERSITY OF MAINE
  B.S. Computer Engineering*   1993
  B.S. Computer Science**   1995
UNIVERSITY OF SOUTHERN MAINE
  B.S. Computer Science**   1994

Maryland

LOYOLA COLLEGE IN MARYLAND
  B.S. Computer Science**   1990
TOWSON STATE UNIVERSITY
  B.S. Computer Science**   1994
UNITED STATES NAVAL ACADEMY
  B.S. Computer Science**   1987

Massachusetts

BOSTON UNIVERSITY
  B.S. Computer Systems Engineering*   1983
MASSACHUSETTS INSTITUTE OF TECHNOLOGY
  S.B. Computer Science and Engineering   1978
  (with or without Cooperative Education)*
  S.B. Computer Science and Engineering***   1994
  S.B. Electrical Engineering and Computer Science***   1994
MERRIMACK COLLEGE
  B.S. Electrical Engineering (with or   1966
  without Cooperative Education)*

NORTHEASTERN UNIVERSITY
    B.S. Computer Science**   1986
TUFTS UNIVERSITY
    B.S. Computer Engineering*   1982
UNIVERSITY OF MASSACHUSETTS AMHERST
    B.S. Computer Systems Engineering*   1978
UNIVERSITY OF MASSACHUSETTS DARTMOUTH
    B.S. Computer Science**   1988
    B.S. Computer Engineering*   1984
UNIVERSITY OF MASSACHUSETTS LOWELL
    B.S. Computer Science**   1990
WORCESTER POLYTECHNIC INSTITUTE
    B.S. Computer Science**   1986

Michigan
OAKLAND UNIVERSITY
    B.S. Computer Science**   1988
    B.S. Computer Engineering*   1979
UNIVERSITY OF MICHIGAN
    B.S. Computer Engineering*   1976
UNIVERSITY OF MICHIGAN, DEARBORN
    B.S. Computer and Information Science**   1997
WESTERN MICHIGAN UNIVERSITY
    B.S. Computer Science   1986
    Theory and Analysis Option**
    B.S. Computer Systems Engineering*   1985

Minnesota
ST. CLOUD STATE UNIVERSITY
    B.S. Computer Science**   1989
UNIVERSITY OF MINNESOTA, DULUTH
    B.S. Computer Science**   1989
    B.S. Computer Engineering*   1989

Mississippi
JACKSON STATE UNIVERSITY
    B.S. Computer Science**   1996

MISSISSIPPI STATE UNIVERSITY
B.S. Computer Science**	1986
B.S. Computer Engineering (with or without Cooperative Education)*	1988

UNIVERSITY OF MISSISSIPPI
B.S. Computer Science**	1990

UNIVERSITY OF SOUTHERN MISSISSIPPI
B.S. Computer Science**	1987

Missouri

SOUTHWEST MISSOURI STATE UNIVERSITY
B.S. Computer Science**	1989

UNIVERSITY OF MISSOURI, COLUMBIA
B.S. Computer Engineering*	1983

UNIVERSITY OF MISSOURI, ROLLA
B.S. Computer Science**	1986

WASHINGTON UNIVERSITY
B.S. Computer Science and Engineering (with or without Cooperative Education)*	1977

Montana

MONTANA STATE UNIVERSITY
B.S. Computer Science**	1993

UNIVERSITY OF MONTANA
B.S. Computer Science**	1996

Nebraska

UNIVERSITY OF NEBRASKA, LINCOLN
B.S. Computer Engineering**	1997

Nevada

UNIVERSITY OF NEVADA, LAS VEGAS
B.S. Computer Science**	1993

New Hampshire

UNIVERSITY OF NEW HAMPSHIRE
B.S. Computer Science**	1987

New Jersey

THE COLLEGE OF NEW JERSEY
  B.S. Computer Science**   1997
FAIRLEIGH DICKINSON UNIVERSITY
  B.S. Computer Science**   1987
MONTCLAIR STATE UNIVERSITY
  B.S. Computer Science   1993
  Concentration in Professional Computing**

NEW JERSEY INSTITUTE OF TECHNOLOGY
  B.S. Computer Engineering*   1996
  B.S. Computer Science**   1986
STEVENS INSTITUTE OF TECHNOLOGY
  B.S. Computer Science**   1986
  B.S. Computer Engineering   1986
  (with or without Cooperative Education)*

New Mexico

NEW MEXICO STATE UNIVERSITY
  B.S. Computer Engineering*   1978
  B.S. Computer Science**   1988
UNIVERSITY OF NEW MEXICO
  B.S. Computer Engineering*   1978
  B.S. Computer Science**   1988

New York

CITY COLLEGE, CUNY
  B.S. Computer Science**   1992
CLARKSON UNIVERSITY
  B.S. Computer Engineering*   1991
COLLEGE OF STATEN ISLAND, CUNY
  B.S. Computer Science**   1989
PACE UNIVERSITY
  B.S. Computer Science**   1986
POLYTECHNIC UNIVERSITY
  B.S. Computer Science**   1988
  B.S. Computer Engineering*   1991
  (BROOKLYN AND FARMINGDALE CAMPUSES)

RENSSELEAR POLYTECHNIC INSTITUTE
B.S. Computer and Systems Engineering (with   1978
or without Cooperative Education)*

ROCHESTER INSTITUTE OF TECHNOLOGY
B.S. Computer Science**   1989
B.S. Computer Engineering (Cooperative Education)*   1987

STATE UNIVERSITY OF NEW YORK AT ALBANY
B.S. Computer Science**   1987

STATE UNIVERSITY OF NEW YORK AT BINGHAMTON
B.S. Computer Science**   1989

STATE UNIVERSITY OF NEW YORK AT BROCKPORT
B.S. Computer Science**   1994

STATE UNIVERSITY OF NEW YORK AT NEW PALTZ
B.S. Computer Science**   1991

STATE UNIVERSITY OF NEW YORK AT STONY BROOK
B.S. Computer Engineering (Option in   1991
Electrical Engineering)*

SYRACUSE UNIVERSITY
B.S. Computer Engineering*   1973
(with or without Cooperative Education)

UNITED STATES MILITARY ACADEMY
B.S. Computer Science**   1997

North Carolina

APPALACHIAN STATE UNIVERSITY
B.S. Computer Science**   1988

NORTH CAROLINA A&T STATE UNIVERSITY
B.S. Computer Science**   1988

NORTH CAROLINA STATE UNIVERSITY
B.S. Computer Science**   1987
B.S. Computer Engineering (with or without   1990
Cooperative Education)

UNIVERSITY OF NORTH CAROLINA AT GREENSBORO
B.S. Computer Science**   1995

WINSTON SALEM STATE UNIVERSITY
B.S. Computer Science**   1995

North Dakota
NORTH DAKOTA STATE UNIVERSITY
    B.S. Computer Science**   1986
UNIVERSITY OF NORTH DAKOTA
    B.S. Computer Science**   1987

Ohio
CASE WESTERN RESERVE UNIVERSITY
    B.S. Computer Engineering (with or without   1971
    Cooperative Education)*
UNIVERSITY OF CINCINNATI
    B.S. Computer Engineering   1987
    (Cooperative Education)*
UNIVERSITY OF DAYTON
    B.S. Computer Science**   1991
UNIVERSITY OF TOLEDO
    B.S. Computer Science and Engineering***   1991
WRIGHT STATE UNIVERSITY
    B.S. Computer Science**   1987
    B.S. Computer Engineering*   1984

Oklahoma
UNIVERSITY OF OKLAHOMA
    B.S. Computer Engineering*   1997
    B.S. Computer Science**   1988
UNIVERSITY OF TULSA
    B.S. Computer Science**   1988

Oregon
OREGON STATE UNIVERSITY
    B.S. Computer Engineering*   1985
PORTLAND STATE UNIVERSITY
    B.S. Computer Science**   1994

Pennsylvania

BUCKNELL UNIVERSITY

B.S. Computer Science**	1991
B.S. Computer Science and Engineering***	1997

CARNEGIE MELLON UNIVERSITY

B.S. Electrical and Computer Engineering*	1989

DREXEL UNIVERSITY

B.S. Computer Science**	1986

LEHIGH UNIVERSITY

B.S. Computer Science in the College of Engineering & Applied Science**	1987
B.S. Computer Engineering*	1987

PENNSYLVANIA STATE UNIVERSITY

B.S. Computer Engineering (with or without Cooperative Education)*	1991

UNIVERSITY OF SCRANTON

B.S. Computer Science**	1990

VILLANOVA UNIVERSITY

B.S. Computer Engineering*	1997
B.S. Computer Science in the College of Liberal Arts and Sciences**	1991

Puerto Rico

UNIVERSITY OF PUERTO RICO, MAYAGUEZ

B.S. Computer Engineering**	1994

Rhode Island

UNIVERSITY OF RHODE ISLAND

B.S. Computer Engineering*	1992

South Carolina

CLEMSON UNIVERSITY

B.S. Computer Science**	1986
B.S. Computer Engineering (with or without Cooperative Education)*	1988

COLLEGE OF CHARLESTON
    B.S. Computer Science**   1992
UNIVERSITY OF SOUTH CAROLINA
    B.S. Computer Engineering*   1994
    B.S. Computer Science**   1990
WINTHROP UNIVERSITY
    B.S. Computer Science**   1990

South Dakota

SOUTH DAKOTA SCHOOL OF MINES AND TECHNOLOGY
    B.S. Computer Science**   1993

Tennessee

EAST TENNESSEE STATE UNIVERSITY
    B.S. Computer Science**   1994
MIDDLE TENNESSEE STATE UNIVERSITY
    B.S. Computer Science**   1994
VANDERBILT UNIVERSITY
    B.S. Computer Engineering**   1996

Texas

BAYLOR UNIVERSITY
    B.S. Computer Science**   1987
MIDWESTERN STATE UNIVERSITY
    B.S. Computer Science**   1996
PRAIRIE VIEW A&M UNIVERSITY
    B.S. Computer Science**   1992
SOUTHERN METHODIST UNIVERSITY
    B.S. Computer Engineering (with or without   1985
    Cooperative Education)*
TEXAS A&M UNIVERSITY
    B.S. Computer Science**   1993
    B.S. Computer Engineering   1993
    (with or without Cooperative Education)*
TEXAS CHRISTIAN UNIVERSITY
    B.S. Computer Science**   1990

UNIVERSITY OF HOUSTON
B.S. Computer Science** 1987
UNIVERSITY OF NORTH TEXAS
B.S. Computer Science** 1986
UNIVERSITY OF TEXAS AT ARLINGTON
B.S. Computer Science and Engineering*** 1983
UNIVERSITY OF TEXAS AT AUSTIN
B.S. Computer Engineering* 1988
UNIVERSITY OF TEXAS AT EL PASO
B.S. Computer Science** 1986

Utah

BRIGHAM YOUNG UNIVERSITY
B.S. Computer Engineering* 1997
B.S. Computer Science** 1989

Virginia

GEORGE MASON UNIVERSITY
B.S. Computer Science** 1995
HAMPTON UNIVERSITY
B.S. Computer Science** 1989
NORFOLK STATE UNIVERSITY
B.S. Computer Science** 1991
OLD DOMINION UNIVERSITY
B.S. Computer Engineering (with or without 1989
Cooperative Education)*
RADFORD UNIVERSITY
B.S. Computer Science** 1992
VIRGINIA COMMONWEALTH UNIVERSITY
B.S. Computer Science** 1988
VIRGINIA POLYTECHNIC INSTITUTE AND
STATE UNIVERSITY
B.S. Computer Engineering (with or 1990
(without Cooperative Education)*

Washington

EASTERN WASHINGTON UNIVERSITY
B.S. Computer Science**   1987
PACIFIC LUTHERAN UNIVERSITY
B.S. Computer Science**   1989
UNIVERSITY OF WASHINGTON
B.S. Computer Engineering*   1988
WASHINGTON STATE UNIVERSITY
B.S. Computer Science**   1996
WESTERN WASHINGTON UNIVERSITY
B.S. Computer Science**   1987

West Virginia

WEST VIRGINIA UNIVERSITY
B.S. Computer Engineering*   1992

Wisconsin

MILWAUKEE SCHOOL OF ENGINEERING
B.S. Computer Engineering*   1988

About the Authors

M arjorie Eberts and Margaret Gisler have been writing together professionally for eighteen years. They have written several VGM Career Horizons books, including three books on careers associated with computing. Maria Olson is a programmer for a Fortune 500 company and has written three books for VGM Career Horizons. This is Rachel Kelsey's second book on computers. She has had extensive experience with computers, especially in word processing and the construction of spreadsheets, and has written several software programs.

Writing this book was a special pleasure for the authors, as it gave them the opportunity to talk with so many fellow computer buffs. It also allowed them to use a new tool in their research—the Internet. Besides visiting many Web sites to gather information, they used E-mail to conduct interviews. And, as you might expect, the authors coordinated this project by using the computer to send files and messages to each other.